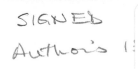

D0405837

The
JASMINE
TRADE

A NOVEL OF SUSPENSE INTRODUCING
EVE DIAMOND

Denise Hamilton

Denise Hamilton

SCRIBNER

NEW YORK LONDON TORONTO SYDNEY SINGAPORE

SCRIBNER
1230 Avenue of the Americas
New York, NY 10020

Design by Colin Joh
Set in Janson

Manufactured in the United States of America

1 3 5 7 9 10 8 6 4 2

Library of Congress Cataloging-in-Publication Data is available.

ISBN 0-7432-1269-X

For information regarding special discounts for bulk purchases, please contact Simon & Schuster Special Sales at 1-800-456-6798 or business@simonandschuster.com

For David

The
JASMINE
TRADE

CHAPTER 1

I heard the ring through fuzzy sleep.

Groaning, I opened one eye and groped for the receiver.

"Hello?"

"Hel-lo, Eve Diamond," said a cheerful voice on other line. "Miller here."

My editor was oblivious to, or else ignoring, my sleep-logged voice at ten in the morning, a time when most reporters were already at their desks, rustling through the daily paper and midway through a second cup of coffee. I swallowed, and tasted chardonnay, now a sour reminder of last night's excess.

". . . slumped in her new Lexus, blood all over the place, right there in the parking lot of Fabric World in San Gabriel," Miller was saying. "Guess the bridesmaids won't be wearing those dresses any time soon."

I cleared my throat.

"Can I have that address again, my pen stopped working."

"Why, suuure," he said. "Hold on, let me see what the wires are saying."

I would hold forever for Matt Miller. He was my hero, known and loved throughout the paper as a decent human being, a trait the *Los*

Angeles Times rarely bred anymore in its editors. Most of the real characters had long ago been pushed out of the profession or early-retired
to pickle themselves slowly and decorously in hillside *moderne* homes.
They had been replaced by gray-faced accountants with more hidden
vices. Funny thing was, Matt didn't seem to drink too much, and he was
happily married.

After a quick shower, I was out the door of my apartment. I lived in
a funky hillside community ten minutes northwest of downtown. Silverlake's California bungalows and Spanish-style homes harkened
back to an earlier era when the neighborhood had bustled with some
of Hollywood's original movie studios. And though the studios had
long ago given way to the same public storage facilities and mini-malls
that infested the rest of the city, a whiff of 1920s glamour still clung to
our hills and attracted one of the city's most eclectic populations—
lately it had been a wave of boho hipsters. They settled down, living
cheek by pierced jowl alongside multigenerational Latino families,
third-generation Asian-Americans, Eastern European refugees from
communism, 1930s-era Hollywood communists, and a smattering of
liberal white yuppies, all of whom somehow managed to get along.
Plus it was freeway close.

Within moments I was chugging along the ten-lane expanse of
asphalt, looping around downtown Los Angeles and heading east on
Interstate 10. Steering with one hand, I flipped the pages of my *Thomas
Guide* with the other, looking for Valley Boulevard and Del Mar. Out
my window, the bony spines of the San Gabriel Mountains were
already obscured by a thick haze. The San Gabes were a scrubby desolate range northeast of the city, from which bears and mountain lions
emerged with regularity to attack the inhabitants of tract houses
gouged from the hills. Each year, flash floods and icy ridges claimed a
dozen or so hikers. You wouldn't think that could happen so close to
the city, but it did. The way I saw it, nature, too, demanded its pound of
flesh. It was only we who called it accidents.

The cars ahead of me shimmered in the heat. The forecast was for
102 degrees in the Inland Valleys, with a Stage 1 Smog Alert. Already,
perspiration pooled in the hollows of my body, and I cursed the fact
that the A/C was out again in my nine-year-old Acura Integra.

Oh, it happened at *that* place, I thought, as the mammoth shopping center loomed into view. It was an anomaly that only the Pacific Rim fantasy aesthetic of Los Angeles could have produced. Built in a Spanish Mission style, with dusky earth tones, the three-story shopping center catered exclusively to the exploding Chinese immigrant community, although on occasion, a looky-loo gringo would wander through, bug-eyed at the panorama of this Asian Disneyland.

At San Gabriel Village Square, a name developers clearly hoped would evoke a more bucolic time, you could gorge on Islamic Chinese food, buy designer suits from Hong Kong, pick out live lobsters for dinner and $700 bottles of French cognac for dessert, or take out a $1 million insurance policy on your cheating spouse.

Or, as seventeen-year-old Marina Lu had done, you could order custom dresses for the ten bridesmaids who would precede you down the aisle the following June, the wedding day Marina had planned for years with the boy she had known since junior high.

Except on this stultifying morning, fate had backed up and pulled a U-turn, and now Marina Lu lay dead, brains splattered all over the buttery leather seats of her status car, the two-carat rock on her manicured engagement finger refracting only shattered hope.

I picked my way past the yellow police tape that cordoned off the murder scene, waving my notepad and press pass and standing close enough to a burly cop so that my perfume-spiked perspiration got his attention.

"Looks like an attempted carjacking that went bad," the cop said, squinting into the sun as he recited the facts. "Witness in the parking lot heard the shot, then saw an Asian kid, about fifteen, take off in a late-model Honda with two accomplices. Fifth carjacking here this month, and the first time they flubbed it. She must have resisted." The policeman punctuated his commentary with a huge yawn that bared his fleshy pink palate.

"And there's why," his partner said, watching the homicide detective retrieve a Chanel bag and pull out a matching wallet stuffed with hundred-dollar bills. "She was gonna pay cash for those dresses. Those immigrants don't believe in credit."

Nudging the Acura back onto the freeway, I headed for my office in Monrovia, a formerly white WASPy town at the foot of the San Gabriels, where the *Times* had established a bureau in the halcyon years when it was busy stretching great inky tentacles into every Southland cul-de-sac. The Valley was gritty and industrial, filled with the vitality of colliding immigrant sensibilities that were slowly squeezing out the blue- and white-collar old-timers. All the big Rim cities were morphing into Third World millennial capitals. But in the San Gabriel Valley, the future was already here. I made a mental note to ask the police reporter from the *Chinese Daily News* out for lunch on the Times Mirror tab. I had seen him again today at the mall carjacking, interviewing madly. Skinny, with bad teeth, he looked like he could use a good meal. And I could use some fresh story ideas.

"Metro wants twelve inches," Miller called out when I stepped inside the fluorescent light of the office, letting the cool air blast my hot skin.

I wrote it up, then dawdled at my desk. Until there were some arrests, it would be just another murder in the City of Angels, which on prickly summer days averaged more than one each hour. Sure, there was the sob factor about the bride mowed down as she planned her wedding, and I milked it for all it was worth. But it was more from habit than any vestigial hope that I would shock readers into doing something about it. The story of the dead woman in the car was no more gripping than that of the two-year-old toddler killed by a stray bullet in South-Central L.A. as he played in the living room. The elderly widow clubbed to death in Long Beach by the transient she hired to weed her lawn. Or the seventeen-year-old honor student in El Sereno whose single mother had changed neighborhoods to escape the gangs, only to have her son shot when his car broke down on the freeway. For reporters and cops alike, a sort of battle fatigue had set in. We had lost our ability to be shocked. My brain flickered to the next story as I ate cold sesame noodles from the plastic *bento* box I packed each morning. Then it was back in the sweltering car to interview a man named Mark Furukawa for an education story.

In a small bureau, everyone wore several hats. I also covered the schools. Frankly, the education beat didn't thrill me. Single, without kids, I couldn't relate to the obsession with SAT scores and dress codes. Now a teacher had referred me to Furukawa, hinting that the youth counselor for troubled kids at the Rainbow Coalition Center could dish up something more spicy.

Their offices were in a decaying mini-mall in El Monte, a small municipality twenty minutes away. A scattering of Asians sat in the waiting room, resignation and boredom etched across their faces. Some filled out forms, while others stared out through the grimy venetian blinds into the parking lot, ignoring the dust that clung to the metal slats and balled in the corners of the room.

Soon, I was ushered into a functional cube of an office. A framed photo of an Asian woman stood on the desk. She was clad in a vintage forties cocktail dress, with a string of pearls and a low-cut *décolletage*. Her hair was done up in long curly waves and her eyes were big and limpid.

Behind the desk were bookshelves crammed with medical journals and psychology texts and a guidebook to Los Angeles County gangs. Wedged in between was a blue-and-white can of something called "Pocari Sweat" whose cursive lettering evoked the Coca-Cola logo.

I checked it out for a while, then glanced at my watch, wondering when Furukawa would show, until a man appeared in the door. He was in his early thirties, exuding an attitude that started with his Doc Martens, traveled north up the jeans to a jutting hip, and ended with ponytailed hair tied back in a colorful Guatemalan scrunchy. A little too street for his own good, I thought, and probably a recovered drug addict or gangbanger to boot.

"Be with you in a sec," the man said, and disappeared. I had been expecting a middle-aged guy with a paunch, not some hipster near my own age. Well. I made my way back to the other side of the desk and settled into a plastic chair, feeling the fabric stick to the back of my skirt. Now I took a closer look at the girl on his desk. She smiled into the camera, her eyes shiny with love. It figured he would have a stunning girlfriend. Nobody displayed a picture like that without intending to telegraph something.

He came back into the room and we shook hands and traded business cards. I told him my predicament and asked whether he was seeing any trends with kids in the San Gabriel Valley.

"There are a million good stories out there, but the real interesting ones, I can't talk about." Furukawa lit up a cigarette. In the San Gabriel Valley, everybody still smoked, and no one asked you to put it out. That would have been going against the culture.

He bit down on a pen and thought for a moment. "I do see a lot more straight-A kids living a double life in gangs."

"In the Asian community, hhmmm. I wouldn't have thought."

"Yeah, that's the problem with us, the model minority myth."

"I didn't mean . . ."

"You're not the first. But dig, most of the kids I see are immigrants. Mom and Dad may live here now but their brains are hard-wired to the old country."

Furukawa leaned back in his chair and described kids caught between traditional Asian values and permissive American culture, and fully at home in neither. The schools sent him all their problem cases and he jive-talked them into listening, which was always the first step, he said. He spoke their language. It didn't matter that he was a *Sansei* and they were Overseas Chinese and Southeast Asian.

"No offense, but I thought the Chinese didn't like the Japanese on account of World War Two."

He appraised me anew.

"This is the New World. We all get along. They'd like Hirohito himself if he paid attention to them."

I scribbled as he spoke, filling page after page in my notebook. He saw I was lagging and stopped, puffing on his cigarette and staring out the window until I caught up. In another, more quiet corner of my mind, I wondered how often he gave this spiel to ignorant whites and how he felt about it.

Soon he seemed to grow impatient and ambled over to the bookshelf to pull something down. Now he turned and lobbed it at me.

"Catch."

I dropped my pen, extended my hands, and found myself holding the blue-and-white can of Pocari Sweat I had been staring at earlier.

"Nice reflexes. You'd be good in a pinch."

He walked back to his chair and sat down, and I wondered what kind of game we were playing.

"What the hell is Pocari Sweat?" I asked. "Do you squirt it under your arms?"

"Japanese sports drink. Think Gatorade. The name is supposed to evoke a thirst-quenching drink for top athletes."

"Who's going to want to drink something called 'sweat'?"

"Exactly." He looked pleased with himself. "No one in America. But it's only marketed in Asia. Lots of stuff has English names. Asians don't get the negative cultural connotation of the English words, so you end up with something that doesn't quite translate."

"I see." I wasn't sure where this digression was going.

"A lot of the immigrant kids I counsel are like Pocari Sweat. Caught in a culture warp they don't know how to decode. The parents are even worse off. They expect their children to show filial piety, excel in school, and come straight home when classes let out. Meanwhile the kids want to date, hang out at the mall, and yak on the phone. They want all the nice consumer things they see on American TV. So they find ways to get them. The parents only wise up when a police officer lands on their door."

"And they're not collecting for the police benevolent fund."

"You got it." Furukawa stubbed out the emphysema stick. "The kids get beaten or grounded for six months. So they run away. To a friend's house to cool off, if they're lucky. If not, to a motel room rented by some older pals from school, maybe a *dai lo*. Where they can drink and party with their girlfriends. And when the money runs out, it's easy to get more. The *dai los* always have work."

"A *dai* what?"

"That's Chinese for older brother. It's a gang term. The *dai lo* recruits younger kids into gangs. Shows them a good time. Takes them out to a karaoke bar when they're underage and buys 'em drinks. Drives them around in a fast car. The good life. It's very seductive when you're fifteen. And these kids feel that once they've left home and disgraced their parents, they can never go back."

He might have been talking about the weather, or how his car needed gas. To him, this was mundane, everyday stuff. To me it was a glimpse into a suburban badland I hadn't considered before.

"What do you mean, there's always work to do?"

"Muscle at the local brothels. Drug runners. Carjackings. You name it," Furukawa shrugged. "One homie told me he gets a thousand for each Mercedes he delivers."

"Carjackings? I was out on one of those today. But it got messy," I spoke slowly. "Young bride who'll never see her honeymoon night. It'll be on the news tonight."

Furukawa winced.

"Can you introduce me to some of these kids?" I tried to keep the hope out of my voice.

"Afraid not, darling."

"Why not? Now that you've told me." I was miffed.

"They're minors. There are all sorts of privacy issues. And these are fucked-up kids. They don't need any more distraction in their lives."

"Yeah, well."

It was a tantalizing lead, but I needed his help to pursue it.

"Wait a minute," I said, "I thought the Vietnamese were the ones who joined gangs. A society brutalized by war, years in internment camps, families torn apart and killed . . ."

"Yeah, they sure do. But they ain't flying solo. You got Cambodians, Filipinos, Samoans, Overseas Chinese. It's the Chinese usually call the shots. Local offshoots of the Hong Kong triads: White Crane, Dragon Claw, Black Hand. They're equal-opportunity employers," he grinned. "And unlike your black and Latino gangs, they don't advertise it with baggy clothing or shaved heads. Your typical Asian gang member dresses preppy. Neat and clean-cut. Sometimes they're even A-students. Total double life, like I was saying. But sooner or later something cracks."

Yeah, like today in the shopping center, I thought. I looked out the window, where the sky was streaked with red and purple.

"This could be a really good story," I told him. "But I would need to meet some kids, then use their stories to illustrate the larger trend."

His eyes swiveled from me to the manila files piled atop his desk, then back to me. He put his hand on the top file, then shook his head.

"I just finished telling you that these are screwed-up kids. And I know that ultimately, Eve Diamond, you don't give a rat's ass about the slash marks on their wrists or the gang rape they suffered at age thirteen. You just want the lurid details. Then after you've gotten them all heated up reliving it, you'll toss the mess back into my lap and expect me to fix it."

"That's why you're a totally *simpatico* counselor and I'm a heartless reporter." I tossed back the can of Pocari Sweat. With an almost imperceptible flick of the wrist, he extended one hand and caught it.

"Of course we'd change their names. We're not intrusive like TV. Think how a *Times* story would get people talking. The Board of Supes might even cough up extra funding." I leaned forward and locked eyes with him. "I can see you're protective about your kids, Mark. They're lucky to have you on their side. But for the record, we're not all automatons."

I stood up.

He stared at me with a look I couldn't decipher.

"Drink?" he said finally. "I know a great Italian place."

"Italian?" I said in mock-horror. "The least you could do after insulting me is offer to take me to a sushi bar you know tucked away in one of these awful strip malls."

"Not too many of those left on this side of town," he sighed. "They've all moved west and gone uptown. Besides, what you got against Italian?"

"Nothing. I just have this thing for *sake*."

He considered this.

Suddenly nervous, I rushed in to break the silence.

"Maybe some other time. You probably have to meet your girlfriend."

"My girlfriend?"

"I pointed to the photo on his desk. "I couldn't help noticing. She looks just like Gong Li."

He laughed. "My mother, who is Japanese, by the way, not Chinese, will be flattered."

"That's your mother?" I hoped my voice didn't show relief.

"Yes. Right after she got married. My father took the photo."

"Sorry," I stuttered. "I just assumed that since it was on your desk . . ."

He was staring at me again. I knew I was turning crimson. I hadn't meant to get all personal. Now he would think I was nosy as well as a heartless exploiter of damaged kids.

"Don't be," he said. "It's there for a reason. There's a lot of transference in my line of work. Some of these teenage girls, they're really searching for their lost daddies but they'll settle for me. So I put Mom here to keep an eye on things. I've found she wards off the weirder stuff."

Now I was doubly intrigued. And oddly ecstatic that he didn't have a girlfriend. At least not one whose picture he put on his desk.

He was all business as he showed me the door.

CHAPTER 2

Unlocking the security gate to my apartment, I could already hear Violetta's dog bounding up the back stairs. I walked through the long hallway and opened the screen door in back. The collie trotted in and began cavorting around the room, whinnying in ecstatic canine song.

"Bon Jovi," I said, as the animal wagged its plume of a tail. "What a goofy name for a dog."

But he was good company and didn't ask for much in return, except for an occasional walk. Strolling past the ramshackle bungalows and crumbling Spanish duplexes of my neighborhood, I always hesitated to call for Bon Jovi when he strayed, lest my neighbors hear and shudder at my bad musical taste, when in reality the fault lay with Violetta, my Hungarian landlady who lived downstairs. Having escaped from communism, Violetta was enamored of all things American.

I poured a glass of red wine into a tumbler with dried sediment at the bottom and walked back out to the porch, where I dropped into the easy chair and surveyed downtown Los Angeles. In the velvety summer air, the towers of downtown sparkled in brilliant reds, blues, and yellows, set off against the black sky like a computer circuit board. It was a million-buck view for $650 a month. So what if you heard gunshots every night and then twenty minutes later, the malevolent buzzsaw of police helicopters swooping down with searchlights, so loud that it seemed they would burst through your window. Guns and choppers, that was just L.A. Or my slice of it, anyway.

Drifting back into the kitchen, I tore open a bag of chips, opened some black bean dip, and poured another glass of wine. I ate and drank at the counter, leaning my belly against the rough Mexican tile, thinking absentmindedly that it was time to start eating healthy.

In the bathroom mirror, I peered at my face. I thought I spied a wrinkle. Big pores, that was for sure. A pale, washed-out face framed by unruly red hair. But not bad for twenty-nine. That poor young bride today, she wasn't even twenty, and now her life was over, snuffed out in a random moment. In that parking lot, victim and assailant had moved toward each other in a macabre dance, one unwitting, her mind on place settings and airline tickets, the other calculating and predatory, intent on the car, the two drawing closer and closer until they collided in explosive violence. Was it preordained? What if Marina Lu had stopped to fill up with gas first? Or sent her sister on the errand, a sister who drove a less flashy car? If I thought about it too much, I'd take to my bed for good. I pictured myself with books scattered across the comforter, face down with their spines open the way the nuns told me never to do. They would walk around, picking them up and closing them with a disapproving snap. Well, I was a big girl now. I would read as I damn well pleased.

With a third glass of wine in hand, I grabbed my book and walked back out onto the porch, stretching out on the chaise lounge. Finally, thank God, a breeze. Summer didn't really start in Los Angeles until August and then often lingered into October. Angling my paperback so the light from the porch lamp fell onto the typed page, I was soon engrossed in *Red Azalea*, a novel about the Chinese Cultural Revolution that I had picked up at the secondhand bookstore. By ten o'clock, when the fat full moon shone luminous overhead, I was doing back-breaking labor on the South China Sea with Anchee Min, singing Madame Mao's revolutionary operas. By eleven, I was asleep.

The alarm woke me up 5:30 A.M. I pulled on a T-shirt and shorts, then boiled water for a cup of instant coffee. With milk. Squinting, I wriggled a Fig Newton free of its plastic casing and bit down, savoring how it yielded to my teeth and dissolved on my tongue amid pools of hot coffee. I took a few more gulps. There. An almost imperceptible adjustment of mood. A quiet flow of wakefulness. I opened my eyes. Much better.

When I swung open the back door, Bon Jovi was waiting to go. He knew the drill, even if I forgot it half the mornings and left him peering mournfully through the window, smudging the pane with his wet nose. The cool air seeped through the folds of my clothes. I liked running in the dawn, clasping tight to Bon Jovi's leash as he trotted alongside me. In summer too, but especially in the winter, when it was so cold I had to go at a fast clip just to get warm. By the time my body started generating heat, I was already into the rhythm, pumping on cruise control. At those times, I lapsed into a fugue state, my mind thousands of miles away, sailing serenely along as my legs traversed steep hills, snapping back into consciousness only when I hit an intersection and saw cars coming at me.

Now, my old tennis shoes slap-slapping the asphalt with each step, I was hyper-aware. I swore I could smell figs ripening on a gnarled tree at the empty corner lot. The anise plants stood like pale green feathers at attention, infusing the air with the tantalizing aroma of licorice. It made me think of Macao, that island off the China coast, near bustling Hong Kong but its sleepy opposite. I had been there with Tim. We would sit in a cafe and pour Pernod into tall glasses of iced water. The water would turn milky when you added the clear, colorless liquid. One could pretend it was absinthe. Tim Waters was a tall boy with curly brown hair and a Southern drawl. Later, we would make love in a hotel room on the top floor that was barely big enough for a double bed, where the eaves came down to the floor and a church bell pealed out the hours we lay entwined.

There was no more Macao. There was no more boy with curly hair. I saw a skunk nosing in the trash. It waddled off as I approached, and I bellowed out a stern "no" to take my mind off Tim and remind Bon Jovi that skunks were off limits. Crossing Glendale Boulevard, I turned to face downtown. The morning freeway traffic was starting, a dull white wall of noise as the city's workers began their daily pilgrimage to the downtown hives. Commodity brokers were already at their desks, scanning their tickers as the New York stock markets opened. Yawning Japanese businessmen on the West Coast were taking advantage of the Tokyo slumber to send memos and faxes to their counterparts across the Pacific. The flower and produce markets were halfway through their day, while the garment workers in the decayed tenements south of downtown hadn't started theirs yet. Bon Jovi whined anxiously. I spun on my rubber toe and skipped down the stone staircase that led to the Silverlake Reservoir. It was a man-made lake that dated to the 1920s, when the growing population of Los Angeles had needed new supplies of drinking water. Surrounded by green parkland and old houses, the lake was calm at this hour, a glistening surface you could almost skate across. The sky was purple and orange now, the sun rising like a ball of fire behind the eucalyptus trees. It soothed me to look down at the lake. I never tired of its depths, which changed color with the light, at times cerulean, then dark green, violet in the dusk, or violently black before a storm. Westsiders had the beach and better air, but over here on the Eastside, folks had their own little patch of blue, and it cost hundreds of thousands of dollars less per lot. The Silverlake Reservoir was the poor man's ocean. It even drew the occasional seagull that circled in confusion, looking for flying fish. A pity they had put a chain-link fence around it in the 1970s, but people had started throwing in trash and wading in on hot days. So now all the joggers and strollers had to hug the fence or take their chances on the cracked sidewalks, whose ancient concrete had long ago ruptured and split as tree roots pushed relentlessly through the soil.

The exercise hounds were doing their three-mile treadmill around the lake. Elderly Japanese couples walked briskly. A wiry Latino with a gang tattoo on his neck sprinted with head held high, bobbing to the beat of his Walkman. A blonde with a fluorescent running bra jiggled past, matching scalloped shorts riding way up her thigh. They walked, jogged, and ran, in pairs or alone. They pushed baby strollers and held tight to leashes. They carried weights, plastic water bottles, and cotton towels to mop up the excess sweat. For some, this was a daily routine. Others looked as though they had just rolled out of bed that morning and vowed to get in shape. I fit neither of these categories. I ran when I felt like it.

On the freeway two hours later, I felt the blood surge through my veins, felt it delivered in hot, sharp jolts to my brain. I breathed in deeply. Freshly showered and fed, I was alert to all possibilities, yet serene like the lake. Whatever mayhem happened in the city today, I could take it.

CHAPTER 3

The office was full when I arrived and the coffee was gone. My good mood evaporated as I thought about what lay ahead—visiting Marina Lu's grieving parents. In J-school, they had taught me that distraught families found it cathartic to bare their souls to a complete stranger. It was modern-day therapy for our violent age. Wouldn't Mom and Dad like to tell the public what a good kid Johnny was, to haul out his school yearbook and awards, to elaborate on the tragedy of his being gunned down/drowned/blown up before his life had barely started?

As a rookie I had risen to the challenge, relishing my skill at getting families to open up, a stealth psychologist who won their trust with my ponytail and freckle-faced demeanor. I had lost the stomach for it. But the more I loathed it, the better I got, sitting primly on some suburban floral sofa, knees and ankles together, scribbling into a notebook on my lap and cooing condolence at the appropriate moments while thinking how in their place, I would have shouted "Go fuck yourself!" and slammed the door hard. But they never did. Instead, they opened the door and murmured 'Please come in' and I did, fastening like a vampire on the sad details of their personal lives.

The Lus lived at 327 Elm Street in San Marino. That wasn't surprising. A bastion of old-money WASPdom, San Marino's leafy exclusivity was now drawing wealthy Chinese who chased the American dream of big homes, good schools, and low crime with as much fervor as any native. In the last decade, the city had gone from all white to half Asian. For years they had refused to let in Catholics, Jews, blacks, and people with accents. Now they were reaping the harvest of their own conservative social politics.

As I neared my destination, the homes grew bigger, the yards more lush with mature trees whose names adorned the streets: Maple, Elm, and Chestnut. I saw Mediterranean Revival homes, Tudor, California Craftsman, and 1950s *moderne*, all in exquisite repair unlike my own neighborhood. I didn't see anyone playing ball or tag on those lawns green as AstroTurf, hushed as a church. There was only the occasional Latino gardener, genuflecting over a flowering shrub.

The Lu family had opted for Tudor. In the driveway of their mansion stood a white, late-model Mercedes with gold trim. I bet *it* had a working air-conditioner. I parked on the deserted street and walked up the long brick pathway. I took my time, letting my surroundings wash over me, and noticing a huge elm tree near the front door that someone had hacked to a barren stump. Its trunk was wide as my car and gnarled like an elephant. From the clumps of earth and spade marks around its base, it looked like the workers would be back soon to finish the job.

So the family believed in *feng shui*, I thought. That means Overseas Chinese, not Chinese-American. I had written about pitched cultural battles between old-time whites and Chinese immigrants here. Because *feng shui* placed great importance on the alignment of objects to create a positive energy flow, or *chi*, the first thing the immigrants often did after moving in was to uproot gracious, 100-year-old trees near the front door because they blocked the beneficial *chi* that brought health and prosperity to the family. This butchery of the local flora incensed the lily-white brigade, who hadn't wanted a bunch of Asians moving into their neighborhood in the first place.

At the front door, I grasped the heavy iron clapper and brought it down hard on the wood, then stepped back to wait, making sure my notebook nestled in my purse. I didn't want to scare them off right away by waving it in their teary faces.

From the corner of my eye, I saw a curtain flutter in the nearby window. A moment later, the door was opened by a tall Chinese man in a sleek, double-breasted charcoal suit. His broad shoulders filled the frame.

"Yes?"

I introduced myself and told him I was working on a story about the tragedy. "We've already spoken with the police, but I'd like to talk to some family members. Would you be her father?"

I smiled tremulously, trying to convey the proper blend of sorrow for the most unfortunate tragedy and duty that compelled me to stand stuttering like an idiot on their doorstep. It occurred to me that Mr. Lu might not speak English.

Behind his gold-rimmed glasses, the man didn't blink. I pegged him at about fifty-five. Smooth-shaven, with graying streaks in his thick black hair that he combed straight back from a high forehead. Rolex on a hairless wrist. I averted my eyes so as not to stare, using the opportunity to check out his shoes. Smooth, supple ebony leather with tiny, detailed stitching marked them as expensive.

"I'm her father."

The voice spoke in British English. I waited. Most people fear silence more than anything and will rush to fill the vacuum, saying things they don't mean or will later regret, valuable things for my newspaper.

But Mr. Lu wasn't biting.

After forty-five seconds, I cleared my throat and continued.

"I know this is a very difficult time for you right now. And you have my deepest condolences. But I would like to ask you a few questions."

Mr. Lu hesitated and gripped the door handle more tightly, as if fighting a private battle with himself. Then his big shoulders rolled back and relaxed. I waited to see which side had won.

"Come in," he said finally, stepping back from the door.

He ushered me through a marble foyer and into a sunken living room laid with white Berber carpet. I sat at the edge of a white brocade sofa and pulled out my notepad and Bic pen while I took inventory. On one wall hung an antique Chinese scroll behind glass. An Impressionist seascape in gilt frame stood watch over the formal dining room and I wondered whether I ought to recognize the artist's name. The coffee table was cut from a single slab of etched glass, delicately balanced over carved Greek pillars. Atop it stood a pale green vase from which a single flower drooped blood-orange petals. The place was decorated with taste and money, but it had the sterile feel of a model home, I thought, one that was meant to be photographed, not lived in.

"Will Mrs. Lu be joining us?" I asked brightly.

"Unfortunately, Mrs. Lu was visiting her parents in Hong Kong when the news came. She is en route now."

I knew he wasn't taken in by my tactics. While I had been surveying his home, Mr. Lu had been studying me, observing the hammered silver earrings, vintage skirt, natural leather purse, sensible shoes. Perhaps he was reassured that I posed no threat to him, with my designerless clothes and rough-hewn jewelry. My smiles and hesitancy. He was a power broker, used to wielding control. I yielded it to him.

"What do you want to know?" Mr. Lu asked, so quietly that I had to lean forward.

I started with general questions, working my way methodically to the specifics. That was another journalism trick. First throw them some softballs. Then, when they're all relaxed and opened up, smile sweetly and go for the kill. Mr. Lu's first name was Reginald. He was a Hong Kong banker who had come to California ten years ago to scout out new business opportunities for his employer. After criss-crossing the Pacific for several years, Reginald Lu had brought his family over with him. He consulted with friends and relatives already in the United States, then bought in San Marino, whose bucolic wealth and spaciousness beckoned as the antithesis of Hong Kong's vertical claustrophobia.

The Lus wanted their two children to attend high school here because they liked the U.S. educational system and had heard that San Marino students scored high on standardized tests. Plus 98 percent of the district graduates went on to college. Mr. Lu wasn't a perfectionist who wanted success for its own sake though. He knew American high schools were less cutthroat than back home. The children would have a better chance of getting into a good American university. Marina had already been accepted into UC Berkeley, Mr. Lu said proudly. She had been a quiet, intense girl who played the violin and had scored a perfect 800 on her English SAT. Yet she was equally fluent in Cantonese and wrote classical poetry she copied into a journal she rarely showed anybody.

"Did the police ask to see the journal?" I asked.

An imperceptible pause. Then, "No, I'm not aware that they did. Why would they?"

"You're right. There would be no reason." I moved quickly onto another topic, making a mental note about the journal.

"Tell me about her fiancé."

Michael Ho was twenty-four, a friend of the family. The parents had known each other for decades. Michael worked for Lu's bank.

"What's he like?"

Reginald Lu flexed his long, blunt fingers.

"I'd rather not get into that," he said. "I don't see what such personal details have to do with your story. He is a fine young man we would have welcomed into our family."

"Well, it just seems so tragic that she was killed while planning her wedding. I wanted to know a little more about him."

Again, "I don't see how that's relevant."

Segueing into something less threatening, I asked about his business in America. Early on, he had realized that all those new immigrants would need somewhere to put their money but that they wouldn't trust American banks. So he started his own. I later learned that Golden Pacific Bank catered almost exclusively to the Overseas Chinese, offering Mandarin and Cantonese-speaking tellers, weekend service, and flexible loans. It drew new business quickly through word of mouth in the insular Chinese community. Lu also exploited a gap in knowledge between American and Chinese culture. Where U.S. banks were loathe to make business loans to Asian immigrants who lacked equity or collateral, Lu loaned like crazy, knowing his customers would work three times as hard as a Westerner to pay off the loans, since defaulting would mean a loss of face. He was right.

Today, Golden Pacific Bank had $800 million in deposits and was a heavy hitter in the Chinese Chamber of Commerce. Lu himself judged the Chinatown Beauty Pageant each year.

Nose in my notebook, I wondered if he took his pick of the prettiest contestants. I didn't doubt he had mistresses. Rich, powerful men usually did. Nothing serious. Very discreet. Exquisite, porcelain-skinned Chinese women younger than his dead daughter. Afternoons at anony-mous hotels, between board meetings. Precious tokens of affection that fit easily into scented female palms. I imagined that beneath the proper exterior hid a man who licked mounds of black caviar off the tan, flat tummies of his girls. I wondered how it would feel to have him spoon out cold caviar as I lay outstretched. I glanced up, afraid he had divined my thoughts, but he was explaining details about global financ-ing. This is the way my mind works after eight months of sleeping alone, I thought with chagrin. And I don't even like older men.

"Mr. Lu, is it usual in Chinese culture for girls to get married at such a young age? I was under the impression that most young women finish college first."

"That's true, but it was a love match and we wanted our daughter to be happy. We were also greatly pleased when she and Michael drew closer, as our families were already linked by commerce. Michael would have made a fine son-in-law. Age is not always important. And now, Miss Diamond, if you're through . . ."

Mr. Lu stood up. The interview was over.

As he shut the door behind me, I felt Mr. Lu watching again from the window but didn't look back. I had his business card and a promise that I could call him if I had any more questions. It was time to find out what Marina Lu, A-student, was like once she left her parents' house each morning.

But I had timed it wrong. Classes were still in session at San Marino High and no students loitered outside. It must be weird to get married barely out of high school, I thought.

As I drove back to the office, I had another idea. If Marina Lu was picking out bridesmaid dresses and making all those wedding arrange-ments you have to do months ahead of time, why wasn't her mother at home helping her? What could she be doing in Hong Kong that was so important? Or was Mrs. Lu perhaps cloistered in an upstairs bedroom, too red-eyed to come down and talk to a reporter? Was Mr. Lu trying to save face with a little white lie? Perhaps that's all there was to it.

The Lavender Latina was at her desk, delicately forking in mouthfuls of smoked salmon penne from a Tupperware container as she flipped through the latest issue of the *Advocate*. Luz Beltran was one of the few openly gay female journalists in the newsroom.

"Hot enough out there for you?" she grinned, exposing a mouthful of big, straight white teeth like you see in a toothpaste commercial. Except that right now, she had a fleck of basil stuck on her eyetooth.

"Luz, go like this," I pantomimed, scraping my tooth with my nail. "You have *hierbas* in your *dientes*."

Luz grimaced and complied.

"Now that I've saved you from ridicule for the rest of the afternoon, will you do me a favor? I need a ride home one day this week. I have to get the A/C fixed in my car or I'm gonna go postal and you'll end up writing about me. They want to keep the car overnight."

"Sure," said Luz, who passed just blocks from my house on her way home to the Fairfax District. We often did each other commuting favors; it was common courtesy in this city where cars were more important than apartments and often served as one in a pinch.

"So. How's your love life?" she asked. "Finally getting over Tim?"

"Maybe. You know Mark Furukawa? He counsels delinquents at the Rainbow Coalition Center. He kind of flips my skirt. I'm thinking of having a drink with him. This morning, I found myself fantasizing about a fifty-five-year-old guy I was interviewing, for God's sake. Very inappropriate considering his daughter just got offed in that carjacking. If he only knew what I was thinking."

I giggled. I wondered if other people were able to compartmentalize their lives so that things didn't seep from one dimension to another at the most disconcerting times.

Luz stabbed at her penne.

"I've run into Mark on stories, and I have one word for you on that action. Player. He's a little too cool for his own good."

"But everyone says the kids worship him."

"Great, so he's got a fan club of fifteen-year-old hoodlums who think he's God. What happens when you don't worship his hipster ass like they do?"

"I would hope he could differentiate between his clients and a woman he sees after hours," I said stiffly.

"You would hope," Luz echoed.

A jingle of keys interrupted us. Then an angry sputtering.

"What do you mean he's not in his office yet? He's a city employee, isn't he? I'm going to call back in fifteen minutes, and in the meantime, please leave a message on his desk that Trevor Fingerhaven of the *Los Angeles Times* is looking for him. F-I-N-G-E-R-H-A-V-E-N. That's right."

Slapping his cell phone shut in a dramatic gesture, Trevor Fingerhaven swept imperiously past and eased into his desk with a soft grunt.

"It's a fuckin' scandal, if they think they can get away with that," Trevor muttered. "Because they can't. I'm on to them. Right."

Luz stuck her tongue out at me. I made a quick gagging motion. So much for any kind of personal conversation. Trevor was a former *New York Post* reporter who had recently transferred into the bureau. Supposedly he had won some big muckraking prize that had been his passport into the *Times*. Weaned on the scandal sheets of his hometown, Trevor saw conspiracies everywhere he looked and interrogated sources at full volume so none of us could concentrate on our own stories. He was tall and stooped and cadaverous, which gave him the look of a municipal streetlight, and he was messy in a schoolboy fashion that was extremely unbecoming as he approached middle age. Despite having a wife and two kids, he appeared to spend all his free time snouting around the edges of corruption, attending council meetings on his own time, lugging home stacks of government documents, and warning us that he was very, very close to cracking a huge and far-reaching "fuckin' scandal."

It rarely came to pass. But occasionally Trevor's subterranean rootings paid off and he unearthed a modest journalistic truffle. Then, to his great dismay, the story would be pried out of his jaws and handed to a Metro hotshot to pursue. Trevor accepted this indignity with little grumbling, as if he knew his limitations. He certainly knew everyone else's, because he was a notorious eavesdropper, sopping up tidbits of intelligence to stash for later use. He also inserted himself into every conversation. No matter what the subject, Trevor was an expert or knew exactly whom to call for the real story.

"Hey, I've been meaning to tell you about this piece I read in *Psychology Today*," Luz said and winked.

"It describes the different ways men and women process language. Linguists say that when a woman doesn't know the answer to a question, she'll say so. But men have an answer for everything. They might know nothing about the mating rituals of Saharan camels, but they'll hold forth for hours. The author says it's because men perceive questions as challenges, whereas women see them as straight inquiries for information."

I inclined my head to the back of the room. "I know a few men like that."

Trevor, who had grown quiet in his cubicle and was obviously eavesdropping, couldn't resist. Soon he ambled over, coffee cup in hand, on the pretext of visiting the kitchen. He stopped before us.

"I'll tell you something about that theory," Trevor smirked. "It's absolutely without merit. A good friend of mine has researched the subject. He teaches psychology at the University of Florida. We've had long discussions on the topic. If you want, I can give you his number and you can call him."

Luz turned to me and burst into laughter.

"What did I tell you."

"Ladies, I'm just trying to help." He gave us a hurt look, then ambled off.

We looked at each other. To muffle the belly laugh that was coming, I grabbed a tissue and blew my nose hard. Luz stuffed her mouth with penne. At 6 P.M., when we left, Trevor was still braying into the phone.

That evening, I cleared off a week's worth of dishes from my kitchen table while Bon Jovi peered in from the back porch, drawn by the scraping sounds of silverware against ceramic plates. "Come on in, boy," I said, and he rustled past my legs and settled with a soft moan onto the kitchen tile, placing himself strategically between table and sink. Still standing in the doorway, I watched an owl wing its way across the night sky then settle into a nearby tree and hoot, mournful and solitary. I listened, perched on the edge of a wilderness within sight of downtown.

Much later, after I had fed the dog all the stale cheese and crackers and spinach quiche in my fridge and let him out, I was jolted awake by another noise, one that always unnerved me. The coyotes were hunting again. By day they burrowed into steep hillside lots, biding their time in the bleached landscape. But at night they came down and loped along the asphalt streets, reclaiming their turf as the town slept. Driving home late once after an interminable city council meeting, I had surprised a big brute in my headlights. He stared solemnly at me, then disappeared into thin air. The first time I dismissed it as a hallucination brought on by lack of sleep. But another night while jogging, I had seen a car approach and a dun thing on four legs that raced madly ahead of the light, diving into a hedge just as the car crested the hill. It looked like a beige dog, but no dog moved that fast or was that silent.

The howls grew louder and more urgent now. The coyotes yipped excitedly and my heart raced. I pulled up the blankets and shivered, despite the heat. Somewhere in the dark, a small animal howled in terror, gave a few yelps and then was still. I imagined a dog caught unawares, or a cat slinking along nocturnally in pursuit of mice, only to find itself cornered by gleaming eyes, slathering jaws. What terror must grip any animal at such a sight.

CHAPTER 4

I t was slow in the newsroom the next morning. Police had no suspects yet on the Lu carjacking murder. School officials weren't
returning my phone calls. So I drove out to San Marino High to
interview classmates of Marina Lu.

I had timed it right. School was out and the campus was clotted with
kids. I strolled onto its immaculate grounds, trying to walk like I fit in.
An English teacher, maybe? The debate coach? I didn't want some
campus security guard strong-arming me off private property. If they
made me go to the principal's office to get permission first, I was sunk.
Those administrators always clammed up tight, invoking confidentiality of school records and reminding me it was against the law to interview juveniles without their parents' permission.

Hesitating before a group of Caucasian boys, I considered that this
wasn't the best place to start. But I flashed my reporter's pass anyway
and began asking questions. They might be more gabby than the Chinese students. Teenage boys always talked to me, since by now, I had
developed the bravura sorely lacking during my own high school years.
They were on their way out to the alley to smoke a cigarette, so I joined
them.

"Are we going to be like, on TV?" asked a boy with a closely shaved
head.

"No, but you might be in the *Times* tomorrow. I'm a newspaper reporter, not a TV reporter. No cameras, see?"

"Awwh, too bad," said a second teen, who wore a Pendleton shirt in the 102-degree weather.

I considered the generation gap between us. Twelve years, but they might as well be light-years. These kids didn't read the paper. No one their age did. For them, nothing was real unless they saw it live on TV. Like the freeway chase after the white Bronco.

"You heard about the carjacking murder of your classmate, Marina Lu? Did you know her? What was she like?"

The boys fell silent. Adolescents could be so tongue-tied at first. It was as though no one ever asked them what they thought, unless it was for a test. They were usually so flattered at being treated like adults that once you got them going, they wouldn't shut up. But getting them started was going to take some prodding.

"So. Was she cute?"

A slow grin crossed Pendleton's pimpled face.

"She was a fox. She always wore real stylish clothes and had long straight black hair down to her butt. But she didn't talk much to us. She was quiet. Studied a lot. I think her parents were from China."

"Did she have a lot of friends? Boyfriends?"

"She was a loner. Sean here thought she was cute. He asked her out once. You did so. You're just mad 'cuz she iced you. She had too much class for you. When I was a freshman, we had some Chinese kids in class. The boys were nerds and so were the girls. The races kept to themselves. Their girls weren't babe material, if you know what I mean. Then the Asian girls started going out for cheerleader and prom queen. All of a sudden, they're cool. A lot of them have white boyfriends. But not Marina. I think maybe she had a Chinese boyfriend."

"OK, guys, thanks a lot." It was clear they didn't know any more.

I moved off, stalking better prospects. Two Asian girls in halter tops and bell-bottom jeans with ragged edges. Tall and slender, with plum brandy lipstick accentuating full lips. Almond eyes rimmed with heavy black liner. I could see the attraction. The robust American blondes looked so insipid by comparison.

"Did you know Marina Lu?"

"We were friends," said the girl with the white halter top. It set off her copper skin. There was no fat on her midriff.

I caught something in her inflection.

"Were? You mean, right up until she was killed?"

"No, we had drifted apart. We didn't have as many things in common anymore."

"How so?"

"I hope you're not here to dig up dirt on Marina," said the other girl, who wore a blue halter with big yellow sunflowers and carried an AP physics textbook. "Because she was a good person."

"Tell me."

"She tried so hard to please her parents. She called them every day. She got straight A's. She took every honors class San Marino offered."

"What do you mean she called them every day?"

Sunflower halter, whose name was Jenny, started to speak. Her friend jabbed her in the ribs.

"I don't care anymore, Alison, she's dead. And I wonder whether this would have happened if her parents had been around more."

Jenny looked away, focusing on a building in the distance.

"Her parents traveled a lot for business."

"Yeah, I know. I just talked to her father. He founded some Asian-American bank."

"That was only one of his businesses," Jenny said. "He spends most of his time in Hong Kong. Marina said he's doing joint ventures in China now because that's where the money is. He would fly into L.A. every four months to see her and check up on Golden Pacific Bank. But he's got someone else running it now, so he doesn't need to live here anymore. Marina told me that mostly, they just talk on the phone from Hong Kong, and ask her what she and Colin ate for dinner and if everything was OK. Colin's her little brother, he's only fourteen, and she took care of him. Marina hasn't seen her mom in more than a year. We used to think she was lucky, because her mom wasn't there to bug her. But it was hard on her. She missed her parents. When my mom grounded me, Marina told me she was jealous. She wanted someone to tell her what to do. She got tired of being a grown-up all the time."

I felt dizzy from the heat. I recalled what Mark Furukawa had told me. It also explained why the mother of the dead girl was in Hong

Kong. Parachute kids: I remembered hearing the term. The kids lived here alone or with a housekeeper, attending fancy schools and home-steading the pricey real estate, while their parents stayed home in Asia. The Lus had been caught with their parachuting pants down. Mr. Lu had probably grabbed the first red-eye, winging eastward to start the damage control. It was still a freak murder of the wrong-place, wrong-time variety, but it would reflect poorly on the Lus if word got out that their pretty little daughter had been keeping house all alone in ritzy San Marino, with only a housekeeper and her fourteen-year-old brother for company.

"What about Marina's fiancé?" I tried to sound nonchalant. "What kind of a guy was he?"

"You mean Michael?" asked Alison, who had decided to talk to me after all.

"We didn't know him," Jenny added.

"Remember when I told you that we drifted apart. Michael was part of that. He was older. He took her out places late at night."

"He picked her up from school sometimes. She would get into his car. It was a black Jag."

"I think she outgrew us," Alison said.

"I think that since her parents wanted her to live on her own, she decided to be as adult as she possibly could," said Jenny.

"When maybe what she really wanted was someone to draw the line for her," Alison added.

"It wasn't like she ever did anything bad," Jenny said. "She always kept up her grades. That was very important to her. She was so smart. She got into Berkeley. I only got into Irvine."

At the curb, a Volvo pulled up. Inside was a suburban-looking Chi-nese mom in a sweatshirt.

"We have to go," they announced, already walking toward the wait-ing vehicle.

"Tell me more about parachute kids," I said, staring across the table into the eyes of a discomfited Mark Furukawa.

Mark tore open his package of chopsticks and began rubbing the long, thin pieces of wood against each other. We had settled on Islamic Chinese cuisine, whose most renowned purveyors had a restaurant smack in the middle of San Gabriel Village Square. If I looked out the tinted window, I could see the parking spot where Marina Lu had been murdered. Maybe even some bloodstained asphalt. Bustling crowds filled the shopping center as if nothing had happened. I heard Mark whittling away with his chopsticks and it reminded me of a grasshopper rubbing its legs together.

"Sure," Mark said. "But why so intense? What's up with you?"

I had called him, breathless, when I got back to the office, leaving five messages until he finally returned my call when I had already given up and packed my bag to go home.

"I was in court all day. Didn't even eat lunch," he said.

"Well, then, how about dinner? It's on Otis."

Otis was Otis Chandler, one of the scions of the *Times* ruling family that had molded the newspaper almost a century ago and still held a large chunk of the voting stock.

"That would be fine. Let me check my calendar and see how this week looks."

Was he being deliberately dense? "How does tonight look, Mark?"

"To-night. Well, um . . ."

I was enjoying this. Smooth-talking Mark was at a loss for words. And I could be as assertive as I wanted. He was just a source with information I needed.

"I guess I'm free tonight," Mark said, regaining his off-kilter poise.

So here we were. There was no pork or booze on the menu. Just heaps of lamb and seafood and fresh-baked bread studded with scallions and encrusted with a layer of toasted sesame seeds. I would have liked a glass of wine; it would have put me more at ease. I was at my most charming and witty after one glass of wine, in the rosy flush of anticipating the second. But I was working tonight. And I drank too much anyway.

"Remember the carjacking story I mentioned the other day? It happened right here in San Gabriel. The victim's name was Marina Lu and she was a parachute kid," I said.

"Really? I thought I read that she lived with her parents in San Marino."

"I went to the high school today and talked to her friends. They said Mom and Pops flew in a couple times a year to check on the kiddies.

They probably left the rest to a housekeeper who doesn't speak English."

Mark whistled long and low. The waitress, thinking she was being summoned, scurried over, but Mark waved her away absentmindedly with his chopsticks.

"Apparently she was a good kid, but she ran with a fast boyfriend. The fiancé. He picked her up after school in his Jag. He was twenty-four. I'm not saying he murdered her but she was no sheltered little Chinese girl."

"Here's the thing with parachute kids," Mark said. "They're emotionally adrift because their parents aren't around, but they can't talk about it because it's illegal for kids to live alone here, they'd get yanked out of school and shipped home. So you've got loneliness, abandonment, lack of parental supervision, and resentment tacked on to the usual adolescent problems, and a terrible pressure builds up inside. Many of them internalize it, focus on school, and do OK. At least so far as the outside world can see. But when they lose it, watch out."

"So what do you think happened with Marina?"

"What do the cops think?"

"No criminal record. A-plus student. Tragedy. The usual. I know the schools bring in shrinks to talk to the kids when something heavy goes down and kids say interesting things. Especially to you, since you're such a pro."

Mark smiled crookedly at me. It was a smile that told me, I am wise to your ways and will not be taken in by you. But I will play along for the sake of both our dinners.

"Even if I *were* counseling anybody involved with this case, I couldn't talk about it."

"Oh yeah, I forgot."

When I pulled out my corporate credit card to pay for dinner an hour later, I watched him from beneath lidded eyes. Was he one of those macho men who squirmed when a woman reached for the bill? But Mark was busy staring at the restaurant hostess, who wore a long white robe and a modified *hijab* wrapped under her chin, like a nun's wimple. She was talking on a cellular phone.

He insisted on walking me out to the car. I didn't mind. The night was balmy. Neon signs in Chinese lit up the parking lot. I smelled sesame oil and expensive perfume. This is what Hong Kong must be like, I thought, and imagined Marina Lu skipping through the streets in her schoolgirl uniform, then later hurtling through international airspace to a new life in America. I pictured her childhood abode in Hong Kong, a walled compound high atop Victoria Peak overlooking the bay, the air always humid with rain, and Mainland China a stone's throw away, waiting patiently to reabsorb its errant colony. I saw the wisdom in preparing an escape route, as the Lus had done. Plant roots on both sides of the Pacific and see which flowers best.

"Ever been to Asia?" I asked, leaning against the warm metal of my car. A private security patrol car cruised by, checking out people who loitered among the rows of Benzes and Lexuses. The rent-a-cop was white. His face looked too red in this light, like he had scraped his cheeks shaving. In this place, whites were the ones with the shitty-paying jobs.

"Just Japan. Did the post-college trip. It was weird. All these people who looked like me, and asked me for directions and shit. When I answered in my halting Japanese, they realized their mistake and gave me a wide berth. All except one man who gave me a stinging lecture. With a face like mine, he said, you should be ashamed not to speak Japanese. Then he leaned in close and whispered. 'You might get mistaken for a Korean.'"

Mark looked at me slyly. "My relatives in Tokyo were really nice. They put me up and fed me great *yakitori*. But their life is so regimented. I would never, ever fit in. I felt more foreign than the *gaijin*."

"That's the great thing about L.A. No matter who you are, you fit in, because no one fits in, so everyone is in the same boat. And it gets more that way each day. Now it's whites who are odd man out."

"Do you feel like that?"

I gave it some thought. "Would I be here in the biggest suburban Chinatown in the country if I did? Would I live in a Latino *barrio*? My mother was Russian. She never learned proper English. People used to call our house and ask me if the maid had answered the phone. We don't have a maid, it's my mom, I would explain. That's how provincial things were in the San Fernando Valley then. They assumed anyone with an accent was a maid."

"Probably still do."

"Yeah. So speaking of other languages, where did you learn Chinese?"

"College. I had a girlfriend who was ethnic Chinese from Malaysia. We went out for three years. At first, I just wanted to learn enough to impress her family. By the time we broke up, I was well into a double major—Chinese studies and psychology."

"What happened with the girl?"

He scuffed his foot on the asphalt. "She fell in love with someone else and went back to Malaysia with him."

"Someone Chinese?"

Mark hesitated, then nodded. "It wasn't anything racial. We were so young. It couldn't have lasted."

"But you wanted it to?"

He shrugged. "It was first love."

I thought of Tim. "Yeah, well, I'd best be off."

"Good night," Mark said.

He didn't move. I wondered what came next. I opened the car door. Nothing did.

I drove off.

CHAPTER 5

For a week, I came into work each day and thought about a dead girl. But when the phone rang, it was always a live person on the other end, wanting me to write about their kid's music recital, the couch dumped behind their alley, or the scholarship their women's club was doling out. Mostly, I let them talk and they felt better. Sometimes I told them to send a press release and I'd see. I didn't hear from Mark and it irked me that I cared. It wasn't like it had been a date, although it was as close as I had gotten in a while. At night I went home and stayed there. I was in a slump and I knew it. Journalists go through that, after the adrenaline rush of a good story. All of a sudden, things go glassy and flat. You tread water and scan the horizon hopefully for the next big wave, and if none materializes, you get out the wave machine.

I called Sgt. Vittorio Carabini of the Monterey Park Police Department. We had worked together on a murder story a few years back, and while he would barely spell his name for me from the station phone, he was happy to yak about his more steamy investigations over a long lunch. Especially if we went to Santori's.

So that Friday, I wheeled the Acura down Garvey Boulevard to our rendezvous. The scenery along the way never tired me. It was dingy and lowslung and breathtaking in its ugliness, a ticky-tacky assemblage of fast-food joints, vacuum repair shops, and sad retirement homes where the windows were permanently closed and the curtains drawn, even at high noon. You never saw any old people cruising around in wheelchairs or shuffling by on walks supported by blue-smocked orderlies. The places had Orwellian names like "Seabreeze Manor" and "Parkview Villa" but overlooked auto body shops.

Almost imperceptibly, the streetscape began to change. First it was just a restaurant here. A hair salon there. English signs giving way to pictograms. Travel agencies advertising specials to Taipei. Then bridal shop mannequins wearing lacquer-red gowns and elaborate head-dresses. More people on the street. Grandmas with parasols to keep the sun off, haggling with street merchants. Men with dirty aprons scurrying to hurl trash bags into Dumpsters. The bustle of commerce that was so missing from the tired, white parts of this dusty valley.

I pulled up in front of Santori's. "Italian home cooking since 1958," read the boot-shaped sign. It was a family-run, red-sauce and white-sauce kind of place that would have been an anachronism in penne- and arugula-obsessed Los Angeles even if it hadn't been surrounded by dim sum and Chinese noodle businesses.

It was a holdout, the lone outpost on the street that hadn't yet joined the Pacific Rim. And I knew it was just a matter of time before Mama Santori died and Fat Tony sold the place out from under his mother's grave and high-tailed it to a more Occidental part of town. You could see it in the sneer on his face as he greeted the Asian customers who trickled in to try his exotic European fare. The children of immigrants make the best racists because they have short memories.

Carabini was already tucked into a red vinyl booth, back to the wall, where he could eyeball the front door for any surprises. Although the sun wouldn't be casting any shadows for hours yet, his hand already curled protectively around a glass of house red. The carafe jug with its white plastic netting stood close by.

"Long time," I said, sliding into the booth and trying not to look at the wine.

"Good to see you, Eve." He grunted and raised his glass. Word on the street was he had been hitting it hard since the divorce. He had always been one for the ladies, and hadn't seen any reason to stop just because of a band of gold. But losing the kids to his ex had been rough.

"Each time I drive by, I'm amazed that Santori's is still open. But it sure packs in the lunch crowd," I said, looking around at the full booths.

"You should see it at dinner. Dead by eight. Used to be you couldn't get a table without a reservation, but those days are gone." The way he said it, I knew he meant more than just the crowds.

"So what are you up to now?" I scanned the menu and decided on the veal. If I was going to sin, I'd just as well do it big-time.

"Boss has me training a couple of new chink recruits for that Valley-wide task force on Asian crime."

I swallowed, torn between telling him off and leaving with the info I wanted. The tightrope that reporters walked each day of their lives. Suddenly, ordering veal seemed like the most venal of transgressions.

"I take it you're none too keen on that?"

"No." He waved the waitress over, asked how her boy was doing in school, and they chatted for a few minutes. Then we gave our orders.

"Why's that?" I resumed when she left.

"You really want to know? You can't put this in the paper."

"Vit, you know me better than that."

Carabini took a big slug of red. He looked up at the ceiling, squinting at the plastic fruit that hung next to bottles of Chianti in blond straw baskets.

"I have nothing against them personally."

There was a long pause. "But I don't trust 'em. You're never sure where their loyalties lie."

"What do you mean? They're cops, aren't they?"

"How do you know they'll pick being a cop over warning their *paisanos* if we take down some triad operation in a raid one night?"

"How do you know that about anyone? You're Italian. Would you warn a Mafioso about the same thing?"

He looked at me with incredulity.

"I'm an American," he said finally, like that explained everything.

"Well, so are they. I bet most of them are second-generation. They have to be U.S. citizens to be cops, right?"

"It's different," Carabini insisted. "If I go with one of these guys to take a statement and he's speaking Cantonese or Mandarin, hell, he could be saying anything and I'd never know. It's uncomfortable. And the boss thinks we have a slow leak. LAPD had the same problem a few years back. Turned out two of its Asian gang guys were on the take."

"I remember that. Weren't several white cops indicted too?"

"Yeah, well, it all started with the slant cops."

I wanted to tell him to stop whining and go learn Chinese. I wanted to ask him how a basically good guy could have such a shitty attitude about people who looked different from him. I wanted to tell him it was too late in any event because the San Gabriel Valley was different now and would never go back, and if he didn't like it, he might as well transfer to an Armageddon militia in rural Idaho. For once, I wanted to talk to someone honestly and say what I thought instead of always remembering the notepad in my hand, the job I had to do.

Instead, I took the low road.

"I'm sure you know better than me," I shrugged. This conversation was not going at all the way I wanted. What I wanted was a good story, and there was something about the Marina Lu carjacking that smelled promising. Maybe it was the high-flying boyfriend. I steered the topic in that direction.

"Speaking of our Chinese brothers and sisters, remember that girl who got jacked on the way to order bridesmaid dresses for her wedding? High school student. Happened in the parking lot at House of Fabrics?"

"Yeah. We're working that one like a big dog."

"Maybe it wasn't a carjacking. Maybe someone she knew wanted to silence her."

He looked at me. "Like who?" The words hung there and sniffed the air.

I kept my voice neutral and gave him my most naive look as he lifted his glass again in solitary communion.

"Oh, I don't know. Her father. Her fiancé. The butler. All the usual suspects. I hear she left behind a diary where she wrote about all her teenybop problems."

The glass came down so hard that wine sloshed out, staining the gingham tablecloth crimson.

"Oops, sorry about that. Been having some rough nights."

I watched his hairy paw mince across the table and dab at the checkerboard pattern with his napkin.

"Maybe you should send one of your Chinese recruits out to see what he can get. The family might be more open to a fellow countryman."

"We don't turn a house upside down searching for clues on a routine carjacking," Carabini said, elaborately casual now. "Unless we have reason to suspect it ain't so routine."

He ran his index finger around the rim of his wine glass real absent-mindedly, as if he didn't have another thought in the world. "Would you know of any such reason?"

"Just considering all the angles," I said.

Carabini propped one arm on the back of the red vinyl booth and grabbed the carafe with the other, tipping the last of the ruby liquid into his glass.

"I think you're bluffing to find out what we know."

"You're right. I don't know shit." My eyes were flat now. "It's just that her friends at San Marino High said Marina's fiancé, a guy named Michael Ho, had been showing her the fast life. Girlfriends were concerned. Of course there might have been a little green-eyed monster at work too."

"Never heard of him." Carabini's voice was mellow, aged with oak.

"Well, there's no reason that you should. He's never strayed onto your side of the fence. So, um, got any suspects in mind?"

"Our informants say White Crane's fingerprints are all over it. They been using young kids to jack the cars. Within hours, they slap on new ID numbers and load 'em into ocean-going containers with a doctored bill of lading that says twenty-five pallets of shrink-wrapped Tide. In Red China these days, they pay three times face value for a Lexus. No more Mao suits."

"You figure whoever did it has a record?"

"Maybe. We're pulling in gangbangers and questioning them. Punks don't know shit. They're scared of something, and it ain't me."

"Did the Chinese cops get anything off them?"

He gave me a look. "Nada."

I squirmed uncomfortably in my seat. No one likes a dead end.

"Vit, did your guys find anything unusual at the murder scene when they searched it? Something the killer might have left behind in his hurry to get out of there?"

Vittorio Carabini swirled the two inches of liquid left in his glass and considered it sorrowfully.

"No," he finally said.

"What about the girl?"

"Ditto."

"Oh."

The wave machine was sputtering.

"Well, that about covers it then, huh?"

"Yup."

We passed on the spumoni ice cream. Carabini didn't blink when I grabbed the bill. Maybe it was all that child support he had been shelling out lately.

After lunch, I headed for the coroner's office to see Marina Lu's report for myself. I thought that reading the cold, clinical language of death might spark something in me that emotion could not.

I drove south through downtown, past sidewalks black with grime, inhaling the cologne of idling buses. Toothless men sat on crates and panhandled while suited yuppies strode by with disdain. Stuck at a light, I looked down a fetid alley where a junkie stuck a needle under his toenail and jammed down the hammer, as oblivious of the passing crowds as they were of him.

I was headed to the sprawling complex of L.A. County-USC General Hospital on N. Mission Road, the place of last resort for the indigent and ailing. Conveniently, the coroner's office was here too, so the bodies could be trundled across the parking lot from the hospital to the morgue.

The office where I was headed didn't smell of formaldehyde—the autopsies were performed two floors away. The clerk took her time about it, laboriously writing down my name and scrutinizing my ID. "Just a minute," she said and shuffled off.

She returned and slid a file across the counter. "You can sit at that table and read it, sugar. Need a complete copy, that's forty-two dollars."

I always feel like a kid on Christmas morning when a city official hands me a file. There is that tingle of anticipation and dread. Will it be what I want, what I've begged Santa for? A big Chinese Santa with a Fu Manchu mustache? I'd even sit on his lap and wriggle if that would help.

I flipped hurriedly through the boilerplate pages, knowing that what I wanted, the coroner's conclusions, lay at the end.

Marina had died of cerebral hemorrhage, DOA at the scene. Two bullets, both still lodged in her gray matter. She had eaten rice cakes for breakfast and had not been sexually molested. She was five foot, three inches tall and weighed 105 pounds. She wore Nikes and jade earrings. I read on and on, the details piling up in a grotesque heap. I started thumbing through the pages, scanning now. I probably would have missed what came next, except for the color. It's not often you read the words "black" and "red" in a coroner's report and they don't refer to blood. But there it was, paired up with "hand." The deceased had sported a one-inch black hand tattoo entwined around a red heart on the upper part of her right breast.

I stopped and caressed the paper. I knew tattoos were hip with kids these days, but since when had the trend spread to nice immigrant Chinese girls? I stood up.

"I'll take a copy of each page," I told the clerk, sliding the file back across, loathe to have it leave my hands even for five minutes but wanting the tangible proof that this official document could provide. For what, I didn't yet know.

Twenty minutes later, I was back on the freeway, the Acura gunning for home like a horse for his feed bag. Right around the time I leaned into the interchange for my final jog into Silverlake, it occurred to me that Vittorio Carabini would want to know about the hand and might even be able to tell me what it meant. Funny he hadn't mentioned it over lunch.

CHAPTER 6

O n Saturday morning, I needed a bracing dose of reality. So I called Babette. She said breakfast at Millie's sounded perfect.

Millie's was a dive diner on Sunset Boulevard, where the waitresses wore cat-eye sunglasses and back-sassed a lot, flicking their unhygienically long fingernails in your face as they sloshed coffee into chipped porcelain mugs and slapped down grease-stained bills.

I like my home fries served up with attitude.

Babette pranced in twenty minutes late, as usual.

Her close-cropped, dirty-blonde hair was fluffed attractively around her face. She wore short shorts, a tank top, platform sandals, and too much makeup. Seeing her, I marveled that we had stayed friends, especially after all that horror when I was seventeen. Perhaps it was the shared experience in Catholic school, where the vigilant scrutiny of the nuns was enough to turn a saint to sin. And Babette kept them pretty busy. Where my immigrant family aspired to and finally bought a small house on a sensible block of North Hollywood, Babette's large clan rented, making their living from a chain of laundromats scattered throughout the city. One time the handyman found a severed arm wrapped in a Hefty bag in one of the dryers. That's the kind of neighborhood they were in. Babette also found interesting things when she helped her grandmother clean out the laundromats. Like biker porn and bags of *sinsemilla* that we would fire up at lunchtime in our uniform skirts, parked high on some canyon road off Beverly Glen.

One day we ditched school to go to the beach, smoking doobies and singing along to Free Bird. When Babette's old Chevrolet Chevelle broke down on the Ventura Freeway, we marched out in our bikinis, walking single file down the shoulder to find a call box.

Before long, a California Highway Patrolman pulled over and told us to get into his car. I was sure he was going to bust us. Our eyes were bloodshot and we reeked.

"But why?" I wailed. "We haven't done anything wrong."

Babette looked at me with disgust, then turned her high beams back onto the man in blue.

"Tell me, Officer," she asked, her voice going all throaty. "Are you going to handcuff us?"

She stretched out two shapely wrists, staring with admiration at the decals on her purple nails. Even at sixteen, Babette couldn't say two words to a guy without giving him the full-on face. Her flirting embarrassed me. I thought it way too obvious. But the men always melted. Problem was, they were usually the wrong men.

"No, miss, I'm not going to arrest you." The officer was excruciatingly polite. "I'm going to drive you to the nearest call box. You girls are going to cause an accident if you keep walking down the freeway like that."

Now, as we stirred nonfat milk into our coffee, Babette was explaining her latest discovery. Dating through the singles ads.

"It's a perfectly appropriate way for busy, professional people to meet," she said, resting her heart-shaped chin in her manicured hand. "Better than a bar or a crowded party. And cheaper than signing up with a dating service. But since L.A. is the serial murderer capital of the world, if you do connect with someone, I would recommend meeting him for a drink in a very public place. Don't let him walk you to your car—he could get your license number and stalk you. Don't give out your home number or God forbid, your address. And take it real easy, sex-wise."

"Oh, I don't know, Babette, it's not my speed."

"There's nothing sleazy about it. You don't have to put an ad in *New Times*. You can send it to the *New York Review of Books*."

I considered. "What would I say?"

"You want to convey your interests in a sort of shorthand, since they charge by the line," said Babette, who had studied accounting in college.

"All right, let's make one up. But I can't do it straight romantic. That would be too obvious."

"Like placing a singles ad isn't?"

"OK, I'll try it. But I'm going to put my own spin on it."

Seizing a paper napkin, I wrote:

"SWF, 29, pretty in an Art Deco way, seeks male running partner, 22-35, for 3-mile morning jogs and perhaps more. I prefer Bryan Ferry and Bach to the Beatles, am post-punk but not post-modern, and most nights crave the delirium of Dostoevsky more than the tedium of TV."

"There," I said. "That ought to scare off the 'long walks along the moonlit beach' types. And men looking for bimbos won't respond. On the other hand, it could attract all sorts of pseudo-intellectuals."

"And fitness Nazis," Babette added sagely. "Are you really going to run with them?"

"Why not? Might as well find out ahead of time whether they breathe heavy and break a sweat."

Now we were warming up to Babette's favorite topic.

"Did I ever tell you about why Michael and I broke up?" She looked up from between spiky black eyelashes.

I had a hard time keeping track of Babette's beaus. She was always falling in love with someone new, then dumping them for slight infractions that she had somehow overlooked in the first glow of courtship.

"No."

"He was really cute and smart, and we laughed a lot together, but when we got into bed, he would sweat. I don't mean your normal perspiration. I mean buckets. It would drip off the tip of his nose and splat onto my face like a leaky faucet until I couldn't concentrate on anything except when the next drop would fall. It drove me crazy. It was like being in bed with the Swamp Creature."

"Oh, that's too bad."

"So you still moping after Tim?"

Everyone asked me that. For once, I decided not to lie.

"I know it's pathetic."

I thought of Tim Waters, whose skin took on a damp, velvety texture when he sweated. He was the only man I had ever met who smelled like milky bread after two days without a shower. We had slid along each other's bodies like two seals in the late summer heat, the kind of heat we were having now. Four years it had been, long enough to grow up together, long enough to take each other for granted, when you were in your early twenties and hungry for every new experience the world could lay at your feet. At least I was. What a fool I had been to leave him. And for a tawdry office romance that had lasted all of three weeks.

Not that he hadn't warned me. "If you leave, it's over. I won't be waiting for you," Tim had said.

He was very Old Testament that way. An eye for an eye. People didn't break the rules. If they did, they got thrown out of the kingdom. And I had broken the cardinal rule. I had been delirious, drugged, and feverish with longing for Stewart, a tall, bookish reporter who had just been transferred from New York. I was entranced with his nasal whine. His literary sophistication. His ability to distinguish between a Gewürztraminer and a Liebfraumilch. I had worshipped a false prophet. Now I had no one to blame for my loneliness but myself.

And Tim was living in Singapore, where we had once gone together to drift across Asia. We had done it cheap, in the time warp between hippies and slackers. Now Tim worked for Sun Microsystems, kept an apartment near Raffles, and dated chic Chinese girls. We didn't correspond. Well, that wasn't exactly true. For months I wrote long letters, trying to woo him back with my words, my sorrow, my wistful descriptions of things we had done together. My eloquence would have moved a stone. But not Tim. From Singapore came only silence. I might as well have posted my letters into the Pacific for all the response they drew.

Humiliated, I had finally stopped. Now I had another tactic. I would be the best reporter the *Times* had ever seen. I would break stories, get noticed, and work my way up the ranks, until I got a foreign posting somewhere in Asia. I wasn't asking for Singapore. Bangkok would do just fine. So long as it was on the same continent. Then we could run into each other accidentally in Jakarta or Beijing and it would begin again.

That was why the Marina Lu story was so important. Each time I scratched the surface, I saw clues to a hidden world where everything seemed connected and obvious to everyone but me. I felt like the blind man groping at the elephant, not sure of what I had found but too curious to stop. If I could break this story, I'd be up for a promotion. A promotion would take me nearer to Tim. And Tim would take me nearer to God.

"Well, at least I'm not sitting home and moping," I told Babette. "I'm trying to date. There's this guy, a source I met through work. His name is Mark. I feel something for him. So maybe the Ice Age is passing. So long as I haven't evolved into a woolly mammoth by the time the glacier recedes, it should be OK."

Babette looked at me shrewdly and tucked the scribbled paper napkin into my purse.

"Stop torturing yourself. It's not a sin to enjoy life. You spent ten years blaming yourself for what happened to your brother and now you seem determined to spend the next ten pining for Tim. I know what you need, and you're not going to find it in a confessional. Now place this ad."

CHAPTER 7

Monday found me back at the office, scrabbling at loose ends. I placed a call to Carabini's office. Before we could connect, I ran into him while covering a jewelry heist. The store was in downtown Arcadia, the kind you would call small and inconspicuous if not for the two armed guards stationed in front like bas-relief statues. I had walked inside once, just to check it out, and a polite young Asian man had shadowed me through the room as I ogled the baubles. Whenever I stopped at a jewelry case, he hovered at my elbow, exuding the clean smell of money. It might have been an Asian thing of wanting to offer service. But the plastered-on smile convinced me he was there to make sure I didn't pry open the double-paned glass and snatch what lay nestled on the crushed red velvet.

The thieves had taken a more ingenious route, breaking into the neighboring shoe boutique at night, then punching a hole through the common wall. They knew exactly what they were after, because they took only imperial jade. None of the cheap, plastic-infused stuff. The old Burmese-Chinese owner suspected it was an inside job. He had recently fired a sales clerk, he said, peering at us.

Carabini frowned and wrote it all down. It took longer than usual because the man's son had to translate every word. Junior wore round, wire-rimmed glasses, slicked-back hair, and an Italian business suit of light summer wool. He stood a foot taller and several centuries removed from his old man, a squat peasant with rough hands and cotton trousers. When slick-boy caught me looking at the old man, he felt compelled to explain.

"My father grew up in the jungles of Burma, where the world's purest, most valuable jade comes from," the son told me. "He apprenticed with the best traders, learned all there was to know about the stone. He looks like a common laborer, it's true, but people come to us from throughout Asia because of his reputation. He can hold a stone in his hand and feel its worth in his fingers."

"So how much would those be?" I pointed to an exquisite pair of teardrop earrings in luminescent green.

"A hundred and twenty-five thousand." He didn't blink. "Clear green is most prized, because it is the purest and most rare."

"Jesus, the shit is worth more than diamonds," Carabini said.

Later, we congregated at the broken wall and I ribbed him.

"What brings you here on such a straightforward assignment?"

"Showing my young pal here the ropes." He pointed to a Chinese rookie.

"Besides," he spoke out of the corner of his mouth, "how do you know this isn't connected with my undercover work?"

"Well, is it?"

"Can't say." He was suddenly coy, trying to yank my reporter's chain.

"Anything new on the Lu case?"

"Not a thing."

"I've got something for you."

He appraised me warily.

"I went to the coroner's office and looked at Marina Lu's autopsy report."

"Is that right? You're really doing your homework. Robert, will you go over and see if the owner's son is around. We need to ask him a few more questions. Put it to him in Chinese, maybe he'll cooperate better."

Carabini winked at me.

"He seems to have been cooperating just fine in English," I said stiffly. I hated it when he got like this.

"You were saying?" he asked nonchalantly as the rookie walked off.

"I was saying the owner's son speaks perfect English, in case you hadn't noticed. Now about Marina, turns out she had a little black hand entwined around a red heart tattooed above her right breast. What do you make of that?"

Carabini's eyes narrowed, and he examined his fingers.

"Does that mean she was in a gang?" I persisted.

"Never heard such a thing. Probably one of those fake ones that washes off in a few days. My son is nuts about those."

"The coroner's report didn't say anything about it being fake."

"Beats the hell out of me, Eve."

"What if Marina Lu was in a girl gang?"

The Chinese recruit was walking toward us.

Carabini chuckled.

"All I know, Eve, is that my kids are crazy about those fake tattoos. It's all the rage in the schools. C'mon, I'll buy you a *mochi* ice cream. Young Robert here has turned me on to them."

Young Robert shrugged and said nothing.

I laughed.

"Vit, isn't that a bit exotic for you? I thought you were a plain vanilla kind of guy."

"I'm finding you can develop a taste for just about anything." Carabini exuded a salacious air that had nothing to do with ice cream.

As we sat in the window seats, watching the traffic stream by, Carabini sent Robert off to look for the owner's son again, then chomped into his ice cream and said through bitefuls that he might be getting his kids back.

"One of the guys at the station has a hotshot lawyer he wants me to meet. Guy gets three thousand just to sit across the table from you. And it goes up from there. But he can get a petition hearing before the judge. Plus I've hired a private investigator, who's turning up some nasty evidence on my dear ex-wife. She's not the angel she claims."

"Few of us are." There was something in his tone I didn't like. If I were an ex-wife, I sure wouldn't want some needle-nosed investigator peering in through my windows, seeing how many drinks I had and who I brought home at night.

"The headmaster at Borwick Academy says they could enroll mid-semester if I get custody."

My eyebrows arched. Borwick was an elite college prep school in Pasadena, known for graduates who scored equally well in the Ivy League and Olympic equestrian events.

"Watch it, Carabini. Your kids will get so snooty they'll turn their backs on a mere detective father. They won't want to eat with you at Santori's anymore."

"Like hell they won't," he growled. "I'm their daddy and I'm making unspeakable sacrifices so they can go to a good school and have a good life and they'll damn well eat wherever I want."

Just then, Robert came up with the owner's son, who had been holed up with his dad, drawing up a list of all the missing items, some of which dated back to the seventeenth-century Ch'ing Dynasty. He pegged the loss at $5 million.

CHAPTER 8

A week passed. The days dripped out of their bottle as slowly as molasses. I interviewed the parents of a twelve-year-old boy who had killed a store owner to get a bicycle he saw in the window. A paramedic who had married the girl he pulled out of a burning car. A man so irate at winning only $15,000 in the lottery that he blew it all on a trip to Vegas.

Eventually, I hacked out a free morning and visited Nicholas Madigan, a teacher at San Marino High. I had written about him when his heavily Asian debate team swept the national championships the previous year. The story gave the public what they clamored for: good news with lots of heroes. Madigan was a personable guy who had the kids eating out of a hand that wasn't much older than theirs. But his rumpled khakis, taped glasses, and unruly hair belied the ambition that coursed in his veins and gave him dreams of pole-vaulting out of San Marino's petty politics and into something much bigger.

Couldn't fault him for that. Everyone was working some angle in this town. The geometry only got you in trouble when your own plane failed to intersect with that of your superiors. Otherwise they slapped you on the back, gave you a promotion, and called it success.

Arriving at break, I found Nick grading papers in an empty class-room. The room smelled like chalk and stale sandwiches.

"Hello, Eve, what brings you to our esteemed campus?"

"I want to learn about parachute kids."

He looked surprised. "You know about them? I have plenty in my classes. There's one young man you might find interesting. Frankly, I'm a little worried about him."

"Why's that?"

"He's seventeen and thinks he's immortal. I call him at home in the morning, wake him up, and tell him I'd better see his skinny ass in fourth-period history or else. They respect it when you ride them hard, though they grumble all the way. But someone else is riding this one harder."

"Can I meet him?"

"Stick around until the bell rings and let's see if he shows up. Then, if you don't mind hearing about Little Big Horn—we're doing Westward Expansion—for fifty-five minutes, I'll introduce you after class."

"Great."

"But keep me out of it. The school board's been gunning for me ever since I mouthed off to the press about budget cuts."

"You can be an unnamed source. But if there's nothing in it for you, why are you putting yourself out on a limb?"

Nick sized up the question like one of his star debaters.

"Because it disturbs me. I know everybody's supposed to sacrifice for the greater good of the family. But parents sitting in safe old Hong Kong have no idea what's going on in our 'nice' American suburbs. They think it's a movie setting. If so, it's a John Woo special, not *American Graffiti*. Guns and no roses, and a thousand and one ways for a kid to go bad."

Nick's last words were drowned out by the bell. In came a torrent of kids, wearing knapsacks and braces. "Morning, Mr. Madigan," they said, taking their seats. A few gathered around his desk, clowning and vying for his attention.

The contemplative Nick of a moment ago disappeared. In his place was Madigan the Taskmaster, quizzing kids about term papers, demanding overdue homework. The students squirmed but only pressed closer, lapping it up. They wanted to please him.

When he shot me a discreet high-sign, I headed to an empty desk in the back of the class. As the students listened to Nick read the moving last words of Chief Joseph, I tried to pick the kid out. By the time the bell rang for lunch, I had him narrowed down to one of two students. He was either the guy slouched by the window, his choppy black hair iced straight up like a punker, or the kid two aisles across, camouflaged in baggy trousers and a backwards baseball hat.

"Eve, come meet Tony Hsu. He's so smart he thinks he doesn't have to study."

I was wrong. Tony Hsu didn't wear it on his sleeve. He was dressed in a white polo shirt tucked into trim 501 Levis, and his hair fell way short of his eyes. It looked like he had shot up six inches in the last year and his frame hadn't caught up. He slouched a little, but so did every other teenager.

Yet this one oozed vulnerability. He reminded me of my younger brother, Matthew, dead these twelve years. All of a sudden, it seemed like yesterday.

We were at a party, one of those big bashes that kids in wealthy Valley neighborhoods threw when their parents went out of town, leaving their offspring with keys to the liquor cabinet and admonitions to be good. Flyers would get printed up and passed surreptitiously from hand to hand: Keg party Saturday. Five bucks and all you can drink. Hundreds of kids would show up, most of them under-age. It was an innocent time compared to today, and one of the few opportunities for Babette and me to meet boys. Back then, we didn't worry about rival gangs arriving to shoot each other. Not in Sherman Oaks. The worst we feared was that a nosy neighbor would call the cops and they'd show up before things really got going. But on some of these estates, the houses were far enough apart that the noise didn't penetrate past the old-growth orchards. And the servants had long ago been dismissed for the weekend.

I was seventeen, and my mother hadn't wanted to let me go. Even though I soft-pedaled it to her, Mom's old-world nose told her that something was up. I must have betrayed too much excitement as I wiggled into my new white Levis and embroidered Mexican top, stopping by the mirror to admire the baby-oil tan that had fused my freckles into an even brown. But I begged and cajoled, and finally she relented.

"Why don't you take Matthew, it would be a nice change of pace for him. And you're much more social than he is."

"Oh, Mo-om," I said.

Long before it was cool, Matthew had been obsessed with computers. At fifteen, he had no interest in sports or girls, but sat hunched over a wood chair in the computer lab at Notre Dame High School all day and into the night, learning to program a large, antiquated mainframe that some rich donor had bequeathed to the school. He might as well have worn a monk's cowl like the brothers who taught him, for all the interest he displayed in typical teen pursuits.

This did nothing to enhance my own tenuous standing in the rigid high-school pecking order.

"He's such a nerd," I complained on the phone to Babette. "Why couldn't he have been born two years ahead of me and taken up surfing at an early age? Then he'd have cool friends, and they would hang out in his room listening to Led Zeppelin and one of them would see me walking around the house in my red frilly top and might fall in love with me."

"Maybe he's just a late bloomer."

"But he doesn't even have any friends."

At that moment, Matthew walked into the kitchen, and I knew he had overheard me, from the way his shoulders slumped. For a tech-head, he was pretty sensitive. But he didn't say anything. Matthew wasn't the type to complain, and that maddened me even more. He just opened the fridge and stood there as it belched out cold gusts of air, his gangly teenaged ears turning slowly scarlet.

I felt sorry for him. Even as I tormented him, I knew I was exorcising some ungainliness I hated in myself. Then, furious at my weakness, I would turn even meaner to assuage my guilt.

And now, the price of liberation for one Saturday night outing was hauling Matthew with me to the party. Well, so be it.

"Did you really want to go?" I asked him as we drove to Babette's house to pick her up.

Matthew shrugged. He was wearing his favorite shirt, the beige cor-
duroy one festooned with cowboy boots and cattle brands. It was nerd-
wear, but I had to admit I liked the mother-of-pearl buttons.

"Kind of."

We didn't say anything more. After Babette clambered into the car,
she filled the stale air between us. As she spoke, she carefully outlined
her lips with a burgundy pencil, then filled in the spaces between with
Midnight Seduction lip gloss. Matthew stared straight ahead. Ball and
chain, I muttered. I might as well be baby-sitting. Babette's running
monologue irked me too. I turned up Bryan Ferry. But his voice, which
usually entranced me, suddenly struck me as arch and melodramatic.

I paid Matthew's entrance fee and then Babette and I immediately
ditched him. The last we saw of him was his stiff, carrot red hair
reflected in a large hallway mirror as he headed upstairs. He would
probably wander through all the bedrooms before they were claimed
by amorous couples, looking for some electronic equipment he could
fidget with. Let him find his own fun.

Babette and I headed outdoors by the pool, where the keg sat in a
wooden tub packed with ice next to the diving board. An acrid smell of
chlorine rose from the steaming blue water, searing my nostrils.

"Let's go inside," I told Babette.

Much later, the cops came and the diminutive hostess, a pathological
liar, assured them her parents were asleep upstairs and her graduation
party would soon be winding down. They left and the party continued
at a lower pitch. By now, everyone was pleasantly stoned or buzzed
from the liquor. Some people were passed out in chairs. I hadn't seen
Matthew for hours and was beginning to feel stabs of guilt for aban-
doning him, although in such a big house, it was conveniently easy to
lose him. And each time I headed out to look for him, someone I knew
waved me over and I forgot all about my little brother. It was almost 1
A.M. when I heard a thud outside, and then a high-pitched scream.

When I pushed my way out back to the pool, the first thing I saw was
that thatch of carrot hair bobbing in the water, with a darker pool of
red spreading like a halo around it. The corrugated edge of the white
diving board was also smeared with red, as though someone had tried
to wipe off a paintbrush against its grainy edges.

"Matthew!" I screamed, but no sound came out.

"Excuse me, excuse me!" I shouted, pushing my way through the crowd of teenagers who stood by gaping, their eyes unseeing as milky-eyed fish. Fucking androids. I shoved violently at them, grunting through clenched teeth, but nobody said anything as they let me through.

"Please, God, please, God," I whispered to myself. "No, no, no. It can't be. Please, God."

As I ran, I looked up, tracing the arc his body must have made as it had fallen. Directly above the pool was a balcony with French doors leading into a dimly lit bedroom. Funny how I hadn't noticed that light before, I thought. Balanced precariously on the edge of the railing was a half-empty bottle of Jack Daniel's.

"M-m-matthew doesn't drink, doesn't drink, doesn't drink," I told myself, and the words echoed like a mantra in my stoned brain as I ran. I felt like a character in a movie, dodging in and out of a rush-hour crowd, running desperately to catch a train, as if my life depended on it. Or his. Why did it take so long? Why wasn't anyone else moving? Would I ever reach the pool?

Finally. With a throttled cry, I leapt off the tiled rim and into the water, legs akimbo. I had to save him. Only I could save him. I groped in the murky water, spewing chlorine, my arms flailing and slashing until they hit something. I pummeled him like a punching bag, grasping for a handhold so I could drag him out of that poisonous pool, forgetting everything I had ever learned in water-safety classes, grabbing brutally at clumps of hair, at the sodden collar of his favorite shirt, finally closing my long fingers around his neck and jerking it violently toward me.

And then I screamed again and almost let go. His neck wobbled in my hand, like a rag doll.

Hands stretched to meet mine as I hooked one leg into the gutter and wrestled my brother over the edge of the pool, heavy and inert. Then I heaved myself up and crouched over his crumpled body, panting and dripping.

"Don't move him," an authoritative voice above me said. "The paramedics are on their way. It looks pretty bad. His head hit the diving board."

I looked down at Matthew. A yellow string of vomit trickled out of his mouth and mixed with the blood dripping from a gash at his hair-line. As I visualized scooping out the vomit and pinching his nose to perform artificial respiration, sirens wailed and the backyard lit up like daylight.

"Hurry," I urged them. "Hurry."

But it was too late. Matthew was already dead of blunt force trauma to the head, a term I came to know all too well years later when I became a reporter and began covering such tragedies. Since no one had seen him all evening, we had to reconstruct his actions. But as far as the forensic pathologists could determine, Matthew had spent most of the party locked in the master bedroom, dismantling the 25-inch color TV that faced the bed and taking slugs from a bottle of booze he found sitting on the bedside table. They found most of the tubes and wires laid out neatly on the Persian rug, a feat that homicide detectives said showed the technical prowess of an advanced electronics engineer. The coroner, who delivered a ruling of accidental death, put his blood alcohol at .19, well above the legal limit for intoxication.

Sometime during the party, Matthew must have grown bored with his solitary task and increasingly drunk from the unfamiliar alcohol. He had wandered out with his bottle to the balcony, drawn by the raucous laughter and music. How long did he stand there, hands gripping the old stone wall, before he leaned forward, tilting crazily from the booze and strange surroundings, spinning and twirling until he finally became airborne? While downstairs, I had let myself be pulled away yet one more time to smoke a joint or flirt with some friend of Babette's who might decide to ask me out.

My mother never blamed me. She didn't need to. I wrapped my woe around me like a medieval hair shirt and wore it against my skin for years. I shunned parties. Living in Southern California, I couldn't bear the sight of a pool. The smell of Jack Daniel's made me vomit. Eventually, I developed a cynical outer shell that even fooled me most of the time. As they say, I put the past behind. With age came the wisdom to know that no matter how much I atoned, it would never bring him back. I had to live my life. But I felt I understood him so much better now. Why hadn't I been kinder to him when he was alive? Oh, Matthew, when will you stop haunting me? I thought, before years of discipline firmly yanked his memory back into a safe compartment of my brain.

I inhaled deeply and was back once more in Nick Madigan's musty classroom. But Matthew's after-image glinted like a hologram behind my eyes. I felt a sudden urge to pull Tony Hsu to me and cradle his head on my chest as I brushed the shiny black hair off his forehead.

"Hello, Miss Diamond," he said in a low voice. Hands jammed into pockets, not looking into my face.

"Hi, Tony."

"Ms. Diamond is doing research on a story about parachute kids and she'd like to interview you. She won't use your real name. You don't have to say yes. It's completely up to you."

Now it was my turn to look away. I felt Tony Hsu's eyes flicker over me with wary interest, then I flooded him with my brightest smile.

"Waddaya say?"

He immediately averted his eyes again. His weight shifted uneasily from foot to foot. A skittish wild animal.

"That sounds OK."

"I'd like to spend some time just hanging out with you. See how you live. What you do in the evenings. Mr. Madigan says you also take care of your sister. Maybe we could talk about that too. If you ever get lonely here in the U.S. Whether you miss your parents. All that stuff."

"Sure."

We made plans to meet Wednesday afternoon after school.

CHAPTER 9

Tony Hsu lived in a ranch house with brick trim that sprawled on a half-acre lot in San Marino. Getting there early, I took in the genteel splendor of houses I would never own, neighborhoods I would never live in. Did the rolling lawns and stained-glass windows look as foreign to Tony as they did to me? When I finally pulled into his driveway, I parked the Acura alongside a BMW and a large Mercedes. Both had the polished, sleek look of new cars.

Tony answered the door on the first ring. He wore another polo shirt and jeans and thick white athletic socks. I noticed shoes on the foyer floor and dutifully unlaced my sandals. I liked this custom. It made sense not to track dirt and crap into the house. It also made things more homey, padding around the inner sanctum in soft footwear.

This was another big, opulently appointed house. Rough, linen-weave sofas. Big leather armchairs. Teak end tables with lamps for reading. A Chinese watercolor on the wall that looked real old.

Tony led me into the family den, which stood in sharp contrast to the sterile perfection of the living room. Here was where people actually lived. In the corner, someone had piled a nest of blankets and pillows. Empty soda cans and plastic bottles of Japanese coffee drinks lay crushed on the floor. A flat cardboard box that once held pizza formed the base of a junk-food pyramid that ended with a small, grease-stained container of Chinese take-out with chopsticks poking out. The trail of detritus led to another teenager who sat at the edge of an ottoman, punching a remote control. I looked up and saw two TV consoles stacked against the wall.

"This is my friend Bruce. He's a parachute kid too," Tony explained. Awkwardly, we shook hands.

From the upstairs bedroom, I heard the unmistakable falsetto of the Bee Gees and a rhythmic thumping on the floor.

"And that would be my sister, Lily, she's practicing her cheerleader moves. Hey, Lily!" he yelled.

From the room came excited female giggles.

"Lil-y," he bellowed again.

The door opened, and his sister, who looked about fourteen, stood in the doorway, her long legs and cheerleading skirt silhouetted in the shadow, another girl peering behind her.

"What?"

"C'mere for a minute."

"Why?" She crossed her arms.

"Dad sent another fax about the report card. Will you please send it to him so he quits bugging us. At this rate he's gonna fly in here next week to find out what the problem is."

The girl pouted. "I'll take care of it just as soon as you buy the Wite-Out."

"I promise I'll pick some up tonight."

"Cool." She disappeared behind the door again. Soon the giggling was louder than ever.

"So this is what we usually do. Boring, huh?" He reached for the remote of his other TV, the one that got Jade Channel and the Chinese Communication Channel. Soon, he turned it off in disgust.

The fax machine started whirring. Tony excused himself and went over to take a look, ignoring an elderly Chinese woman with the face of a shar-pei who padded silently into the room in embroidered silk slippers and gave us a disapproving look.

I smiled tentatively in her direction. "Is this your grandmother?"

"Are you kidding? She's not part of our family, she's a servant from back home. She's supposed to watch us, but I didn't want her spying on us all the time, so I made her go live in the guest quarters out by the pool. She can't tell us what to do. She doesn't even speak English.

"Why don't you go eat some chicken feet?" he jeered at her in English, showing me what a modern American he was.

The old woman caught the tenor of his voice if not the words. She shot him a baleful look, then shuffled off.

Tony brought the faxes over to where I sat.

"One of these is from my father, see, it's about Lily's report card. This one's from my mother. She says please remember to pay the mortgage on time. I forgot a few months ago and it turned into this big deal."

"How often do you see your parents?" I asked, trying not to appear too stunned.

"Oh, maybe once every six weeks, when my dad comes here on business. He's got factories on the Mainland and the Philippines so he's pretty busy."

"And your mother?"

"She hasn't been out in four years."

"Do you miss her?"

He shrugged again. "In the beginning I did. But now I'm used to it. I saw her last year when I went back to Hong Kong for summer vacation, so it's not like it's been four full years."

"I see." Even his nonchalance was studied. "So what do you do for fun?"

"Go out to eat with friends. Play computer games. Watch TV."

As a child, he said, he had liked historical dramas about the Ch'ing emperor and the intergenerational family soap operas that Taiwanese audiences couldn't get enough of. Now it all struck him as vapid.

"Being so far from home, maybe you find it hard to relate to a big bustling family," I suggested.

"Naw, I just think they're boring."

But in five minutes, he clicked the soap back on. Maybe a big, dysfunctional TV family was better than none at all.

Tony and Bruce and I talked aimlessly as a Hong Kong soap called *We're All in This Together* unfolded on the screen. I wanted to let the line unreel slowly, gaining their confidence so they would forget I was a reporter.

When I began asking questions in earnest, they responded with the innocence of those who have not yet felt the media's scorching glare. They had no idea what their words would sound like on paper, how a reporter might twist their identities, damn their parents, and send social service agencies scurrying after them "for their own welfare and protection."

The words came rushing in torrents, like an unplugged dam. Had I asked, they would have told me how often their parents slept together. But they didn't know—their parents were six thousand miles away. In Hong Kong and Taipei they were called "Golden Youth," Tony explained, the offspring of the new elite who were off making fortunes in the new factories of Mainland China and Southeast Asia. They gave their children everything but time. And once the children hit school age, the parents often packed them off to Southern California so they could eventually get into good American colleges instead of competing in the cutthroat Asian academic worlds. At first the whole family would fly in to inspect houses in a choice neighborhood with good public schools. Places like San Marino or Hacienda Heights that had once been all-white bastions of exclusivity. Now whites were fleeing to safer, more sanitized suburbs, and it only took money to get in. After enrolling the kids in school and ensconcing them in new homes bought with cash, the parents flew back to Taipei or Hong Kong to continue running the family business. The kids who had parachuted in stayed behind.

Bruce explained that he lived in a condo with an imported Chinese cook he had taught to make hamburgers and milkshakes. Perhaps he and Tony wouldn't have become friends back home. But there was something about being parachute kids that drew them together.

"What do you think about life in the United States? Do you see yourselves as more Chinese or American?" I asked.

"We look and act like American teenagers but inside our hearts, we are Chinese." Tony was solemn now. "We believe in traditional Chinese values."

"Can you give me an example?"

"We respect our families. Young people here don't obey their parents. They treat them with disrespect. To us, that's wrong. I get mad at Lily sometimes, because she's becoming so American. She rarely calls our parents anymore. She doesn't spend time when they visit. Her Chinese has gotten so rusty she can barely understand them. Instead, she makes jokes in English about 'our father the ATM machine.' That's not right."

The teenager who had jeered about chicken feet had receded, leaving a petulant old man who griped with dismay about the shortcomings of the new generation.

"Do your parents give you an allowance?"

"We get three thousand per month for ourselves. That's after we pay the mortgage, but it's hard to stay on a budget. Sometimes when I run short, I tell my dad, 'You put us here. The least you can do is make sure we have enough money.' He usually sends a check the next day."

By the time the summer sun had set and a new moon came out, we were ravenous. "Let's go out to eat," the boys said. "You want to come in our car?" I hesitated. What if I wanted to make a quick exit as it got late? What if I didn't like the company they kept? Should I put myself in their hands or break the spell and take my own car?

I clambered inside the Benz.

And was glad I had. Bruce pulled out smoothly and slipped a Chinese pop cassette into the sound system. We spun past the lights of Valley Boulevard in a cocoon of cool air and swirling music. They spoke between themselves in fast Cantonese and laughed. I wondered whether it was that nervous laugh some Asians use to cover up embarrassment, or did it spring from real humor? Switching to English, Bruce told me the Mercedes belonged to his father. It was too big and ostentatious. What he really wanted was a Mazda RX-7 he could trick out with tinted windows, fat tires, and lowered suspension.

"My father will buy it for me," Bruce boasted. "All I have to do is make him feel guilty for leaving me here."

The words glittered at the edge of my consciousness. I knew I should write them down, but they slipped past and were lost in the night. Cruising through the San Gabriel Valley with these two, in this car, I felt very young and exalted. The pop music was so familiar, yet different, with its Asian lilt and inflection. On the street, people moved in slow motion under neon signs lit up with Chinese characters. In front of a storefront restaurant, a man with a stained white apron and chef's hat squatted on his haunches, smoking a cigarette. He held the white stub between his thumb and forefinger and inhaled deeply. Dizzy from hunger, I dangled between two worlds on a thin filament and felt it fray.

The Benz pulled up at Ocean Clipper Restaurant. Although it was late, the parking structure was full of cars. I saw scores of slim Chinese teens in designer clothes handing off their late-model Japanese cars to the waiting valets.

We were in Monterey Park, where it had all started in the 1970s, the vast wave of Overseas Chinese immigration that would turn this small town in an industrial valley into the Chinese Beverly Hills, the only city in the continental U.S. where the majority of residents were of Asian descent.

"We're going to take you to a banquet-style place that has good seafood," Tony explained. "Their chef is famous, from Shanghai. Next time, we can go to a small Hong Kong–style coffee shop. So you can see the two extremes of our food. OK?"

So there would be a next time. They liked me. They wanted to show me their world. I was strangely pleased to have won their confidence. I would surrender and let them be my guide. Part of being a good reporter was knowing when to be aggressive as hell and when to turn passive and go with the flow.

"This place is huge," I murmured as the smiling hostess led us through mirrored rooms with varnished wood paneling, each filled with large round tables of chopsticks-wielding diners.

Waiters with faces furrowed in concentration scurried through cavernous halls, bearing steaming plates of lobster and shrimp, red-glazed suckling pig, and platters heaped with wilted green vegetables drizzled with a brown oyster sauce. The place echoed and clattered with voices and carts that rolled past, bearing sumptuous dessert platters.

Sometime after we had demolished the hand-pulled noodles but before we could tuck into the roasted eel, I thought I noticed a surge in the noise level of the large dining hall. Other patrons must have caught it too, because the place grew still suddenly, as everyone cocked an ear and looked blankly at each other.

Yes, here it came again. It was not the satisfied hum of conversation brought on by a full belly and a circulation soothed by warm snifters of brandy. It was an angular, agitated pitch.

A double door burst open and a group of men streamed in like a line of maddened bees, hands tugging at shirttails and covering their privates. Each one of them lacked their pants. They jumped up in the air in indignation, bellowing in Chinese. Behind them crowded fully clothed wives and girlfriends, decked out in velvet and silk. One older man, red-faced and sweating, was waving a gun and bellowing.

"What in the hell is going on?" I whispered to Tony and Bruce, inching my chair closer to theirs for comfort. I looked around quickly, trying to size up the situation. I contemplated sliding down my chair and under the table so I could crouch on all fours, hiding. But the tablecloth, that damn pink pastel polyester-blend tablecloth, wasn't long enough to cover the floor. It offered no concealment.

"What are they saying?" I repeated urgently. "Is this some kind of a raid? Are they filming a movie?" I concluded hopefully.

"Wait. I'm trying to hear what that man's saying," Bruce said.

"He's yelling something about bandits. Thieves," Tony said.

Now the diners began to push back their chairs and run to the pantless men, surrounding them in little clusters to hear their story. One man wearing jockey briefs calmly yanked a pink tablecloth off the nearest table, upturning the chili oil and renderings that puddled onto the lacquered tabletop while he methodically knotted the pink thing into a sarong around his waist. In the back, a woman screamed loudly and hysterically. A waiter darted through the crowd, yelling into a portable phone.

Now a stout man waded to the center of the room. He brandished a bullhorn. I wondered where on earth the Chinese restaurant had gotten hold of a bullhorn.

The stout man held his arms up high and brought them down slowly, as though urging the crowd to stay calm. Then he spoke into the bullhorn, reaching into a back pocket with his free hand and fishing out a paper napkin, which he dabbed dramatically against his brow.

"What *is* he saying?" I pleaded. Now that it appeared the danger had passed, I was feeling like a reporter again. If only I understood this blasted language. What a formidable barrier stood between these people and me. I was helpless on their turf.

"OK, hold on, here's what I can make out," Tony said. His eyes widened and he looked apprehensively at Bruce.

"All those people, they were in a wedding party, OK, and they were celebrating in one of the banquet rooms, OK, and then . . ."

Tony gulped. His face was ashen.

"They got robbed. A group of guys dressed as waiters came in, pointing guns, and they lined the people up. They made the women take off all their jewelry and forced the men to hand over their wallets and take off their pants. The groom resisted so they pistol-whipped him. After they were through, they made everybody lie face down on the floor, and they locked the door to the banquet room and took off."

"The owner, that's him there," Bruce pointed to the heavyset man, "is telling everybody to stay calm. He says the police are on their way."

A waiter staggered into the dining room, teetering under a huge load of pants, many with leather belts still dangling from finely stitched loops. The men of the ill-fated wedding party, their pale hairless legs moving like the stalks of prehistoric insects, made their way to the heap to sift through the slacks and pull on their own. A heavily made-up young woman wearing an ornate headdress and red silk Chinese robe plunged a napkin into a glass of ice water and daubed at the face of a young man covered with eggplant-colored bruises. One eye was swollen shut. From the other streamed a steady flow of tears.

Diners were now heading for the exits of Ocean Clipper, leaving behind barely touched lobsters and bottles of Chivas. Tony stood up too, tossing five crisp ATM twenties onto the table.

"Let's get out of here."

He trembled violently. Beneath the shock of black hair, his face looked like a Kabuki mask.

"Let's get out of here," he repeated, as Bruce shoveled in one last eel, oblivious to his friend's distress.

"Tony," I said. "Are you all right? What's wrong?"

"I'm OK," said Tony, his teeth chattering.

I cursed the fact that I hadn't brought my car.

"You guys go home. I'm going to stay and interview these people. Here," I said, tucking forty dollars into his hand. "My paper won't let you pay for me. I'll take a cab back to your house when I'm through and pick up my car. We can continue our discussion another evening. I'll call you to arrange it. But right now, I think there's a story here and I'd better stick around."

They left, and I strode after the owner, only to realize I had forgotten my notebook in Bruce's car. Winding my way out of the restaurant and through the parked cars toward the Benz, I heard the sound of retching, then Tony's voice.

"I know who hit Ocean Clipper tonight," he was telling Bruce. "Jimmy Lai called me earlier this evening. He wanted my help. Rich wedding banquet, he told me. Ripe pickings. He didn't say where. I told him I had plans. I didn't tell him I was meeting with that reporter. But it looks like it was my fate to end up at Ocean Clipper Seafood tonight, one way or another. You can't go against your fate."

I heard him hawk and spit, then open the door. As the big engine purred to life, I crouched down low so they wouldn't see me. I would have to find something else to write on.

It was after 2 A.M. when I got home, wound up and unable to sleep. Tony's words kept echoing in my brain. He was dancing with the dragon, deep into something doomed to spin out of his control. If only I could get him to open up about it, maybe I could talk some sense into him. But how to do that without letting on that I knew?

As the minutes bled into hours on the red digital clock by the bed, I tossed and turned on my rice husk pillow. Each time, it scrunched comfortingly, a sound I have always liked. Because the robbery had occurred so late and because no one had been killed or injured, the night city editor had busted my big scoop down into a four-inch brief. "Armed gang holds up patrons at popular Monterey Park restaurant; more than $1 million in cash and jewelry stolen."

I had dictated it from my cell phone right on deadline as the owner hovered anxiously, still dabbing at his brow.

"This publicity is very bad for us." He wrung his plump hands.

"These things happen from time to time in our business, especially here, but nobody is hurt. Never anyone hurt."

"Is that right?" I paused to take in the implications.

In midstream, I amended my dictation to say that the robbery was not an isolated incident but one of a number of hits that occurred at Chinese restaurants in the San Gabriel Valley "from time to time," according to the owner.

I beckoned him over again.

"What was your name?"

He pulled out a thin silver case and handed me a business card with a flourish. I squinted. "Kee Luck Yun, manager, Ocean Clipper Restaurant," it said.

"Hold on a minute," I told the city desk.

"We don't have all night," came the exasperated voice at the end of the line, who wanted to get home to his family after a long shift.

"Hey, I thought you were the owner?" I asked Kee Luck Yun.

He stood there thinking. "I am both," he said finally. "But sometimes I am just the manager. No trouble that way."

Yeah, I thought, like when the local gang comes around, trying to extort protection money. Or when the IRS dropped by, wondering why you hadn't rung up every $150 dinner paid with cash.

I spelled the owner's name out slowly for the night city editor. It would look bad if we got it wrong. Just more proof to the paper's Chinese readers that the *Times* was too lame and ignorant to get their names right.

CHAPTER 10

The next morning, I wanted to call all the local cop shops to find out more about these restaurant takeovers and how prevalent they were in the Chinese community. If Asian organized crime was involved, did they also do carjackings? Would the trail lead back to Marina Lu?

But Miller had other plans. "San Dimas High School students are going on strike to protest the dress code. They claim it's unconstitutional that they can't wear baseball caps and Raiders jackets. I need a story by four P.M.," he called from his corner office.

So I listened to student complaints and chased down school officials cloistered in endless meetings. I knew it was silly, but I also scanned the hallways for Mark Furukawa. What a coincidence, I'd say, I didn't realize you counseled kids from this school. But I soon grew disgusted with my reverie. It only distracted me from the story I really wanted to do, the one about parachute kids. Before I went home, I sketched out what I had to Miller. When I started in on the $3,000 allowances and faxing over of report cards, he got a predatory gleam in his eye that meant he was hearing a good story.

"Details like those will make this story sing," he said. "You need to spend more time with these kids to get it right."

"If you say so." I tried to hide my delight. The next day, I called Tony and asked if we might meet again.

"What do you want to talk about this time?" His voice was more curious than hostile.

"Oh, I just want to hang with you some more."

I had my telephone headset on so I could scan through the Calendar section as I waited for his response, turning each page gingerly to avoid a telltale rustle.

"I guess that's cool."

In his family room, we drank green tea and kept things light. He asked me why so many American teenagers wanted to live on their own. To him, it was no picnic. Even if you could eat midnight feasts at Ocean Clipper whenever you wanted.

"That reminds me," I said. "That heist at the Ocean Clipper. Was that a gang thing?"

"Yes," said Tony. "That's a typical way Chinese gangs get money. They got two and a half million that night."

The owner had said $1 million. Maybe he had lowballed it to me. Maybe the Chinese papers Tony read had printed a more accurate figure. Maybe I didn't want to think about the obvious.

"What about your own involvement with gangs?"

"I know a few *dai los*." Tony averted his eyes from me like he did that first day we met. "But I mainly stay clear of them. I don't want to cause my parents any hassles."

Upstairs, a door slammed and Tony jumped.

"Sorry. I guess I'm a bit twitchy."

"Oh, yeah? Why is that?"

Tony took a deep breath and opened his mouth. From the staircase, a girl's high wavery voice sang a song by Hole called "Doll Parts," the words wafting down the stairs in a disembodied chant. Then, with a loud thump, Lily leapt the last few stairs and landed in the living room. She smiled, revealing a mouth with more steel braces than the Vincent Thomas Bridge in Long Beach. Lily had long straight hair and longer legs, the gamboling limbs of a colt tucked into white tennis shorts. She advanced into the room, twirling in a series of ballet pirouettes, her glossy black hair whipping as she turned.

"Lily, this is Eve Diamond, she's the reporter who was here the other day."

"Pleased to meet you," Lily lisped politely, continuing her pirouettes.

"Those are some pretty smart turns, Lily. Your head is snapping around perfectly, which is what keeps you from getting dizzy."

She stopped. "You know about ballet?"

"My great-great-aunt was in the Kirov, back in Russia, before the Revolution."

Lily gave me her undivided attention.

"In Hong Kong, where we are from, my first teacher was an old Russian ballerina," Lily said. "You want to see my ballet scrapbook? It's upstairs."

Still humming under her breath, Lily leapt up the steps, two by two.

Gamely, I followed. Her room was white on white, with lace-trim curtains and white stuffed animals clustered on the white down bedspread—a polar bear, an Arctic wolf, and a white lion that looked like Kimba, from the Japanese children's cartoon.

The discipline that such whiteness must have required seemed at odds with the rambunctious energy and eclectic tastes of a fourteen-year-old girl. But Lily had been on her own for a long time. Maintaining control over her environment—if only in the color scheme—probably had psychic ramifications that I could only guess at.

She climbed onto a chair and began pulling down volumes from the shelf above her desk, rummaging for the one with photos of her Russian teacher. The discarded books were strewn in a heap. I picked one up. "Private Moments," read the ornate gold script. It was a cheap thing, the binding already starting to fray. A girl's journal. How many lonely secrets would it reveal about Lily, the truth behind the bright mask she turned on the world? The journal of a parachute kid. I wanted to read it so bad I could taste the words, savor their sorrow. But I proceeded slowly.

"What's this, your diary?"

Lily stopped, her forehead scrunching up.

"Not mine," she said, after a moment of recollection. Her face grew somber. "My friend Colin gave it to me to stash. It belonged to his sister. She died. Colin didn't want his parents to find it. So now I've got it."

"How sad."

Lily straightened her back like a good ballerina and stood perfectly still in fifth position.

"Yes. She was murdered."

For a long time, we stood there looking at each other. My fingers stroked the gold letters, tracing the words, caressing the embossed script. If I did it long enough, I might buff it out completely.

"What did you say your friend's name was?" I could barely breathe.

"Colin. Colin Lu."

"So this is Marina Lu's diary?" I held it up.

"Yeah, that's right." Lily was puzzled. "You knew Marina?"

"No. I only wrote about her after she was dead. The *Times* covered her murder. It was so senseless and tragic. You know, her getting killed before she was due to get married and all. I interviewed the cops. Witnesses. School friends. Her father. They live in a big place, not too far from here."

"Colin hates that house. He says it's too big. Spooky and empty, especially at night. They're like us, you know. They're parachute kids. That's why Colin and I became friends. We understand each other."

Her face softened as she spoke of Colin. They were geo-orphans, huddling close for comfort in this grave new world. But who had given Marina safe harbor?

"This diary is important. If the police knew you had it, they might want to take it. They'd want to read it for clues. In case there was any evidence."

"Evidence of what? She was killed by a carjacker. It was random. It could happen to any of us," she said softly.

Funny how quickly immigrants pick up our awful new vocabulary, I thought. Words like carjacking that had been unknown until the 1990s. Now it had entered our lexicon of violence.

"Still, it could show us her state of mind in the weeks leading up to the murder. At the very least, it would make a compelling story. The last days of a normal girl planning her wedding, unaware that her life was about to end. I'd like to pay Marina the honor of describing her life. Her dad won't talk to me much and she can't. But this," I said, holding up the diary and flipping it open randomly, "this right here could be the key. The window into Marina Lu's psyche. Will you let me read it?"

"Oops," I added, as a chunk of pages fell out. Quickly, I stuffed them back inside and shut the diary, but not before I saw spidery writing webbing across page after page. Crammed so tight with words that you could barely see any white.

Lily looked troubled.

"I don't know, Ms. Diamond. I don't know if that would be right."

She ended in a question, as if waiting for me to convince her. And so I did. Of course it wouldn't be right. But it would be journalism. If I had wanted that slim volume initially, when I thought it held Lily's inner life, I was transformed with longing for it now that I knew it was Marina's. So I smiled into Lily's eyes and seduced her with my word pictures into giving me that murdered girl's diary. And in the end, it shamed me how easy it was to win her over. All I had to do was appeal to her sense of the dramatic.

Stepping in close, I grabbed her arm, as if overcome by a brilliant idea.

"Lily, what if there are clues in here to Marina's murder? Maybe somebody knew she had money. Maybe someone was following her and Marina wrote about it in her diary. We could solve this together. We could find the killer. Like in the movies. Wouldn't Colin want that? Then at least, Marina wouldn't have died in vain."

"Yeah," said Lily, visualizing the scenes. "He would."

I left the ranch house twenty minutes later, the diary tucked safely into my tote bag, with a promise that I would return later that week to take Lily and Tony to lunch. Driving back to the office, I couldn't resist taking a peek. I spread the pages out on the passenger seat and read when the car stopped at a red light:

Feb. 18. don't know anymore about this marriage. (OK, I'm just whining) but he's so insistent. Things have sure changed since Hong Kong. He's more distant. And he's working 24/7. Is this what I have to look forward to? Alison says I should have a fling.

She's even got the guy picked out. Tall blond Eric from 4th period. I told her no way, but last night, I dreamed about him. We were in a Jacuzzi. I'm not even gonna write it down. Triple X!

Marina's ambivalence was odd. Could her fiancé have killed her for threatening to break off the marriage? I flipped forward several months and read:

April 8 . . . I borrowed his car to go the mall. It was raining and I left the lights on. When I got back, the engine was dead. A nice lady said she'd give me a jump if I had cables. So I looked in his trunk. He had them. He had something else, too. Three boxes of condoms!!! I freaked. What is he doing with 50 pounds of condoms? Is this some kind of sick joke? We don't even use condoms since I went on the pill. When I brought it up, he laughed and said it was no big deal, why was I so upset. One of his bank customers who owns a condom company and ships them to Mainland China gave him several boxes. I'm like, yeah, right . . . But he kept insisting. "Marina, why else would I have 1,000 condoms in my trunk? For my own personal use? Get real." So then I didn't know what to think. Then he asked if I was getting my period. I got so mad I ran into my bedroom and slammed the door. After a while I heard him leave. Sometimes I think I'm going insane.

A car honked angrily and I realized the light was green. I pressed on the gas. I wanted to reach out across the freshly dug cemetery earth and reassure Marina that she wasn't insane. Michael's explanation sounded like a line of jive the Grinch would use on Cindy Lou Who.

Stashing the slim volume back into my bag, I concentrated on my driving. I had to get back to the office. I knew I should turn the diary over to the police, but I wanted to pursue my own agenda: the killer story I was formulating about the secret life of Marina Lu. The term "withholding evidence" floated into my head. Was it even a real crime or something I had read in a book?

CHAPTER 11

T he Rainbow Coalition Center is having a cross-cultural parenting conference this evening," Miller announced as I walked into the newsroom. "They're teaching immigrant parents how to discipline their kids in American ways. Apparently lots of the parents beat their kids when they bring home B's and C's, then get slapped with child abuse charges. See if we can send a fotog," he added.

What I wanted to do was go home early for once. But then I brightened. There was the possibility I'd see Mark. Bon Jovi would have to do without a run this evening.

Even though it was 7:30 P.M. when I arrived, a sad assortment of immigrants still sat in the lobby's plastic chairs, waiting to see counselors or get referrals to other social service agencies. One elderly man shuffled along the linoleum in rubber thongs, bent over almost double and muttering to himself. Was he a survivor of Cambodia's killing fields? Next to him was a young pregnant woman, so skinny that her body was almost concave, except for the pooching belly. She wore a stained housedress and smoothed back the hair of her two-year-old with absentminded motions when he tugged on her hem. A four-year-old squatted next to her chair, surveying the room with hostile eyes. On one leg was a large purple welt, as though he had fallen from his tricycle repeatedly on the same spot.

Twenty minutes later, we all shuffled into a classroom where an energetic young Vietnamese teacher demonstrated the "time-out" disciplinary technique as an alternative to spanking. While a center staffer translated into my ear, I looked to see what impact her words were having on the pregnant mother. She stared listlessly.

"She's attending this seminar by court order," another voice whispered in my ear. "Her husband was military, killed by the North Vietnamese. She spent seven years in a camp on the Thai border before getting permission to immigrate here. She's remarried now, with new children, but there are problems at home. Those kids aren't the only ones with bruises."

I spun around and saw Mark Furukawa, grinning broadly at me.

"How can you tell me that horrible story and stand there smiling?"

"If I didn't smile, I would cry, and I can't cry all the time, Eve. That would get old after a while."

My indignation melted into something warm and liquid that shot through my veins. Why did Mark have this effect on me? It didn't help that he pronounced my name in that half-caressing, half-mocking way that was so intimate. I imagined him saying it over and over again in other circumstances, with the lights turned down low. No wonder I lost my train of thought.

"I'm here to do a story on your parenting seminar," I said lamely.

"Good, we need all the publicity we can get."

Another Cheshire grin. "This winds down at 9 P.M.. Then maybe we could grab a drink and I'll be happy to answer any questions."

Two hours later we stood in the parking lot, sparring over whose car to take.

Valley Boulevard was almost deserted. Facing north along the broad street, the dark shadow of the San Gabriels loomed ahead of us. The moon was out, lighting up half of Mark's face. He looked pensive.

"Where are we going, anyway?" I asked.

"Bahooka Palace. It has a campy Tahitian theme, looks like it was designed by blue-collar white guys in the 1950s. We can get huge pink frothy drinks in hairy coconut shells. You'll love it. It's like the Jungle Cruise, but with liquor."

"A lot of liquor," I added thick-tongued, some time later, as I finished my third Bahooka Bazooka.

We had compromised and taken two cars, since I worried it would send the wrong signal if we went in his car.

"I don't think I've drunk any rum since high school when we used to sneak a pint into the movie theater. I'd better eat something."

But the industrially breaded shrimp that arrived in a melted red cough syrup sauce didn't clear my head. I was floating, and it felt good to be here with Mark.

I told him about my big plans for the Marina story and explained that I had just that day uncovered an important document—a diary that the police had overlooked. He spoke about his dream of opening up his own counseling center one day and his worries that being the boss would keep him from hands-on work with kids. We worked our way through Asian culture clashes, families, and old loves. I got the feeling that the talk of old loves was really a way to telegraph what we had been like in past relationships so as to better navigate the future.

Mark was watching me. Maybe he felt sorry for me, that I'd had one too many. Well, let that be my guide. If I had drunk too much, I couldn't be held responsible for my actions, could I? Squeezing out of the turquoise-vinyl booth, I moved around the table to the other side and slid in next to Mark, making sure that my thigh slammed up against his.

I stared at the coconut shell for a full minute, waiting. I sensed what would happen next.

"Eve," he whispered into my ear, as he enveloped me with his arms.

I leaned back into them, but continued to stare straight ahead. I didn't trust myself to look at him. It had been so long since I had felt a man's arms around me that I wanted to prolong the moment. Locked together, we drifted along in our own separate worlds. I marveled at the huge, shellacked swordfish mounted on the wood-paneled wall before us, the conch shells and starfish caught in ocean-going nets in the corner. Waitresses sailed out of the kitchen, bringing flaming dishes to tables full of late-night salesmen and gaggles of secretaries celebrating somebody's birthday. At eleven, the joint began to close up for the night. Things ended early in the suburbs.

"I live right around the corner," Mark was murmuring. "Come home with me, Eve?"

So there it was. I felt submerged under warm, tropical water, ebbing and flowing around us.

"All right," I said after a pause. This time, I let him drive. I couldn't have managed it anyway.

At the front door, he fumbled for the key to his bungalow. Inside, the hardwood floors gleamed in the moonlight, smelling like freshly polished lemon wax. A cat warbled a greeting, then fell to the floor with a heavy thump and made its way to him, winding around his legs.

I wanted to be the cat, rubbing up against him, purring with a strong motor as he petted me.

"Gotta feed the cat," he whispered with an apologetic look back, as he strode off to the kitchen. I heard the cat food pouring, gravelly pebbles clattering against a plastic dish.

Looking around, I saw a spare black sofa and a delicate watercolor that looked as if it might have come from ninth-century Kyoto. I have always liked a darkened house. It feels somehow restful. Now I moved slowly through the room, running my hand along the furniture, fingering a small carved ivory *netsuke* that glowed dimly on the bookshelf. Had this been handed down by Mark's grandfather? Or purchased on impulse at a Tokyo flea market a century later? Would I ever know him well and long enough to ask? I wondered, before moving on to the books themselves. Mishima, of course. Kobo Abe. Kerouac, deeply underlined from when he had devoured it at nineteen. The collected short stories of Anton Chekhov. Laurence Durrell. Jorge Luis Borges. So many things for me to savor. I wanted to stay here until I had read each and every one of them. Our relationship could be measured not in years, but in novels.

"There. I locked him up in the kitchen."

Mark was at my side again, looking like a flushed little boy.

He put an arm up tentatively and brushed a lock of hair away from my face, tucking it behind my ear.

"You have beautiful eyes," he murmured, without withdrawing his hand.

He leaned in delicately, a connoisseur of eyes, his face moving into mine, his hand now cupping the back of my head.

Dizzy, I closed my eyes.

His lips were warm against mine, full and yielding. I took a tiny step closer, into the crook of his body.

We kissed for a long moment, neither one of us wanting to be the first to let go. Our mouths opened.

Now he gripped me harder. His breath came faster.

He took my hand and led me into the bedroom. I flopped onto the bed with a sigh. I felt like a rag doll. He tumbled against me, collapsing into the hollows of my body. Now I was paralyzed, passive. I couldn't even meet him halfway. He would have to make the moves. I had forgotten how.

He slipped off my blouse and unhooked my bra. He unzipped my skirt, then slid off my panties, shucking off his own clothes in the process. I felt him press up against me from behind. Felt his hands along my shoulders, massaging my skin. With one hand he cupped my breast, which strained suddenly against his hand. He squeezed it gently, feeling the nipple pressing sharply into his palm, while his other hand snaked down my body and slid between my thighs. All the while, his head was nestled in the crook of my neck.

I felt a flush of wetness between my legs. I strained into him, feeling him grow harder against my haunches. He cupped me like a spoon. It was both intimate and deliciously anonymous, and in the end, it was I who turned halfway in his embrace, so that I could look upon his face, the face I had been afraid to stare into all evening, knowing it wasn't Tim's face. Now that no longer mattered. What mattered was this man here beside me, who was not Tim and didn't need to be.

"Are you tired, Eve?" he whispered.

"No."

"You sure?"

"Yes. Yes Yes Yes."

He smiled lazily and turned me around to face him, fitting his body against mine. When he slid into me, we both shuddered, and I grabbed his buttocks to pull him in deeper still. He moved against me, as inevitable as the tide, looming above me like a dark angel, his movements smooth and sure.

Then he eased slowly onto his back, grabbed my hips and drew me up onto him. Now it was I looming above him. He moved me back and forth, finding the rhythm, until we moved together inside it. Then the world exploded in light and sound and I thrashed and gasped for air like a floundering fish and collapsed atop him, sobbing in emotion and wonder.

Much later, he asked again.

"You tired, Eve?"

"No."

Finally, we slept.

CHAPTER 12

Light was creeping into the room when I woke. I propped my head up on one elbow. Through the window, the sky was molting purple and orange.

Mark was lying next to me, one bare leg slung over the comforter. His skin was buffed olive, with faint constellations of hair. The exposed limb made him seem vulnerable, but that wouldn't last long. It was time to go. I didn't want to face any awkward breakfast routine, looking him in the eye and having to relive last night. I wanted to save that for later, when I was by myself. Plus I badly needed a shower and a change of clothes. Men were such sound sleepers that I figured I could slip out the door, hop into my car, and be home before he even woke up.

My car.

My damn car was at Bahooka's. I had let Mark drive me here. This was what happened when I abandoned my vehicular principles. I pictured myself sitting primly beside him as he drove me back to that Polynesian restaurant, the magic vanishing in the bright light of day, both of us too embarrassed to say much.

I would walk. It wasn't far. Hadn't Mark said he lived around the corner? I would retrace our steps.

I tiptoed around gathering my things. The cat padded in, looking hopeful, and I threw him a handful of dry food so he'd stay quiet. Standing on the porch, I pulled the heavy wooden door shut behind me, hearing the sliding click as it closed. Bye, sweet.

Across the street, an old lady crouched in a flower bed, pressing down wet soil. Hoping she wouldn't look up, I walked briskly to the sidewalk and turned to the left, as though I did this every morning. For two blocks I walked, past single-family homes that had seen better days. Many were California bungalows like Mark's but, unlike his, the wood had been stuccoed over.

In the driveways, trucks and vans advertised small businesses. Lopez Gardening. Lucky Painting. A-1 Carpet Cleaning. Inside all these houses, people were stirring. The self-employed started their days earlier than the office drones and ended them long after the suits had mixed the evening's first cocktail.

A screen-door slammed, and a Latina girl dressed in the blue-and-gray plaid of a Catholic uniform emerged with a sleepy-looking German shepherd on a leash.

"*Nos vamos en cinco minutos, Lupe,*" a maternal voice yelled from inside the house.

I smiled at her and looked beyond to the broad, open boulevard that rose ahead of me. I'd be gone in five minutes too. If my bearings were right, this would be Rosemead Boulevard. As I neared, I saw the pink and blue Tahitian tikis that announced Bahooka's. Mark was right, it did look like a little corner of Disneyland had been plunked down in the San Gabriel Valley. The parking lot was deserted at this hour except for my car. I made a beeline, not noticing the broken glass until I was scrunching it underfoot.

Gee, someone had an accident, I thought. Then I glanced up. The remains of my car window gaped in jagged shark's teeth. I leaned in and looked for the stereo. Miraculously, it was still there. So were the novels I had bought at a used bookstore near the Pomona courthouse last week. Literary thieves they were not, I thought to myself, already visualizing how I would turn this misfortune into a funny story at work.

Work. My stomach lurched. Firecrackers went off in my head. My tote bag. I had thrown it into the backseat when I left work yesterday for that seminar. Now all I saw was that wide, empty expanse of stained velveteen seat. The thieves had stolen my tote. And inside, next to my turkey jerky, my reporter notepads, and a bag of granola, was Marina Lu's diary.

A wail escaped me. Stupid, stupid girl. How could I have left it in my car? And how could I have been so bamboozled by Mark's attention that I agreed to meet him for drinks instead of going straight home to read the dead girl's journal? Where were my priorities?

A chill went up my spine. I turned slowly around in a 360, scanning the lot for prying eyes. A worse realization was now nagging at me. Was this a random theft or could someone have known I had Marina Lu's diary? And had that person followed me, waiting for an opportunity to steal it?

Could Mark be involved? Was the social worker gig just a front? What if he had conveniently lured me away from my car at a crucial time?

I could imagine my mother's voice clucking to friends over coffee and rum babas at the kitchen table: "Eve has such a *vivid* imagination. Morbid for a young girl too. Always making up such tragic stories until she begins to believe them herself."

Get a grip, I told myself. Breathe in deep. No one is after you. This is only a coincidence. And you are going to be late for work if you don't hurry.

The wild beating of my heart slowed. Satisfied that no one was watching, I used my purse to sweep aside the glass in the bucket seat. The car actually started. I turned and drove home.

After a shower and a strong cup of coffee, I headed back to the car with a dustpan and a brush. I swept away the crinkly shards of blue glass, then reached for the used books. The top one slid into a crack between the far seat and the door. As I groped to retrieve it, I pulled out a sheaf of bound paper.

The pages of spidery handwriting must have fallen out of my tote when I had thrown it into the backseat. The thieves had missed it. I held the last remnant of Marina Lu's diary. I prayed that these were not the entries I had already read that told me Marina was ambivalent about her upcoming marriage to a fiancé who drove around with boxes of condoms. My hand trembled, as it sometimes did in the morning before coffee. I started reading.

bugged that I was asking him so many questions. I'm not jealous. But how can he work so late? Last night he never called, and
I watched Leno and waited for him and next thing I knew I had
slept through my 8 a.m. class . . .

I pictured Marina sitting up in bed writing, then falling asleep over the journal. I looked up. A scrub jay was chattering in the oak tree. The mailman was pulling up to the curb. I took the precious pages into the house before something else happened.

Who was bugged? I wondered, as I went back inside. Had it been her father? No, she wouldn't have been jealous of her father, would she? It had to have been Michael again. From these brief pages, I would have to construct a life. And if the car theft wasn't just a random occur-rence, I had to find her killer before he realized that he had left an important clue behind and came back to get it, and me.

CHAPTER 13

It was 9 A.M. by now, the sun blazing. I was not going to make it to work today. My conscience was clear as I called in sick. They owed me. I had gone in enough times when I was ill. The odious task done, I slipped into bed, laying the diary entries out next to a yellow legal pad and two pencils. Like a good reporter, I would take notes on what I found. This wasn't voyeurism. This was a puzzle. I knew I was missing key pieces, but what else was new in my life.

February 5, the next entry read:

Father will be proud of this report card. Sometimes I think he's more fond of Michael than I am. Just because he drives a Jag and is a good businessman. I wish we could go to that Hong Kong–style cafe Lucky Noodle with Alison on Friday night. But Michael says he's too old for kiddie hangouts. He likes that discotheque on Garvey, where the smoke's so thick it makes you gag.

Feb. 7. I'm worried about Michael. He's so secretive about what he's up to. I wonder if it has something to do with all those condoms? Alison thinks I should follow him to see if he has another girlfriend. I'm insulted she could think that.

Feb. 10. Colin is getting all A's in school. He doesn't miss Mother and Father anymore. He used to wake up whimpering in the middle of the night and crawl into bed with me and I'd hold him and tell him how much Mother and Father loved us. But then I'd cry too. Now he never comes into my room anymore. And he just shrugs when he hears Father's voice on the answering machine. I guess he's growing up.

March 1. I can't even have a date with Michael without his work horning in. Last night we were at the mall watching the new Star Trek movie and he got a call on his cell phone. Pretty soon he was hustling me home. I was still on the front porch wondering what was going on when he zoomed out of the driveway and down the street. He could have at least waited til I got in the house.

April 15. Maybe it wouldn't be a bad idea to follow Michael. All I want is a regular boyfriend who will eat green tea ice cream and watch 90210 with me. And Michael's not like that anymore. He sneers and says it's for losers. And that he's a do-er. I'm afraid he's going to become some rich hotshot like Father and I'll never see him anymore or have a normal life after we're married.

April 22. Alison and I spend our lunches planning out the spy thing. She said I have to get my car windows tinted and we'll both buy wigs and fake glasses. She knows a place in Glendale. She'll even go with me. What a friend.

May 1. Alison said we need to stake out his condo. My job is to make sure the car has gas and to get CDs to play while we wait. Hers is to pick up the diet Coke and rice cakes. Even the flavored ones only have 15 calories.

From far away, the phone rang. Its insistent shrieking slowly rousted me from Marina's world. I laid down the frail pages and slipped out of bed for the second time that morning.

"Eve?" It wasn't work. It was Mark. I looked at my watch. 11 A.M. Suddenly, I was miffed it had taken him that long. "I called work and they said you were sick. Are you OK?"

I detected concern, which was nice. But I had to think fast. I was only a good liar at work. There I could lock eyes with a source and ooze sincerity that even I sometimes believed. But personal fibs were harder.

"Yeah, I'm OK. I woke up early and didn't want to disturb you so I just walked back to the car. Someone broke into it. I'm spending the day getting it fixed. Besides, I wasn't in the mood to deal with the San Gabriel Valley school budget crisis today."

"That's terrible. Why didn't you come back and get me?"

He was indignant. But was he upset about my car, or that he had missed his cue to rescue the damsel in distress?

"It's OK. I just drove the car home. My insurance will pay for the window."

"You sound really weird. You're not upset about last night, are you?"

"Oh, no," I lied. At least, I hadn't been upset until I realized that Marina Lu's diary was gone and Mark might have had something to do with it. I mustn't telegraph my confusion. The evening with him had been sweet, if expensively bought. I realized I should say more about last night. But for the second time in twenty-four hours, I wanted him to make the first move.

"*Je ne regrette rien*," he murmured, before signing off. "I'll call you in a few days."

The receiver clicked before I could formulate the appropriate French reply. "*Moi nonplus.*" Or was it "*Moi aussi*?"

Stumped, I wandered into the kitchen and opened the fridge, not really seeing the Tupperware containers and Styrofoam plates full of leftovers. I'd heard that kiss-off line before: Call you soon. On the other hand, there was his sexy French palaver. I reached for a container and popped it open. Pasta with pesto. I grabbed a fork and ate it cold before heading back to my paper nest on the bed.

I would allow myself five minutes by the digital clock to think about Mark. Although it was 100 degrees outside, I burrowed under the covers and wrapped my arms around myself. The weight of the blankets felt good. And sweating reminded me of last night. Slowly, I pulled a freckled forearm up to my mouth and pressed down hard with puckered lips. Had I remembered how to kiss, or could Mark tell that I hadn't done it in a long time? At least I might live to kiss again. Unlike the girl whose troubled words unfolded before me. Suddenly, I was glad that Marina hadn't been saving herself for marriage. I hoped that she and that night-crawler boyfriend of hers had joined in wild passionate sex in each room of her big empty house. Because it was sure too late now.

I fingered the diary leaves. There weren't many left to go. I rubbed my eyes and plunged back into Marina's world.

June 17. Sitting in a car for so long is really uncomfortable. We didn't really find out much, either. Michael left at 9 p.m. and hadn't come back by the time we gave up and headed to Lucky Noodle. That was at midnight.

July 22. This time we'll get there at midnight and stake the place out til dawn. When I wrote those words just now, it sounded so dramatic. Imagine, me doing something dramatic. Well it's back to my boring old form Friday night. Michael's taking me to the Backstreet Boys concert. I used to like them so much and their songs remind me of my youth. Sometimes I feel so old here.

September 14. Last night we followed him to a house in a skanky neighborhood, with houses and auto body shops jumbled next to each other, nothing like San Marino. Alison drank so much diet Coke that we went to the gas station twice so she could pee, which majorly screwed up our plans to watch the door til he came out. Alison really got on my nerves too, whining about how dirty the bathroom was. But I didn't rag on her or anything. Basically, I was happy she was there. She's such a good friend, even if she thinks Michael treats me like *merde*. If the situation were reversed, you can bet I'd help spy on her fiance.

It was depressing to look at the front lawn, which was about all we could do from the car, it was all yellow and dying. Maybe they can't afford a gardener and the disrespectful teenagers who live inside won't help out their parents. There were three nice cars parked in the circular brick driveway and more on the street, with lots of people coming and going. But not Michael. He stayed put. I know because his car was still there each time we came back from pee patrol. Maybe he really does have a girlfriend, although she must be boring if she lives in a place like that. I know I shouldn't be spying on my fiancé. But I can't stop now until I know.

September 19. Damn. Alison can't go with me tonight. She's retaking an AP test and wants to cram. Then she's off to Hong Kong. I'm on my own. This time, if he's at that house again, I'm going to go knock. I'll say I was driving by, saw his car and decided to surprise him.

There were no more diary entries. That was all the fates had tossed my way. Enough to let me know Marina Lu had unusual boyfriend problems. Well, little sister, didn't we all.

Ten at night found me brewing a pot of Cuban dark roast coffee and scrutinizing my wardrobe. I settled on a crushed black velvet cocktail dress with a big bow on the side. It wasn't retro, it was the real thing, five dollars at an Alhambra thrift store, from a more genteel era when men wore hats, women donned gloves, and young brides-to-be didn't get shot full of lead for no reason.

In the car, a breeze skated across my skin from the windowless window. I headed east on Interstate 10, watching the skyscrapers of downtown L.A. recede in my rearview until they shrunk to the size of a glittering toy inside a snowdome. Somewhere near Monterey Park, the familiar signposts disappeared altogether, and I knew I had crossed some invisible demarcation point. I was back in the San Gabriel Valley.

The New Avenue exit came up on the big green board ten minutes later. I took it. As I cruised slowly, looking for an Asian nightclub, I wondered where Tony was tonight, and whether I would pass him on the boulevard, headed out for a night of aimless teen partying with his friends.

I was headed to a more grown-up place. From what I had gleaned about Michael Ho from Marina's diary, he would go for something slick and expensive-looking. Something money. Soon, I saw it. A green canopy inscribed with Chinese characters and English. The Jade Dragon. Underneath stood three tall, burly security guards in black tails, their hands clasped casually in front. But I knew they were packing. I drove by twice. Then, just to make sure, I cruised the length of Garvey, until it petered out in an industrial strip. Then I turned the car around, pulled up to the jade canopy, and handed the keys to a valet. The parking fee would find its way onto an *L.A. Times* expense report sometime soon.

The security guards were white guys. They looked at me with neutral eyes, but something passed between us that wasn't pretty. The one nearest the front door pawed inside my purse, then two more guards wearing headsets motioned me through an airport-style metal detector. But these hired muscles eyeballed me a lot more carefully than the $5.50-an-hour guards at LAX. The weather around here must get awfully turbulent, I thought.

Inside, it was dark and humid, lit only by red candles that flickered against the walls. The air was thick with cigarette smoke. The music was deafening, Chinese pop spun by a young Asian DJ encased in a glass booth. There were no Caucasians here. The men were in their thirties and up and wore expensive suits. The women were in their early twenties, wearing slinky dresses and lolling on the arms of their dates. This was the kind of place where a bottle of cognac cost $300 and an evening's company could easily bump you into four digits.

I made my way through the throngs and hopped up on a suddenly empty bar stool. With little chance of blending in, I made the most of my difference. Soon, word would get out about the stranger. An emissary would be sent.

At times like this, I almost wished I smoked. I needed a prop until the alcohol arrived, and the ritual of lighting up, inhaling, and blowing out that first mouthful of smoke would have done handily. When I went to pay for the scotch, the bartender inclined his head and said it was paid for. Engrossed in polishing a glass, he didn't meet my eyes.

"By who?"

"House," I thought he responded.

I sipped my scotch, took in the scene, and waited.

"I'd like to buy the house a drink," I finally told the bartender, realizing that I was violating every social taboo in the Orient. But I was a *gwai lo*. A female barbarian. I couldn't be expected to know their protocol, and I used that flaming ignorance to my advantage.

The bartender disappeared, then returned.

"Mr. Young Se is coming," he announced in my ear.

I smelled his cologne before I saw him. Subtle. Expensive. Then he was at my elbow, a clean-cut bespectacled man of forty, much too polite to betray his inquisitiveness.

"Thank you for your kindness, Miss —"

"Diamond. Eve Diamond. And it's I who must thank *you*, Mr. Young Se. For the drink. Could we talk?"

"It would be my pleasure."

I followed him up a carpeted staircase past a series of closed doors. He opened the last one and ushered me in, and we sat across from each other at a wooden table decorated with a single flower bud in a vase and a bottle of very old, very expensive-looking Napoléon brandy.

"It is unusual to have such a pretty young lady enter this club unaccompanied," Mr. Young Se said once we were settled and the liquor was poured into cut crystal glasses. He spoke faintly accented English.

"Well, I was driving by and the sign caught my eye."

"We are honored." His mouth creased into a smile but his eyes watched me without blinking.

"Michael Ho once told me that the Jade Dragon is as stylish as any Hong Kong club. I see now that he was right."

Mr. Young Se's eyes narrowed at the name, but the smile stayed pasted on. He took a delicate sip of brandy and cleared his throat.

"We don't need any girls right now." He held the glass outstretched for a minute and considered. "But my colleague in Rowland Heights . . ."

"You misunderstand me," I said quickly. "Michael and I were friends in Hong Kong. I haven't seen him in several years, but . . ." I turned to him and blushed. "We have some, uh, unfinished business."

He gave me a more appraising look. With those last words, I had moved onto an entirely new plane. Now he took his time, assessing me as a horse trainer takes the measure of a new animal that may earn him a lot of money but also kick him upside the head if he isn't careful.

"He rarely visits us during the week."

I made a quick calculation. It was only Monday night.

"I know you'll get the word to Michael," I said. "He'll be so pleased. But it may anger him to hear about the others who tried to keep us apart."

Mr. Young Se quickly poured himself more brandy and sipped it thoughtfully.

"Of course I will do everything in my power."

"I know you will, Mr. Young Se. I can tell you're a good man."

I finished my drink, shook his hand vigorously, and left. The clock on the dash shone luminescent. It was 3 A.M. I didn't even take off my eye makeup before tumbling into bed.

CHAPTER 14

E ach week we had a staff meeting. They were long, boring affairs and it never failed that just as things were ready to adjourn, Trevor cleared his throat and asked some arcane question. Today, however, the receptionist interrupted his half-posed question when she ran into the conference room, waving a piece of paper.

"The wires just moved a story about a cop shooting in Temple City and downtown is screaming for copy."

Miller stopped in mid-sentence, punched in the number of the city desk, jotted down a few notes, and hung up, looking to see who was free.

"I'll volunteer." I was glad for any excuse to leave a staff meeting early, even though it was Luz's birthday and I'd miss the Sacher torte we had chipped in to buy. I didn't have any plans for later, either. Mark had called to say he'd be out of town for a week at a conference on the psychopathology of juvenile offenders. He said he'd be in touch, but I wasn't holding my breath. That night between us had already receded into fantasy.

In the car, I checked the address. It was in a low-rent neighborhood. With the office cell phone I had wrenched from Trevor on my way out, I called the L.A. Sheriff, since I knew Temple City rented its cops from the county instead of maintaining its own force.

"We're not releasing any more details until next of kin has been notified," the media relations flack intoned, then coughed up a few anyway. The cop had been found dead in his apartment, two bullet holes to the head. They thought it was more than a straight robbery-murder. How come? I wanted to know, but the flack had a ready answer: Cash stashed throughout his apartment had been left untouched.

"How much?" I asked. "Isn't that unusual, considering cop salaries?"

There was stiffening on the other end of the line.

"The investigation is continuing, and that's all the information we have available for the media at the moment."

As I turned onto the dead man's street, I saw TV vans and reporters milling around, held back by grim-faced cops who stood, battalion-like, behind barricades of yellow tape, mourning one of their own. The deceased had lived in one of those garish, 1950s apartment complexes festooned with what looked like reject props from the *Kon-Tiki* movie set.

I groped in my purse for my dog tags and hung them around my neck, making sure the fluorescent-yellow photo ID faced outward.

Even with all that copflesh around, I locked my car. They had other things on their mind today. I was glad, too, that I'd gotten that window replaced. As I walked past the TV lights where the on-air reporters were adjusting their earpieces and applying more foundation as they waited for their twenty-second sound bites, I spied the skinny, frenetic *Chinese Daily News* reporter joking with a young Asian policeman. That's where the action was.

"What's up?" I asked, nodding to the cop. I hoped they might feed me some juicy bits while the pack panted elsewhere. "What info do you have on the dead brother-in-blue?"

The reporter's name was George Ling. He leaned in close. I could smell the garlic on his breath and the oil in his hair.

"He says it was a gang hit," Ling said.

"Which gang?"

Annoyance rippled across the Asian cop's face and he stared at my chest, reading the tags to make sure I belonged there.

"There's a press briefing at 1600 hours where you can ask all the questions you want."

I tried a different approach. "Say, is Vittorio Carabini here? He'll know something."

Now the cop looked positively apoplectic. It dawned on me that Carabini probably didn't have a lot of friends among Asian officers in the San Gabriel Valley, where word of his racism would have traveled fast. The San Gabriel Valley was like a village when it came to that.

"I'm going to ask you to defer all questions until the press conference," the cop repeated.

"Right. Hey, George, how about we go knock on some neighbors' doors and get the 411 on the dead officer?"

"Give me five minutes," George answered, and I knew he wanted to pump the cop for details so I made myself scarce and let the man do his job. Then, since they wouldn't let us inside the apartment complex, George and I strolled to the back and waited by the underground parking garage until a car pulled up. We sprang, thrusting our IDs in front of the driver, whose startled look told us she had no idea what was transpiring fifty feet away at the front of her building.

"There was a policeman who lived in your complex, ma'am. A white guy, in his late forties," I shouted at the sixty-ish white lady who was frantically rolling up her window. "He's been found dead in his apartment. We're reporters. Did you by any chance know him?"

The woman pantomimed no, raised her hands in the universal "sorry" gesture, and drove in.

"Sooner or later we'll find one who knew him," I assured George.

We didn't have to wait long. A tattered Lincoln pulled up. Inside was a hard-bitten blonde with two kids. This time, I let George unreel the spiel while I hovered at his elbow.

"That sounds like a guy I used to see by the pool," the blonde said. "I'd been having trouble with my old man. He split and owed me tons of child support, and I broke down one day on the chaise lounge talking to this guy. He had a beer belly, would that be the one? Ruddy complected? He told me he was a cop and offered to lean on my ex, tell him the DA was investigating him for non-payment. I wasn't sure whether to believe him. You hear so many lines. But I hope it wasn't him. I liked him. My sons liked him too. He played football with you, didn't he, boys?"

"Ma'am, what was his name?" George Ling asked. I have to admit I had gotten kind of lost in her story of their concrete-and-chlorine attraction.

"Why, I don't think I ever asked," the woman said. "Johnny, Timmy, what did you call the man?"

"He had a long name, Momma," the boy said. "He told us just to call him Vit."

"Vit?" I said, my voice as high as the prepubescent boy's. "Was that short for Vittorio Carabini, by any chance?"

"We never knew his last name," the other boy piped up. They had identical brown hair and freckles and looked about eight and ten.

"He was just Vit," the first one said.

"Wait a minute," said the woman. "He gave me his card once. I may still have it." She rummaged through a faux Prada bag, pulling out hair spray, bills, and tampons.

"Here." Triumphant now, she handed over a filthy, crumpled card.

"Vittorio Carabini, Monterey Park Police Department," I read, then turned it over. She had used the back to blot her lipstick.

I sat down on the curb, still holding onto the card, and stared up at the Lincoln, noticing the rust-eaten underbelly. They weren't from California, I thought blindly, they had just washed up here at the Kon-Tiki like everybody else.

"Are you OK?" I heard Ling whisper.

"Yeah, I'll live. It's just that I sorta knew him. We'd have lunch . . . I didn't know he lived here."

"It's not a bad place," the blonde said. "The kids love the pool. I hope to Christ it's not him. And now, miss, if you'll give me back that card, I've got to cook dinner for these hungry boys."

"Of course, and thank you very much, ma'am," I heard George say as the car drove off, belching big gusts of exhaust that brought me back to reality.

"No wonder that cop went ballistic when I asked about Vit. He was in the Valley-wide Asian crime unit, you know. One of the senior dudes. I bet he got whacked 'cuz his cover got blown." I checked my watch and felt a shameful tingle of victory mingle with sadness. There were no pure emotions anymore. "They'll probably announce his name at the press conference, but we got it first."

I thought of Vit, drinking his wine at Santori's, regaling me with yarns of a recent operation, how they had set him up as a pinkie-ringed high-roller who hung out at the Asian gaming tables in the casinos of Southeast L.A. County. The cover story was he had picked up a taste for smack and mah-jongg in Nam, and while he had bucked the former, the latter still held him in a vise grip. For all I really knew about Vit, it might even have been true.

"Last time we had lunch, in fact, Carabini told me about an undercover assignment that might have easily gotten him killed."

I sketched it out for Ling, who nodded. "There's white guys, they get a taste for it, they're worse than Orientals."

"George, get with the program, Oriental is just for food." Ling shrugged. The *Chinese Daily News* hadn't been hit with political correctness yet, but he humored me anyway.

Before we walked back to the front of the building and rejoined the other reporters, I called the office and fed them Vit's name so the library could pull up a bio and file photo. It wouldn't be a scoop, but at least everyone might get home a little earlier tonight.

As I heard it announced officially, the thrill of the chase receded and I was left with the numbing reality that Vit was dead. I wasn't sure why I was so torn up about it. He was just a source, not someone I invited to my house for Sunday brunch. But he had seemed genuine and unafraid to express his biases, even when they were ugly, and I appreciated his honesty. I would have to visit Santori's and eat a plate of *linguine alle vongole* and kill a bottle of red wine in his honor, I thought, wondering if I could entice Luz to come with me. It was so retro she might find it campy.

Now the cop announcer was regurgitating most of what the sheriff's flack had already told me. He didn't describe Carabini's undercover gambling assignment, so I winked at George, whispering that we might have a scoop on our hands when it came to the motive. It would send the wrong message if Ling saw me getting all weepy over the demise of a racist cop.

George whispered back that he had a friend on the Monterey Park Police Department who might talk off the record about Carabini. We headed for the privacy of my car, where George called him from the cell phone and they spoke in Chinese for a long time. Then he handed me back the phone.

"My friend Stephen Zhang knows all about Carabini." George hesitated. I could tell he didn't want to speak ill of a dead man.

"And?" I probed. Delicacy be damned.

George looked uncomfortable. "He wasn't well-liked by some of the Asian recruits. My friend said he made ethnic slurs. He always did it as a joke, but no one was laughing."

I made a face. "Yes, that sounds like Carabini. I'm sorry he was a jerk to your friend."

"He complained a lot about money problems and thought all Chinese were rich. But in the casino, he played rich man. He wore diamond bracelets on his wrist and a recording device around his chest, my friend says."

"Was he afraid someone might be on to him?"

"My friend says it was hard to tell. Carabini was very macho."

"But how could he infiltrate a Chinese organized crime ring, big white guy like him who doesn't even speak Chinese?"

"But every week he was there. He saw people come and go, money change hands. He heard things. Chinese aren't the only ones gambling. Filipinos, Japanese, Vietnamese, Koreans. Even whites. Sometimes English is their common language. And Carabini became part of the scenery. No one would suspect such a loud, obnoxious American could be a cop. It would be too obvious." There was thin contempt in George's voice.

"What does your friend think?"

"He thinks Carabini ran out of luck."

"No shit. Maybe I could meet your friend sometime. I need some more cop sources."

"I can arrange that."

"Great. Let's work together again real soon, George."

"May it be under happier circumstances."

"We're in the news business, George. There are no happy circumstances."

CHAPTER 15

A week later, I followed up. I wanted to cast my net wide and see what the tide was bringing in, and a Chinese cop source sounded especially promising. George suggested meeting for lunch so I let him pick the place and damned if we didn't end up at a Chinese joint right across from Santori's.

Officer Stephen Zhang looked to be in his late twenties. He was stocky, of medium height, but already he had that stiff-legged cop swagger. He walked slowly, scanning the room like he was expecting an ambush. George scuttled crablike behind him, his glasses askew, wearing the same bouclé sweater and polyester pants as the day of Carabini's murder. They sat down awkwardly. As the tea came, George told me he had been with the *Chinese Daily News* for five years now. Before that, he'd been an ace at Xinhua News Agency in Beijing, jetting around with Li Ping to summits in Moscow and Berlin.

"How was that?" I sipped my tea in what I hoped was a demure, pre-Revolutionary fashion.

"Very tense. We printed only good news, and that was sometimes difficult. But I was so happy to see the world, I didn't care."

"You're getting an eyeful now."

"Yes." He beamed. "America is a wonderful place."

I looked up at Zhang, who looked away, embarrassed that I had

111

caught him staring, so I said: "George tells me you're first generation too, Officer Zhang."

Zhang shifted uncomfortably. "I was born in Taiwan, but I've been here since I was ten," he said in unaccented, colloquial English. "I graduated from Mark Keppel High in Alhambra. My parents wanted me to be a doctor, but I've been drawn to the force ever since the DARE officer visited our classroom in sixth grade and warned us to stay off drugs. I was only a kid, but I looked at that white policeman in his shiny black uniform and thought, yeah, that's gonna be me. By now, Ms. Diamond, I'm just as American as you."

He raised his chin in a very un-Chinese way, as if daring me to disagree.

"Maybe even more so," I murmured.

I backed off the all-American and thought about what a strange pair they made, the loud, extroverted Mainlander and the excruciatingly reserved and assimilated Taiwanese-American.

I was dying to quiz Zhang, but restrained myself for now. Instead, over bowls of fragrant soup, I proposed to George that we trade information. I knew we missed a lot of good stories because no one in our bureau could read the Chinese papers.

"That is a splendid idea." Ling took off his thick Dexter glasses, cleaned them carefully, then slid them back over his nose, ready for our first collaboration.

"So what has the *Chinese Daily News* written about the Marina Lu murder?"

Officer Zhang's eyes snapped into focus. I could tell he didn't approve of two civilians casually discussing an open murder investigation.

"That story is too sad." Ling clicked his tongue. "Her father is well-known in the Chinese community. Very powerful man."

"So I hear. Did you talk to him?"

"Yes. And the mother too, once she arrived from Hong Kong. Mrs. Lu told our readers that Marina had changed in the last few months. That she was becoming too American. I wrote a front-page story about the dangers that await Chinese young people in the United States."

Damn. I hadn't been allowed near Mrs. Lu and now I knew my

hunch had been right. Parachute mom had been winging it over on a plane when I called. It was stuff that the Chinese audience would take for granted but that should be kept from the American reader who might jump to the wrong conclusions about why a seventeen-year-old girl and her fourteen-year-old brother were living alone.

"What about her fiancé?"

George Ling sipped his soup long and lustily and said nothing.

"Did you interview Michael Ho too?"

"It was not necessary," he said. "Mr. Ho was not a family member. We Chinese give more privacy to people than you do in America."

"But what do you know about him? Is he a good guy?"

"Michael Ho has good connections to not-so-good people," Ling said. "If he complains to Marina's father that I am annoying him, I am losing my job. Our publisher is good friends with Mr. Lu."

"I see."

"We're not like your Woodward and Bernstein," he said.

"Do you mean that Michael Ho is involved with organized crime?" I looked right at Zhang as I said it. If he had worked at all with Carabini, then odds were he knew a lot about this murder that had not made its way into the papers.

Zhang remained poker-faced. But George Ling looked around fearfully. He was probably glad nobody had overheard the loud-mouthed foreign she-devil.

George shook his head. "I write ten stories a day sometimes. Very busy. Maybe I heard something once about Mr. Ho. But now he is a businessman."

"What do you think, Officer Zhang?"

"We can't discuss open murder investigations." He plopped a piece of barbecued eel studded with toasted sesame seeds into his mouth and I looked on with admiration. The damn things always slithered off my chopsticks.

I wanted to tell him that I was trustworthy and that Carabini would vouch for me. But then I remembered that Vit was dead. And that Zhang would be less apt than ever to trust me if he knew we had been pals.

I tried a different gambit. "Did you ever interview Reginald Lu?"

Zhang shook his head. "Carabini said it was too 'sensitive.' "

"That's funny," I said. "Vit told me the Chinese cops tried but didn't get anything new."

"Maybe you are misinformed."

I speared an eel and fishtailed it up to my mouth before continuing. "By the way, what does it mean if a Chinese person has a black hand and red heart tattoo?"

George looked at me, his chopsticks two parallel ivory lines against his thin face.

"I don't know. Why?"

I paused. Here was the moment of truth. Was I really willing to share my toys?

"Marina Lu had that tattooed on her right breast," I said. "I thought it might mean she was in a gang too."

"Never heard of that," George said. Zhang was silent, but his eyes flickered again. It would take a lot more than one lunch to pry anything out of this cop.

As the waitress cleared the plates, George Ling grabbed for the check and I had to wrestle it from him. Which wasn't too hard. He was skinny and wiry but I was fast and took vitamins. I won.

CHAPTER 16

The lawn had long since degenerated to dirt, pounded into a hard carpet by small scabby legs. Even for a cheap stucco box, this apartment building had seen better days. Three of the windows were patched with duct tape. *Banda* music thumped from a ground-floor apartment. Someone upstairs was cooking with sesame oil, and the smell mingled with car exhaust at the building entrance and unfurled like a stale welcome.

I found the apartment I was looking for and knocked. The door was plywood, as if it had been kicked in once and hastily replaced. From inside, I heard noise and got my *Times* photo identification ready. South El Monte was about as far away from San Marino as you could get, income-wise, but the good citizens of both towns wanted to see ID before talking to a stranger.

I was here to follow up on the parenting story I'd begun several weeks before. Teachers had noticed bruises on the boy who lived here, and the father, a former colonel in the South Vietnamese Army, had been charged with child abuse. But a sympathetic social worker had tipped me off that there was more to it.

Col. Harry Nguyen fingered my laminated card, handed it back, and invited me in. I took off my shoes and stepped onto a green shag carpet.

Nguyen's back was stooped, the legacy of ten years spent in a communist re-education camp after the North Vietnamese had overrun Saigon and methodically hunted down everyone who had worked with the U.S. Army. Nguyen beckoned me to a chair that wobbled when I sat down. I set my purse on a coffee table branded with cigarette burns and hoped the innards wouldn't spill out, revealing my cache of gum and pepper spray. As Nguyen's teenage daughter brought a steaming mug of tea, I took in my surroundings. Someone had patched the stucco walls with primer. They were bare, save for a calendar of Vietnamese teen idol singing stars. In the corner, two lit candles paid homage before a makeshift shrine to the ancestors.

I sipped gratefully. When I swallowed, a sad realization rushed through me. These people are so poor that they bring me hot water to drink instead of tea.

"Thank you for agreeing to talk to me," I began, as Harry Nguyen eyed me anxiously. "Can you tell me what happened last week with your son?"

"My daughter, she very good English, she translate," Nguyen said. He launched into a torrent of Vietnamese that his doe-eyed daughter dutifully translated, inspecting the shag fibers as she spoke.

It had started with a note sent home by the teacher. The Nguyens' eight-year-old son was fighting on the playground. The teacher discovered that his classmates mocked his threadbare clothes. So she sent a note home about a church that would be happy to donate newer ones.

"We are not beggars," Nguyen's daughter translated, "but with this behavior the boy brought shame on our family. So I beat him with a stick. Up and down his legs," the girl said, bringing her arm down in a chopping motion. "My son must be punished for fighting."

I looked up from my notepad and met the confused eyes of Colonel Nguyen. Now it was becoming clear. The boy had gone to school the next day with bruises and the horrified teacher had called the police.

"Father says if he doesn't discipline his son, who will?" the daughter was saying. "We want him to grow up to be a good American. So tell me, please, Miss Lady Reporter, why they punish us?"

As she finished translating, the abuse victim peeked out shyly from a hallway, then ran to crawl into his father's lap, where he squirmed happily. Nguyen looked down with a doting expression. It seemed spontaneous, not like a circus act staged for my benefit. The colonel's hand rested on the boy's shiny black helmet of hair.

"I love my son. It is my responsibility to raise him right."

An hour later, I stood up to go, a good story jotted into my notebook. No wonder the county had just added twelve social workers who spoke Lao, Hmong, and Fukienese, in addition to the more garden-variety Asian languages like Mandarin and Tagalog. My hand was poised on the Nguyens' doorknob when an insistent knock sounded. Out of habit, I opened it.

And stared. Five Asian teenagers crowded around me. Their body language was menacing. One quickly tucked something into the waist-band of his khakis and pulled out his shirt. Another strode forward to Nguyen and shoved him backwards with the palm of his hand, murmuring in Vietnamese. The teenage daughter gasped. Nguyen whirled around and barked an order at her and she was silent. He put his hands together and spoke Vietnamese to them in pleading tones.

Was this a home invasion? But there was nothing to steal. They were focused malevolently on Nguyen, who was growing paler by the minute. I felt selfish relief that their venom wasn't directed at me. After one last burst of Vietnamese, the leader threw down his cigarette butt, crushed it slowly and contemptuously into the shag carpet, and headed out. Each of his lieutenants cast a last intimidating look at Nguyen as they filed out behind him.

"What was that all about?" I gasped.

"They're collectors," she stammered. "My father took out a loan so he could buy some sewing machines and set up a little business with his cousin. They make sports jackets. But there was a fire. It destroyed the workspace and we can't pay the loan back. They want the money."

"Golden Pacific Bank is terrible," the daughter said. "It's not like a regular bank. If you don't pay, they send gangsters to collect."

With a staccato burst of Vietnamese, the father hushed her and ushered me out the door.

Something was nagging me as I got in my car. Nguyen's daughter had said Golden Pacific Bank. Wasn't that the name of the bank that Marina Lu's father had started?

It was time to pay Reginald Lu another visit. I got on the freeway and headed to the headquarters of Golden Pacific Bank.

The gleaming steel-and-glass building on Garvey Boulevard was typical of the new construction built with Overseas Chinese money. The bank was growing fast—twenty-two branches in just seven years—a far cry from the old days, when Asians were prevented by thinly veiled racism from chartering and owning banks in America. Now the global marketplace beckoned to anyone with cash.

The place was cool, air-conditioned, and professional. Suited tellers glided around on the ground floor. The corporate offices were on the fifth.

"Eve Diamond to see Mr. Lu," I told the receptionist.

"Do you have an appointment? He's in a meeting."

"Please tell him it's regarding his daughter."

The woman scowled, but did as she was asked. She returned, closing the door behind her.

"Mr. Lu will be right out."

Twenty minutes later, Lu ushered me into his inner sanctum. I saw no signs of a meeting. His desk was bare. Maybe it was a telephone meeting.

"Ms. Diamond, what is this all about?"

"Do you know a Mr. Nguyen?"

"Name means nothing to me. That's like Smith in Vietnamese."

"What do you do with loans that you can't collect on?"

"We have a very low default rate. Perhaps you don't know this about Asian people, but when we give our word, it is sacred. We will work two or three jobs to pay back the loan on time. But a funny thing happens. The longer that an Asian immigrant has lived in America, the more likely he is to forget the importance of his word. Then he becomes more like your average American."

Lu's eyes glinted briefly, then faded back to opaque.

"But what about the few loans you do get defaults on?" I asked.

"They go through the usual channels. All these procedures are laid down by state law."

"What are those?"

Exasperation crept into his voice.

"If after ninety days we are absolutely unable to collect or reach an agreement, we sell the bad loans. And now can you please tell me what this has to do with Marina?"

"Sell them where?"

"To a variety of places. One of our subsidiaries, for instance, specializes in bill collecting. This is one of the fields in which Michael has proved simply outstanding."

"Michael?"

"Michael Ho. He was Marina's fiancé. Now, Ms. Diamond, will you please tell me what this has to do with Marina?"

"Marina's fiancé ran the Golden Pacific Bank subsidiary that collected on your old loans?"

"That's right, and he's had terrific success. Sharp boy. He put in a new computer tracking system that has worked wonders."

And the snub-nosed revolver didn't hurt either, I thought. Either Lu didn't know the way his protégé collected on the debts, or he was lying. Proceed carefully, I thought.

"I came to find out whether you've received the coroner's report yet," I said. "I was afraid you wouldn't take my call."

"Yes," he said wearily. "Gunshot wound to the head."

"Thank you, Mr. Lu. I'm sorry to disturb you. I hope they find whoever did this."

"So do I, Ms. Diamond. But I don't have high hopes. Your society is a violent one, where strangers kill each other for nothing."

"Well, the police—"

"—are doing their best." He gave me a rueful smile. "We should let them do their job. It's time to move on to other stories. I know something about your business. Just last week I attended a luncheon in your paper's so-called Picasso Room. Perhaps I could bring up your name next time I visit and tell them how impressed I am with your reporting skills. I can be a great help to you."

Or a great hindrance, I thought, finishing what he left unsaid.

We said good-bye uneasily. Why was Reginald Lu threatening me with his pathetic *Times* connections? Why did he want me to stop asking questions about his daughter's murder? This wasn't the first time a source had tried to pull rank on me. But this was a murder. And it seemed like everyone knew a lot more than they were telling.

CHAPTER 17

On the freeway that night, my easy reverse commute turned into a nightmare because of what the radio announcers like to call a SigAlert involving a jackknifed big-rig. I sat in traffic for an hour and it occurred to me that this was reality, in this car, on the freeway by myself. Reality wasn't the hallucinatory world of the immigrant communities in the San Gabriel Valley where I drifted through the day like a pale ghost. That was all brief flashes of Technicolor brilliance, a place whose very lure was its "otherness" from mine. Being able to lose myself in that uncharted territory liberated me, brought out sides I hadn't much explored before, and took my mind off the two missing men in my life. But in the car, I regressed to boring old Eve Diamond.

Sometimes I drove so many miles in one day, crisscrossing the sprawling suburbs, that I could have traveled to San Francisco. On those days, I would go batty. Stuck in traffic one day, I began noticing that a lot of the businesses had switched *K* for a *C* in their names, places like the Kool Kat Liquor and Kwik Kleaners. Then I started thinking about the history of these places filled with white midwestern immigrants; Iowa by the Sea, as Carey McWilliams had called Long Beach.

They had romanticized Southern California, building rough-hewn places like the Loomis House in the Arroyo, which now squatted in the buzzing shadow of the Pasadena Freeway, but many of them had been bigots all the same. What if the *K* was a code way to signal they were Ku Klux Klan sympathizers? You know, everyone else thought it was cute, but it was really like a wink or a secret handshake. Then I started spotting the *K* businesses all over. Krazy Kar Wash in Temple City. Kotton Kandy Florist in Arcadia. And I began to get really paranoid.

When I got home, I checked the machine. No calls. Damn. I poured myself a glass of red. Christ I was drinking a lot lately. Women like me didn't go out to bars at the end of the day to let off steam with their buddies. We went home and drank alone, with only the blinking, indifferent cat as witness. It's no wonder there were so many secret women alcoholics. They died of cirrhosis of the liver at forty-seven and their coworkers would say, gee, she rarely missed a day of work. I never dreamed she had a problem.

I switched to Pellegrino. Then I laid out the bits of my puzzle.

On one piece of paper I wrote *Michael Ho*. On another, I wrote *Jade Dragon*. On the third, I wrote the name of Marina's friend *Alison*. On the fourth, I wrote the *strange house* where Marina and Alison had followed Michael. On the fifth, I wrote the *diary* itself. Off in the corner of a blank page, I printed the word *Mark*, followed by a question mark. Where did he fit in and why was he intersecting between my personal life and my professional one? After shuffling the pages aimlessly, I gave up and went to bed.

I woke up refreshed at 6:30 A.M., grabbed my Marina Lu file, and drove to Du-par's in the San Gabriel Valley for my favorite breakfast— buttermilk pancakes and scrambled eggs with strong coffee. I liked the vinyl booths, the anonymous blue-collar types who read the paper and gabbed with the waitress. The Studio City Du-par's drew actors who read *Variety* and circled the day's auditions, but I was miles away in Temple City, where people scanned the want ads under "mechanic" and "secretary" and checked the race results at Santa Anita to see if their horse had come in.

Why was I so consumed by this case? Was it just *pasatiempo*, something to do because I had no interior life and the profound futility of my days got to me if I thought about it too long? My one-night fling with Mark was an antidote, but I didn't know how far to trust him either. I wanted so much to lay my head in the crook of his neck and confess my fear, but I knew instinctively that with this one, walking away from what I wanted most was the way to get him.

Miller was just pulling into the *Times* parking lot, clicking off his cell phone, as I drove in. He looked right at me and he didn't look happy. I looked at my watch. I wasn't that late.

"You can put that key back in your ignition," he told me. "There's been a triple murder at a Pasadena video arcade. Bit of a scuffle, then one carload of kids left, came back an hour later, and shot up the place. Led by a teenage girl. Probably Southeast Asian."

He breathed heavily. Even in L.A., this was a lot to handle at ten in the morning. "Luz is hitting the school and Trevor's on cops. You've got some good sources at that counseling center. Find out if these were gang kids."

"Let me see if my main contact is back in town yet." I reached for his phone and dialed Mark's number, which might as well have been tattooed above my heart. Miller looked on, impressed at such dedication to the job.

"Eve." Mark sounded happy to hear from me.

So he was back. But he hadn't called me. In that case, I wanted to make clear this was strictly business.

"Did you hear about the Pasadena video arcade shooting last night? Three kids dead and two more critical. Police say the suspects are gangbangers, and get this. The shooter was a girl. So what I want to ask you is . . ."

What I really wanted to ask him was did he want to see me again. And could we skip the frothy drinks this time.

". . . whether you've heard anything about gang activity at that arcade," I continued smoothly.

"Oh no, that's awful. Well . . ." He broke off, sounding disappointed. "Jesus, Eve, that's bad news. But here I thought . . . OK, I confess. I just got back last night. And when I heard your voice, I hoped you were calling for something more personal."

"Not this morning, Mark. I've got a big fat journalism headache."

"And I've got something that works better than aspirin."

"What I need right now is some information."

"Yes, I know." He made a long noise of exasperation. "I'll be free at eleven. Why don't you come down and we can talk. About all of it."

CHAPTER 18

We were in bed again, limbs splayed across the white sheets, no longer moving.

Just an hour ago, I had been at home, sitting cross-legged in front of the stereo, reading the lyrics on the back of an old Frank Sinatra album as I unwound from the long day, the tense jousting with Mark, the complicated story that needed to be written on a forty-five-minute deadline. Then I had driven home. So anyway, Frank was crooning "Blue Moon," and it must have been the heat or something, because suddenly I felt so light-headed with longing that I gasped out loud.

It was 11 P.M. And I had gotten into my car and driven to his house, barely conscious of getting on the freeway. On the passenger seat I had thrown a report from the County Gang Task Force that he had loaned me that morning. Giving it back was the thinly veiled pretext I had dreamed up for showing up at his house near midnight.

When Mark opened the door, he wore only green khaki shorts. He stood in the portal, leaning on one arm, and it seemed the most natural thing in the world to step into the arch of his body. The report slid from my hand to the floor and he didn't ask. Talk seemed superfluous.

Now, I lay spent, staring at the cracks in his plaster ceiling. Slowly, I transferred my gaze to the square of framed indigo cloth that hung as the sole decoration on his wall.

"Once, when I was in Kyoto, a friend arranged for me to tour an indigo factory," I said. "The same family had owned it for many generations. All their hands were permanently stained blue, I'll never forget that, especially the grandfather. He wore a homemade straw hat as he stirred the vats of liquid."

My nose twitched at the memory. "The indigo smelled like seaweed and hay mixed together. A vegetable smell. It wasn't unpleasant. I wanted to dip the tail of my white cotton shirt into the vat to see what would happen. Or ladle some into a bowl and sip it like some exotic soup."

I got out of bed and walked naked to the bathroom, where I looked in the mirror and saw that my face was flushed, my cheekbones pronounced. Spending time with Mark agreed with me. Maybe that's why his words hit me so hard when they came.

"You just like me 'cuz I'm exotic."

I sucked in my breath. Mark's delivery was ironic, but the words hinted at generations of distrust.

I sat on the closed toilet seat and calmly traced the tiny white hexagonal tiles with my bare toes, toes that were gnarled and knotted from too many childhood years of tight shoes. Now my cheek felt feverish, and I lay it against the cool porcelain sink until its graceful curves indented my skin.

"Exotic?" I finally asked. "I think *you're* exotic?"

I studied myself in the mirror. My skin was pale, and my red hair fell in loose curls over my shoulders. My eyes were green, with flecks of hazel and gold. Now, they narrowed almost imperceptibly like my daddy's had when he was angry. I had his Central European flair for the dramatic, infused with the melancholy of my Russian immigrant mother.

I stormed back into the bedroom, rooting around for the clothes I had cast off so feverishly, collecting them in a clenched fist.

"I am one hundred percent more exotic to you than you will ever be to me," I started. "If I wanted exotic, I would have gone for some Italian-suited Hong Kong businessman here in L.A. trying to set up a branch of the family business."

I thought of Reginald Lu and blushed. Mark took it for embarrassment and his face softened. I turned to stomp out of the room, but before I got too far he tackled me, pinning me to the ground, wrestler style.

I howled and scratched at him.

"Let me tell you something, Mr. Third-Generation Asian-American, with your Levis and your college-educated parents and your hipper-than-though attitude. Your grandparents were already homeowners here in Los Angeles when mine were fleeing penniless from the Russian Revolution and Hitler's new world order. You never had to be ashamed of your mother's broken English or afraid to bring your friends over because of the weird relatives who were always sitting at the kitchen table, getting drunk and singing songs in a language no one understood, with all the curtains drawn at three o'clock in the afternoon."

Mark put his face next to mine and held my gaze with his eyes.

"I didn't mean it like that."

"Let me up," I struggled, then screamed with impotent rage as I realized he wouldn't. "You did so mean it. It's that PC crap, that because I'm white, I will have to atone into perpetuity for what people who look like me once did to people who look like you. Well, for one, that's bullshit, because my ancestors were busy escaping persecution just as yours were. And besides, I am not my grandmother."

"OK. OK. Sometimes I just wonder. That's all."

I scowled at him. "You think I'm that shallow?"

"I think you're very deep, Eve." He drew me to him again and I relented, an instinctive response far from my brain.

There would be time enough to curse the uneasiness that now lay before us, the Pandora's box of race.

The next morning, I didn't sneak out of bed before he awoke, but lay there as he slumbered and thought long and hard about what he had said. Those hateful seven words. Why had I reacted so strongly? Was it because I recognized the kernel of hidden truth? Why else would I plunge headlong into this world that I didn't understand, that didn't particularly want me to understand it? Was it a pretend fantasy, second best to exploring the real Asia with Tim? If exotic adventure wouldn't come to me, then I would go and find it, right here in L.A.

As I swung my legs onto the hardwood floor and made to stand up, Mark's eyes opened.

"Where are you going?"

"To the bathroom."

"Will you come back?"

"For a while."

I was anxious to get home, if only to prove that I still existed apart from him. But he wouldn't let me leave without eating breakfast. We drifted into the kitchen.

"I make a mean French toast," he announced, carving the air with a plastic spatula. "No vohn cahn reseest zeez Frenchie toads."

"Yuck," I said, picturing him skinning a wriggling amphibian, then pounding its tiny legs with a mallet.

He ignored my outburst.

"And you can help me with the syrup." He dragged a chair to the kitchen cupboard. "Hop on that and get down the Grand Marnier, brandy, and port. Should be on the third shelf."

"Aunt Jemima's gonna have one hell of a hangover."

"You'll see, Miss Smartypants."

Mystified, I lugged down the booze. He instructed me to pour a third of a cup from each bottle into a saucepan, add a cup of orange juice, three tablespoons of sugar, and two of lemon juice.

"Let it boil down for twenty minutes, stirring frequently, until it's the consistency of thick syrup. You want a morning snort, just lean over and sniff the fumes."

From the other end of the kitchen, he started whistling. Above the rattle of pots and slamming of the fridge, I made out the "Ode to Joy." Mark did a jazzy shuffle, then pulled out a griddle, followed by buttermilk, a loaf of crusty bread, cinnamon, vanilla, and eggs. He must have planned this, I frowned, not entirely displeased but trying to figure out how.

In between all the beating, dipping, and flipping, he set the table and brewed a pot of coffee. The room filled with the aroma of java and heating cinnamon. Tethered to my burner, I stirred steadily and stole secret glances as he padded with wildcat grace across the small kitchen.

We sat across from each other at his breakfast nook and I let him serve. He tapped powdered sugar on my toast, then ladled on the liquid amber dotted with bits of orange pulp. My saliva glands started firing. I took a gulp of the strong coffee to keep from drooling, then took a bite.

My mouth exploded with sensation—the citrus tang of the sauce, the velvet dusting of snowy sugar on my tongue, the eggy batter giving way to the thick chewiness of the bread inside.

He was watching me. It was the same look he wore in bed.

"You were right," I told him, eyes rolled back in bliss. "This is intense."

And suddenly, I wasn't talking about the food anymore. A profound sadness gripped me. Here we were in his sunny kitchen, sipping our coffee and eating brunch and doing all the domestic things a normal couple does on a lazy summer weekend. Then why did I feel like such an impostor in my own life? Was it because I knew this was not my destiny? That I knew from past experience that such bliss couldn't last? From somewhere far ahead in time, I looked back on this idyllic morning and wept.

He sensed my mood plummet.

"Don't you like it?"

"Oh, but I do. Too much," I whispered. "Much too much."

Then enjoy it, fool, a voice inside me urged.

I smiled at him through damp lashes. "It reminds me of something my grandmama used to make, and for a moment there, I got all sad."

Then the old urgency seized me, and I got up as if in a dream, went to his side, and slid into his lap, winding myself around him like a boa. His fork clattered to the floor.

Later, we reheated the remains of the breakfast and ate with the gusto of the truly famished.

CHAPTER 19

The phone rang as I stood outside my front door and groped for the keys. I fumbled the chiseled metal up to the lock and rammed it in, flung open the door, and ransacked my living room for the portable that never seemed to be where I had left it the night before.

"Hello?" Whoever was on the other end wasn't saying anything. I thought I heard faint, scratchy music in the background, like an old-fashioned gramophone. Finally, I put down the receiver.

That night, I prowled the house for something to do. Gravitating to the back porch, I perched moodily on the chaise lounge and contemplated the view. Downstairs, Violetta was indulging in her filterless French cigarettes, and smoke curled and hung in the eaves above me. I wrinkled my nose in distaste, but the odor drew me back to the jade-canopied nightclub where I had played cat and mouse with Mr. Young Se. Damn, it was Saturday already. I considered what I knew about Michael Ho: Marina's fiancé, rising Golden Pacific Bank star and Reginald Lu protégé, someone admired but feared throughout the Chinese immigrant community. Clearly, what George Ling had told me was less important than what he had left out. Ling was scared, pure and simple. This guy exerted some dark power over everyone who uttered his name. I had to go back to the Jade Dragon and find him.

This time, I felt like an old hand. When Mr. Young Se arrived to lead me up the stairs, I took them two at a time and graciously accepted his offer of a glass of cabernet. After one sip, I puckered up. Should have stuck to scotch like last time. What did the Chinese know about wine?

Mr. Young Se said Michael Ho was expected soon. We spoke about the nightclub business and he kept looking at the door. It got really late. My eyelids started to droop. I hadn't been sleeping enough. I raised my arm to check my watch, but it felt like lead. The numbers swam crazily on the white face.

The next thing I remember, I slid forward. I just need to put my head down for a moment, I slurred apologetically to Mr. Young Se. My cheek settled against the freshly starched linen tablecloth. When I swam back into consciousness, two heads were peering over me. They asked questions and I responded like a marionette whose strings are pulled. Then there was nothing but blackness. A dull but nagging pain brought me to. I was in my car, slumped over the gearbox, and it was digging a hole in my side. I moved into a more comfortable position and passed out again. This time the damp woke me up. My body was stiff. My head was foggy and my mouth had a terrible taste. I moved my limbs one by one. Next, I focused on the reassuring sounds of my own breathing. Gingerly, I moved my hand down my dress and then up my inner thighs. My nylons were still on. I slid a cold hand underneath the elastic and down into my panties, filled with dread. I knew what could happen to women who drank too much at bars, then passed out. I groped myself, feeling for stickiness. Nothing. My underpants were dry. They weren't on inside out or backwards. Was I sore there? I flexed. No. So I hadn't been raped.

But neither had I drunk too much. The last thing I remembered clearly was sipping my cabernet with Mr. Young Se and waiting impatiently for Michael Ho to arrive. The wine had been bitter. My brain fastened upon that tidbit, then seized up and refused to function anymore. My head throbbed. The windows were fogged over. The door was unlocked. Someone had done something to me, then shoved me in my car and left.

The sun was coming up now, and when it hit the damp windshield, some clarity returned. I rolled down the window and inhaled deeply of the pink dawn. My purse lay beside me. I opened the wallet, sure I had been cleaned out. Nope, the eighty dollars I had withdrawn from the

ATM the night before was still there, as were my credit cards and my car keys. Gratefully fishing them out, I tried the engine and drove slowly around the deserted nightclub parking lot, testing my abilities. Bad, but OK to drive home. I got on Interstate 10 and navigated fuzzily back to Silverlake. Twice I had to pull onto the shoulder because I was seeing double. I felt dirty and violated and increasingly alarmed that I couldn't remember what had happened.

Pulling up in front of my house, I stumbled up the steps and into the duplex, shedding my clothes as I went. It seemed my bra was missing, but before I could make sure, I slept. I woke in the late afternoon, still feeling hungover and nauseous. My limbs were jerky. My eyes rolled backwards in my head. Slowly, an image swam into focus. It was of a well-dressed Chinese man. He wore a patchouli-tinged aftershave that smelled nice and I wanted to put my arms around him and kiss him. I tried to struggle up, and there was laughter. I felt him fondle my breasts, stroke the nipples until they became hard. There were two other men in the background. One started asking questions. Mr. Young Se had evaporated.

"Why are you so interested in Marina Lu?" one asked.

I told him all about Tim and my plans to get promoted. I explained that Mark and I were solving the mystery together. Significant glances passed between them. I focused again and they were grilling me about Marina's diary. Had I read it all the way through? They were very insistent.

I started crying. Why are you being so mean to me? I told them about Marina's boyfriend problems, the boxes of condoms, and how she had followed Michael to a house.

"Where is the house?"

"I don't know," I stuttered.

"What about the girls?"

"You mean Marina's friends?"

"The girls at the house."

"What girls at what house?"

Finally, they seemed satisfied. The handsome man came in real close now. I could smell the pomade coming off his hair. It was rank, unlike the rest of him.

"Stop asking about Marina Lu," he said, then winked at another man, who covered his mouth with his hand and laughed like a hyena. Several pairs of arms now heaved me up and carried me down the fire escape out back. From inside, the techno music thumped. A dim red light flashed danger in the back of my mind. They are going to kill you. I heard a door slam, then passed into oblivion. The next thing I remember was waking up in my own car.

This evening, after showering, eating a bowl of cereal, and drinking a cup of strong coffee, my brain began to clear. I knew now what had happened to me, knew where the bitter taste in my wine had come from. I had written about the phenomenon of date-rape drugs, listened to stories of tearful, angry women who had met men for a drink in a public place, passed out, and woken up in their beds, violated. Rohypnol, the ultimate date-rape drug. You move in a dream state, doing as you're told, then don't remember well enough to testify afterward. But the guys who had drugged me hadn't been after my body. The fondling had been gratuitous, I realized, recoiling at my involuntary physical responses. That's what date-rape drugs did. They stripped away every inhibition. You'd take off all your clothes if someone suggested it. You were helpless, an insect pinned wriggling to their specimen board. Ingest too much and you'd die. Oh, no, it wasn't my body they had wanted, but my brain, what I knew about Marina. There was something in her diary, in that house she had seen, in the manner of her death, that someone didn't want exposed.

I got back into bed and pulled the covers tight. Rational thought gave way to limpid, liquid fear. They could have killed me in there. They could have made me disappear forever. I rubbed the soles of my feet against the comforting cotton sheets. Somehow, I must have passed their test, told them what they wanted, and it had been paltry enough to spare me. Perhaps they weren't brazen enough to kill a reporter yet. Perhaps they just wanted to learn what I knew, then frighten me, knowing I'd be too afraid and embarrassed to report them. And if I did, Mr. Young Se would smile and say it was unfortunate the young lady had drunk too much and had to be escorted to her car. A search of the Jade Dragon would turn up nothing. The drug had slipped out of my urine already, leaving no trace. Any sediment on the wine glass would long have been washed away. Mr. Young Se would have witnesses to testify to his whereabouts that entire night. I knew I should report this to the police, but what exactly would I say? I didn't even know my inquisitioners, and any publicity would just drive them further underground.

Yes, I had been violated. The very core of my being had been stolen, picked over, then stuffed roughly back into my body. My stomach began to churn. If they thought this would make me back off, they didn't know me very well. It had only whetted my interest. The pieces were there before me. All I had to do was figure out how to put them together. Instead, I slept.

CHAPTER 20

The bougainvillea scraped out a sad lament against my bedroom window. Deep in the bowels of the old house, timbers creaked and moaned. Warm gusts of air blew tumbleweeds big as cars down from the mountains and beached them on front lawns, a prickly reminder that this was a desert, and our lush greenery as illusory as any Emerald City.

I slept poorly, as I always did when the Santa Anas blew into town. The hot winds often set me on edge, and gave me narcotic dreams. Now the Rohypnol leaving my system heightened the effect. I was in a darkened building. Unknown menace lapped at my feet, then slunk back into the shadows. I was afraid to move, but it was equally danger- ous to stay put. From far away, I heard music playing, tinny yet recog- nizable. It was a folk song from Central China, a woman's mournful, high-pitched voice. Don't ask me how I knew the words. Dreams aren't logical. But it went on and on, that voice, singing about lost children, the children who were gone and would never come back. Where are the children? the woman sang, her voice ancient and reedy. And then with a loud slam, the song stopped entirely.

I startled back into consciousness. My body felt rigid. I waited for my spirit to slip back inside and reclaim my limbs, calm my heart. The door slammed again.

Now I eased silently out of bed, toes groping prehensile until they found the comfort of my furry slippers. I didn't feel drugged anymore. It was still dark but the wind had stopped. How long had it been quiet? Hugging the wall, I moved through the bedroom and into the hallway that led to the back of the house. Warm air eddied around me. I made my way along the passage and saw that the rear door had come open and was gaping promiscuously. Right before I reached the door, a last blast of wind tore through the house and the door banged against the wall, repeating the noise from my dreams.

The wind must have blown it open, I thought, and it's been slamming half the night. But I remembered locking it. I wasn't that stupid, after what had just happened. I closed the door and turned the lock, checking it this time. Sure enough, the deadbolt hadn't engaged. The old house had shifted over the years and the jamb wasn't exactly flush with the door. I jiggled until it slid in. I felt better, but prudence led me through the house just in case, turning on lights, peering behind doors, jabbing my umbrella into closets. No, there was no intruder lurking here. Only my ever-fervid imagination, crouched like a chattering monkey on my stiff shoulder.

Wide awake now, I sat at the kitchen table and stared out at the tall spires of downtown, illuminated as always. No, not always. For seventy years this window had looked out onto cow pastures and the lone, white steeple of City Hall, the tallest building in the entire city. It was only in the last twenty-five years that a real L.A. skyline had arisen, as the corporate giants congregating downtown had vied among themselves to build the tallest monument to their greed. Soon the brawlers of glass and steel had elbowed aside City Hall, which now stood off to the left, a prim pale stone dowager dwarfed by newer, flashier players. Well, I still liked the old lady best.

I put on water for tea and made a selection from my extensive stash. Oolong. As my hand closed around the packet, I stopped. Oolong. China. Folk songs. A woman's voice. Missing children.

Where are the children? the woman had sung.

The parachute children. I should find the parachute kids.

I looked at my watch: 4 A.M. I couldn't call Tony and Lily until it got light. My hands closed around the ceramic mug, fingertips touching. Warm steam filled my nostrils. I lifted up the mug and peered underneath. Made in China, it said. Within the last few years, someone had snuck into my house when I wasn't looking and stamped those three words on almost everything I owned. From kitchenware to sneakers to T-shirts. Made in China. All roads led back there. One day I might travel there myself. In the meantime, China had come to me.

Tony sounded happy to hear from me. Or maybe he was just bored, rattling around in that big old empty house of his. I wanted to get him outside, where the sunshine could shower down some Vitamin D he was missing with his late-night, fast-food diet. I wanted to tell him to stay away from Jimmy Lai.

Soon, we were squatting at the edge of a koi pond at the Huntington Gardens in San Marino, marveling at the fabulous estate Henry Huntington had built a century ago to lure his mistress west. The fish were bright orange and gold, with speckles and stripes. They were as big as cats and swam right up to be petted.

"We had koi in Hong Kong," Tony told me. "My grandmother and I fed them every morning."

I pictured the ritual. A white-haired grandmother gliding into the room, sitting at the bed, and stroking the child's face as he woke. They'd walk to the pond, and he'd tug at her papery old hand to go faster. The boy fed them balls of sticky rice. They nibbled it out of his hand and he'd squeal with fear and delight when those cold wet fishy lips grazed his fingers . . .

Tony took a stick, squatted, and poked at the lotus leaves floating on the pond's surface. He looked like a child again, one who wore short pants and a sailor top and went off to school with a bookbag strapped to his back.

"They were her pets," he said. "Some of them had been around when she was a little girl, and they were really old and huge. She gave them names and spoke to them like children. There was one big orange and red dude she scolded when he swam around, ignoring her. Another one had rare tiger-striped markings and she'd praise him and tell him how handsome he was. Koi can be really expensive, you know."

"I learned that when I wrote a story about koi disappearing from Descanso Gardens in La Cañada."

Tony looked up with interest. "What was up with that?"

"One night, guards saw an Asian man raking a net over the koi pond but he scaled the wall and took off before they could catch him. The cops blamed it on the boat people: First they steal and slaughter our dogs. Now they're so hungry, they're eating our fish. I was just a rookie reporter then, and cops talk like they know everything. Luckily, I found an Asian petstore owner who explained that there's a big black market for koi. They end up swimming around in suburban backyards. That made it a better story."

Tony stood up and hurled the stick into the far recesses of the pond.

"Most Americans don't understand Asian culture." His eyes followed a pale gold monster that swam serenely around his dominion.

"It's true that Americans think the world revolves around them. A lot of people from big countries make that mistake. Didn't the Chinese believe that the Middle Kingdom was the center of the universe?"

"That was in the old days, before they knew about the rest of the world."

A couple of punks were crossing the bridge, and I stared, trying to figure out if I knew them from somewhere. When I turned back, Tony was tearing up leaves and hurling them into the pond. His lips were clenched tight. Although he stood taller than me and didn't want my sympathy, I put my arms around him and rested my forehead against his. He smelled like soap and hamburgers. Like Matthew used to smell. I hadn't been there for Matthew when he needed me. Maybe this boy would be different.

"You close to your family?" His voice came out like a croak.

"Yeah, the ones that are left. I had a brother but he died. You remind me of him. He didn't have a lot of friends and he was searching for his way in the world."

"How did he die?"

"I took him to a party and he got bored and lonely and went upstairs and drank too much and fell out of the second-floor window into a swimming pool and died. He was only fifteen. It was my fault. I should have known he wasn't having a good time and taken him home."

There, I had said it. I had confessed my sins to a seventeen-year-old boy. It was a relief to let it out after more than a decade of pretending it didn't exist.

"It wasn't your fault. It was an accident. I know what you're thinking, but you don't have to worry about me."

"Even though you're kicking it with Jimmy Lai?"

I barely knew this kid. Yet I felt something for him, something I thought had died with Matthew.

Tony edged away. "How do you know him?"

"I heard you talking to Bruce the other night. I left my notebook in your car and was heading back to get it but changed my mind after that."

"Jimmy and I just hang out. Talk about girls. Do a little job here and there." Tony hugged his arms and shivered.

"Such as?"

"Mainly I'm the driver." A note of pride crept into his voice. "I made five hundred dollars last week. I don't want to be a rich kid and just lie around all day."

Then, in the dappled shade of the big green estate, Tony laid it out for me.

He was upstairs at the San Gabriel Mall one evening, doing his homework at the Golden Star Café, when Walter, a kid from school, had swaggered in with an older guy. Tony quickly shoved his calculus book into his bag and pretended he had been reading the *Chinese Daily News*.

"We were there a long time, laughing and smoking and ordering up a ton of food," Tony said. "When we got up to go, they walked to the door and I said, 'Hey, we haven't paid yet.' The older guy, that was Jimmy Lai, just raised his hands like they do in old American gangster movies and said 'My money's no good here. C'mon.' He grabbed my arm and out we went. I half-expected the waitress to run after us waving the bill but we just zoomed off into the night. And I felt like I had gotten on a gut-wrenching Disneyland ride that would never end."

"Where exactly did you zoom off to?"

"Lucky Strike," Tony said. "It's a karaoke bar in San Gabriel. It was midnight when we got there. Jimmy introduced me to another guy. He wanted me to help him do a carjacking. I made some excuse and left."

Tony looked up for my reaction. "Smart boy," I said.

Tony frowned. "I didn't see Jimmy for a long time after that. But one afternoon, he was waiting outside San Marino High for me after school. He said he was hungry but didn't like going to restaurants by himself. Did I want to come along? So I did. For a couple weeks, we just hung out. He's from Hong Kong too, but he's a lot older, maybe even twenty-five. I don't know why he wants to be friends with me, but he does. It's amazing. Wherever we go, the bar girls all know him. We never get carded."

I rolled my eyes. Tony looked up into the sky and squinted, watching a red-tailed hawk floating on an air current.

"Then one night, Walter and Jimmy showed up again. And Jimmy asked me for a favor. He wanted me to drop Walter off at the West Covina Mall and wait while he jacked a car. I didn't have to do anything, just drive. It was no big deal, and Jimmy had been so nice, so I said OK."

"We took my Beamer, and the whole drive over, all I could think of was Jimmy saying: 'You're under eighteen. They catch you, they let you go with a warning.' "

High above us, the hawk was circling now, looking for food. I pictured Tony and Walt driving silently up and down the aisles, casing the expensive cars, looking like kids out on a joyride until you noticed the bulge in Walter's waist where the gun protruded. Something made me think of Marina Lu. I listened carefully.

"Jimmy told us Accords were the most stolen cars but to go for the Lexus or Mercedes because that's what everyone wants. 'Very hot,' " he said. "Drive them right to a chop shop and within hours they're dismantled, serial numbers filed off and ready for resale with no questions asked."

"So we get to the parking lot and Walter points out the lady he's going to jack. She's older, Asian."

I exhaled with relief. So he wasn't about to confess Marina's murder. Still, I wondered whether there was a connection. How many carjacking rings could the Valley sustain?

"It was late and the lot was almost empty and she's walking toward some parked cars, a red Toyota Corolla and a cream-colored 450 SL Benz. I hoped Walter might have gotten it wrong, but I knew the type, and I knew there was no way in hell she owned the dumpy Corolla."

"My heart was beating pretty loud. I thought everyone could hear and that would blow it for Walter, but there was no one around. So Walter gets up behind her and . . ."

Tony's voice trailed off, shutting down the concrete crime tableau unfolding in my head. I looked up and saw a family approaching along the gravel walkway, mother, father, and two little kids running ahead, shrieking with delight as they spotted the flashes of color in the pond and realized these were big fish. Tony bent his head toward mine, lowered his voice, and went on.

"He jacks her and tears her out. It takes about twenty seconds, and it's over.

"But she's down on the ground and I wonder, is she dead? Did he kill her? I didn't hear any gun. I start up the Beamer and drive off, staring straight ahead, hoping I can make it to the exit before the security guards swarm me. I'm thinking I'll tell them I came here to buy a pair of Levis for my sister's birthday and I didn't see anything out of the ordinary, and it's true, I didn't even see the gun. Like Jimmy said, I'm clean."

"Clean as mud," I muttered, standing up again. The hawk was circling lower and lower.

"It wasn't until I pulled onto the freeway and headed west that I realized Walter could easily have killed that old lady, wouldn't have thought twice about it," Tony said. "Or a security patrol might have swung by and noticed something. I pictured Walter firing his gun, then racing back to the safety of my Beamer for the getaway.

"And then I lost it. I was shaking so hard that I had to pull off at the next exit. I was somewhere in Baldwin Park. Kids playing ball with their fathers on the front lawn of their tract houses. I crossed my arms over the steering wheel and cried. I wanted to crawl into my mother's arms like when I was a kid in Hong Kong.

"But just thinking of that made me stop blubbering. I had to be strong. My parents were counting on me to do well in America. I was a big boy. Then I thought of something else. I had five hundred dollars coming to me, the first money I had ever earned. And that made me proud."

"Nobody got hurt, see," Tony adds, his eyes still glued to the koi both of us were pretending to watch.

Now it was my turn to tremble. I dropped to where he crouched by the pond and shoved my face up against his.

"That's some shark-infested water you're swimming in," I said quietly. "Can't you see he's just using you underage kids to do his dirty work?"

Tony didn't look up. "I'm not going to shoot anyone. I'll be careful."

"And what about Chinese respect for their elders, that song and dance you were giving me the other day? Is this why your parents sacrificed to send you to America, so you could carjack little old ladies?"

Tony looked miserable but didn't answer. I grabbed his arm.

He gave me a look that said he had already checked out. I let go. Oh, why couldn't you pass on knowledge and wisdom the way you could viruses and blue eyes?

"You've got to get away from them before something really bad happens," I said.

But his back was to me and he was walking, then loping away, retracing his way to the entrance, where a handful of yellow taxicabs idled at the curb. Soon, the one at the head of the line zoomed off with a fare.

CHAPTER 21

I was sipping some cheap office sludge when the phone rang. It was a cop I had been cultivating, from the Asian Organized Crime Unit of the L.A. County Sheriff's Department. They were doing a brothel raid and the briefing was at noon. He said I wouldn't want to miss it but hung up before I could get any details.

The cops often invited the press on these busts. With TV cameras whirring and reporters trailing, they'd burst into some massage parlor, hauling naked johns out of back rooms, pillows clutched to their privates, the men's terror contrasting comically with the sullen, resigned looks of the young women. Then the groveling really began, as the johns begged everyone not to publish their names or show their faces on the evening news. One john I recalled had kept switching the pillow from his groin to his face, unsure which would be most damaging to reveal. My instinct had been to fetch him a second pillow but the Girl Scout reporter in me had prevailed and so I kept my distance and merely recorded the scene in my notebook. In J-school, they teach you not to get involved, and it had taken me time to learn that objectivity doesn't preclude compassion. Now, I would have reached over and tossed him that pillow without thinking twice.

Wheeling the car out to the sheriff's headquarters in Temple City, I considered that life was divided into two parts. There were those brief spurts of reality when you interacted with other people, punctuated by long segments of suspended animation when you were alone in your car or apartment, wrestling with your own puny thoughts. You might be hurtling through space at sixty-five miles per hour but life was really on hold until that next interaction. It was a lonely way to live. No wonder serial killers could lurk undetected for years, committing their crimes not so much in secret but in isolation. If you had no intimate relations with other human beings, who would know how unhinged you had become?

At the sheriff's station, the clerk hustled me into a room where thirty plainclothes cops milled about. Some looked like bikers, with greasy jeans and ponytails. They all wore oversized jackets, despite the heat, and large fanny packs around their waists to hide their guns. Off in the corner, I spied Vittorio Carabini's supervisor, John Latham, and waved. He raised an eyebrow and went back to what seemed like an intense discussion. I sensed that this was no ordinary massage parlor bust. There was a wildcat energy in the room that fired my own nerves.

I spotted my reporter pal George Ling, animated and unkempt as usual. I smiled and he waved back. But before I could make my way to him, the crowd had jostled me toward Carabini's former boss instead.

"Get your pen ready, Latham, I'm about to announce those addresses you were so hot for ten minutes ago," the supervising lieutenant Phil Redman was saying. "We can't have you knowing ahead of time, or one of the other jurisdictions might cry foul, say I'm favoring Monterey Park. Right? Now here it comes."

The ruddy Sgt. Thomas Latham flushed an ever-deeper red once he realized I had overheard Redman dressing him down.

"Aw, Chief, I just wanted to brief my men."

But Redman had already turned away. "Here we go, folks," his voice boomed through the crowd. One hand held a clipboard. The other rubbed thoughtfully at his dishwater gray beard.

"We are going to three locations identified by surveillance as Asian brothels, possible slavery operations. They call it the jasmine trade. Our raid is coordinated for 1400 hours. You are to secure the houses and detain all individuals found inside."

His voice boomed on, explaining that this was a joint operation involving the FBI, the INS, U.S. Customs, and various local jurisdictions. Special agents from the FBI who spoke Mandarin and Cantonese would interview all non-English speaking suspects. The raid was part of a multi-agency investigation into an international organized crime syndicate. Officers were to inventory everything found inside the homes, including telephone books, letters, credit cards, and even scraps of paper with phone numbers, as all of those things might prove helpful in their investigation.

"Listen up, men, I'm going to read off each location, followed by a list of names assigned to that operation. Write it down, folks. Directions will follow."

I felt a tingle of excitement. This was great stuff. Then a shadow briefly crossed my mind and was gone. I shouldn't dwell on the girls. Probably a bunch of drug addicts and sleazeballs without the imagination to consider another profession.

I flowed out the door with a group of officers headed for Rosemead. Our destination, a beige stucco home with a red tile roof, was typical of the thousands of tract houses that had sprung up in the western San Gabriel Valley in recent years. It had a two-car garage, lots of bedrooms, and pre-fab cathedral windows. Several cars were parked in the driveway.

The police car I was in cruised the location, then doubled back to a parking lot behind a convenience store, where the cops shimmied into bulletproof vests and checked the bullets in their guns. Then we drove slowly back to the house. The officers piled out, heads scrunched into their necks, bodies hidden behind plastic shields like riot police use. I took cover behind the car and watched the cops advance across the street and cluster at the door.

"Police, open up."

When nobody responded, a small, skinny guy repeated the command in Mandarin. No dice. With a great shout, one of the officers pulled out a chisel and forced the door open. The men poured in. Once it was clear there would be no shooting, I trailed behind at a reasonable distance.

I heard doors slamming, people yelling in Chinese, and feet pounding upstairs. The living room was spare and modern: a coffee table with overflowing ashtrays, a large-screen TV tuned to a Mandarin channel, and a couch with four Chinese men smoking nervously as the police went through their wallets. They were johns.

I moved into the dining room, where a surly Chinese youth with a shaggy mop of black hair who looked like a hip Hollywood punk was telling police he had come here from New York three months ago.

"What's your name?"

"Steven."

"You live here?"

"No."

"What are you doing here?"

"Visiting a friend."

Steven said his head was splitting. He asked the police if he could get an aspirin.

Why not? the cop said, following him to a kitchen cupboard, hand on his gun, as Steven pulled out some Chinese herb pills.

He gulped his treats with lukewarm tea, then sat back down to light a cigarette. The cop looked at me and smirked.

"Yeah, right, he doesn't live here. Then how's he know where they keep the aspirin?" The cop settled back in his chair, pleased with his deduction.

"Is he a john too?" I asked.

"Naw. He's a gangbanger. The brothel boss hires these kids to guard the girls. In exchange, they get to crash at the pad—a lot of them are runaways—and stash their loot and guns where no one will find it. There's another one just like him upstairs."

In the kitchen, a sheriff's deputy was pawing through drawers.

"You wanna see something?" He beckoned to me. "These places all look the same, that's how you can tell they're brothels. Look here," he said. "Barely any dishes, silverware, or food. Empty cupboards. They want to be able to clear out in a hurry."

It was true. Except for a few bottles of plum sauce, soy sauce, sesame oil, and Steven's herb pills, the kitchen was bare, as if the real tenants had yet to move in.

On the counter, where a housewife might store her canisters of flour and sugar, someone had set up a Buddhist altar, all red and gold, to honor their ancestors. There were sticks of incense, lit red candles, and a hammered copper bowl that held offerings of persimmons and grapes. The effect was unsettling. Here, in this whorehouse, worship was juxtaposed with hundred dollar bills, cases of condoms, and K-Y jelly.

"We find those at each house we raid," the cop said. "They don't seem to care what we rifle through or confiscate. But if we damage their shrine, then all hell breaks loose."

I noticed the smell of cooking food. Walking to the stove, I peered into a still warm wok where barely seared pieces of chicken lay heaped, the flesh still a translucent pink. On the counter was a bunch of bok choy in a plastic produce bag.

They won't be eating lunch today, I thought. For one insane moment, I imagined turning the burner back on and finishing the stir fry, maybe shredding that bok choy like confetti. I hadn't eaten lunch. Wrenching my mind off the food, I wandered upstairs.

I had to pick my way past two girls who sat on the carpeted steps, their sad bird faces averted. They seemed to be in their teens, with straight black hair down their shoulders. One wore a short purple velour robe and kept tying and untying the belt with her fingers. The other wore a man's pajama top and lacy black underwear. Their thighs were as small as my arms. Smooth and hairless.

"They don't speak English," said a cop who was standing guard over them, as if to make conversation. He looked bored.

Meanwhile, George Ling was pulling a crumpled-up sheet of paper out of a planter. Lord knows how he thought to look in there. It was covered with delicate Chinese characters.

"What does it say?" I hoped he wouldn't get territorial. Our papers didn't exactly compete. I needn't have worried. With much dramatic throat clearing, he began:

> Once when I was young
> I had a dream
> To fly forward
> Over mountains and water
> But when I arrived
> I can't go back.

Now I see
That love is far away from me
I am at another end of the sky
And I realize that after love and hate
The last to come is regret.
If you don't have a broken heart
You'll never understand my pain
If you see tears in my eyes
Never ask me for who I cry
Please let me forget all about this
And give me just one night without sorrow.
Let me go through rain and wind
Until I see my home again
Maybe I will drink to ease this heavy heart
But you will never see me shed a tear.

"I guess I'll have to shed one for her then," I said, wiping the corner of my eye with my shirtsleeve. "That's pretty intense. You think one of the girls wrote it?"

"It's a classical Chinese style," Ling said. "But it's written in a very simple Mandarin characters, like someone who is not very educated. The dialect is common to Fujian province. That's where most of the Mainland Chinese immigrants are smuggled from."

He handed me the sheet.

I continued my tour. The first bedroom was also starkly impersonal. The closet held two skimpy outfits and several pairs of cotton shoes— tiny sizes. A mattress and box spring took up most of the room. A vanity table held cheap perfumes, paper flowers, makeup, packets of condoms, lubricating jelly, white hand towels, Kleenex, and an economy-size bottle of mouthwash. I saw a crumpled Alhambra police citation for prostitution and a dog-eared copy of *Teen* magazine. The image of these young girls fantasizing about beauty makeovers and fall fashions as some pock-marked, sour-breathed john pounded into their ninety-five-pound frames on that creaky box-spring mattress was too much to bear.

In the bathroom, FBI special agent Tom Kosovsky was talking to a girl who looked comatose. Suddenly she clicked into life and said something in Chinese. When she finished, Kosovsky straightened his spine and began ticking something off on his fingers. He must not have convinced her, because the girl lapsed back into silence.

I waited a decent interval, then asked.

"What are you saying? What language are you speaking?"

His eyes filled with disgust.

"Mandarin. I told her we won't hurt her and she won't be arrested if she cooperates because we're after the kingpins. But we need to know who brought her here and if she's being held against her will."

"And what'd she say?"

"She was smuggled here from Mainland China and forced to do this. She asked how we can protect her if she cooperates and I told her about the witness protection program. I told her if she doesn't cooperate she'll be in jail by evening."

"And?" I asked, already knowing the answer.

"That's all she said. The other girls don't know jack. They all got here two days ago. A friend has their passports. They don't know his name or where we can find him. They don't know anything about prostitution. They came to this house to visit a friend."

He looked at me thoughtfully. "All these girls are afraid."

There was one more bedroom to inspect. I almost skipped it. In some ways, I wish I had. Because when I turned the knob and walked in, there was a policeman guarding the usual gaggle of sad-looking girls. And next to them, looking disconsolate as hell, stood Tony Hsu.

I reeled, stepping back against the wall to steady myself.

"Tony."

The word flew out of my mouth before I could catch it and stuff it back. I saw with apprehension that he was slowly and almost imperceptibly shaking his head and mouthing "No." This parachute kid was clearly in big trouble. He had been lucky with the carjacking episode, but it looked like his luck had run out.

The cop rousted himself and walked over.

"You know this scumbag?" He shoved Tony and the boy staggered forward.

My hands were at my sides. I pressed one into the cheap stucco wall and the other on the cop's shoulder.

"I'm sorry. What did you say? I'm a little dizzy. All these poor girls. May I please sit down?"

I started to cry. I threw open the sluices and sobbed for all I was worth, clutching the policeman's shirt like a toddler hanging onto his mother.

The cop shifted nervously. He looked confused.

"Did you say Tony? Punk isn't talking, a big, slant-eyed cat has got his tongue. You hiding something, we bring you in along with him."

"Tony? Who's Tony?" I was babbling now, hoping he would take me for just another spacey broad.

"I just realized that I left my car radio back at the police station. I've had two radios stole so I never leave it in the car. It goes right in the briefcase, but with all the excitement, I forgot. It's a Sony. But I didn't think I said it out loud. Could I please sit down now?"

He laughed. "No one is going to steal your car radio from headquarters, Ms. Diamond. But let me see if I can get an officer to ferry you back with a few boxes of evidence."

Moments later, I slid into the unmarked police car. On the way back to the station, I took out my notepad and asked the young officer where the suspects would be held until they were arraigned.

"What about the juveniles?"

"Eastlake," he told me. L.A. County's Juvenile Hall.

I underlined it twice in my notebook, then flipped the pad shut and settled back for the ride.

CHAPTER 22

Yeah, they're holding the kids at Eastlake. I thought you'd want to know. OK, Father Wong. See you then."

I flung off my headset and rubbed my eyes. Father Harry Wong was an Episcopal minister in the Good Shepherd Church of San Gabriel. Wong was a third-generation minister, not a social worker, but in millennial Los Angeles, he found himself straddling God's work and the government's. For months now, he had been visiting captured illegals in INS holding pens, where he delivered church literature, referred them to immigration lawyers, and offered to contact relatives already in the U.S. Now, at my request, he agreed to visit Tony and said I could tag along.

We rendezvoused at a greasy-spoon diner, where the smell of frying food reminded me that I hadn't eaten all day. I ordered a hamburger to go, dribbling ketchup in the car.

In L.A., all the social workers, cops, and reporters knew Juvie Hall as Eastlake after the street it squatted on. The facility, long overdue for expansion and remodeling, was near East L.A., surrounded by barbed wire, uniformed guards, and a palpable aura of neglect. As we approached the entrance, Wong cleared his throat. He was a soft-spoken man whose gentle demeanor belied a steely ability to get what he wanted for his flock.

"This will only work if you don't identify yourself as a reporter," he murmured, as we approached the guard booth. "They won't let journalists in. But I don't think they will ask. Just follow my lead."

Deception made me uncomfortable. But I had to see Tony. Why? I wanted to ask him. Why why why why why. But I realized that the important thing now was getting him out of Eastlake before anything worse happened.

Wong's plan worked and no one questioned why a middle-aged Chinese minister had a young white woman in tow. I hovered deferentially, handing Wong pencil and paper just like a real assistant.

A guard led us into a small institutional room with chipped plastic chairs. Another guard brought Tony in, then positioned himself at the door, pulled out a pair of clippers, and began trimming his dirty fingernails. The intimate click of metal against nail echoed depressingly in the hollow room.

Wong began a gentle probing in Chinese. Tony never let on that he spoke English too. On the other side of the room, the guard passed gas and kept clipping. Pulling my notepad out of my purse, I scrawled a note across the lined paper and handed it to Wong.

"Does he want me to do anything?"

Wong furrowed his brow, adjusted his spectacles, and held the notepad at arm's length. Then he read Tony the question and got a long answer.

"Time's up." The guard walked over, slipping the shiny clippers back into his regulation pocket. He examined his handiwork. The tips of his fingers looked red and raw, with crusts of dirt now exposed to the air.

Under the guard's now watchful eye, I pretended that Tony was just another bit of human jetsam whose statistics would be filed alphabetically in a metal church cabinet. Tony's face was a mask too. Hands clasped, he bowed a farewell to Father Wong as we walked out. It was a poignant gesture, here in this locked facility where dignity and respect were checked at the door. The little gangbanger hadn't altogether lost his filial piety.

Walking down the hall, I wouldn't have noticed the handsome well-dressed man in the hallway flanked by two Asian teenaged boys, except that he stopped as we passed, fumbled with a silver lighter, and lit up a slim, expensive-smelling cigar, observing me thoughtfully all the while. He was Asian. His two companions hovered protectively. They could have been a father with his two sons, except that the age gap wasn't wide enough. Then I was past them. As I turned to watch their receding backs, I thought the handsome one seemed vaguely familiar. Or did I find it hard to distinguish one Asian face from another?

At the guard booth, another officer was on duty and he peered into our car suspiciously, as though we might be concealing runaway juveniles.

"IDs, please," he intoned.

I froze. Wong showed his, and I pulled out my driver's license and gave it to the guard, praying this was just a formality and we'd soon be on our way. It wasn't.

"Your name sounds familiar." He stared at me. "You the reporter who was calling earlier, looking for a kid?"

My scarlet face gave him all the answer he needed.

"Who gave you permission?"

Cheeks burning, I opened my mouth, wondering what words would come out.

"I'm calling my supervisor," the guard said, before I could say anything.

The car idled at the gate. So close to freedom, yet so far. I pictured Father Wong slamming down on the gas pedal and our busting out of there like some multi-culti Bonnie and Clyde. Instead, we were escorted out of the car and into the office, where a very angry supervisor interrogated us both, then photocopied my ID and pried out of me the name and number of my editor before allowing us to leave.

"We try to be straight up with you guys. We know you have your newspapers to publish and your TV shows to broadcast. But these kids are juveniles, and their cases are confidential. Your boss is going to hear about this tomorrow morning, young lady."

This time, I cried for real. I slumped against the door of Father Wong's car and bawled like my heart would break. I had gone too far. I had gotten Harry Wong into trouble. Not only that, but I would be fired. Tony would never get out of Juvenile Hall. No other respectable newspaper would hire me and I'd have to crawl to the *National Enquirer* and beg for a job, then spend my hack nights camped out under shrubbery, waiting for some politico to emerge from his mistress's house.

"Why didn't you just let me handle it?" asked the ever-calm Father Wong.

"I didn't want to lie," I said. "I couldn't masquerade as your assistant if they came right out and asked. That would have been crossing the line."

"You crossed it a long time ago, Eve. Still, in this case, I think a little lie would have been forgiven. Now tell me, please, what is this boy to you? I saw you looking at him. This is more than just a story."

"Tony?"

The question went to the heart of the matter. What *was* Tony to me? A symbol of an earlier loss? A link to a good story and possible promotion? A troubled youth I wanted to help? And why? Since when was I Lady Bountiful?

"I . . . I don't know, Father. I'm still figuring it out myself. But you're right, he is important to me. So please, tell me every word he said to you in there."

"Your friend is very scared," Father Wong began. "His 'friends' want to make sure he doesn't talk and they're applying pressure."

"What was he doing at that horrid brothel? This is part of a gang thing, isn't it?"

Wong paused. "It is complicated. Your friend worked at the brothel, guarding the girls. But he didn't do a very good job. In fact, he helped one escape. She is hiding at his house now and Tony is afraid his bosses will find out. He was planning to quit the day the raid happened. He couldn't stand it anymore."

Inside, my heart exulted. "Anyone can see his heart wasn't in it. But good Lord, now what?"

"The Lord is good indeed. Tony is more worried about this girl than himself. He wants you to check on her and his sister, Lily, and make sure they're OK. And he wants his friend Bruce to post bail. He says you know him from dinner last week. Bruce has enough in his checking account."

"But juveniles can't post bail. They're stuck unless their probation officer releases them to the custody of their parents. Oh, God. Tony's parents. They live in Hong Kong. They think their son is a shining A-student at San Marino High who's in bed by ten each night."

"If Tony's a parachute kid, he'll have a legal guardian. It may be a real aunt or uncle, a business partner of his parents, or someone just hired to act the part. We've got to get that person to plead Tony's case before a judge. Our church can write a letter of support."

"This is a good kid, Father. He's just run into some trouble."

"They're all good kids. Sometimes they just masquerade as Satans." He winked, then threw open the car door, and I slid out into a bright puddle of streetlight that illuminated the diner parking lot. It was midnight. As I stood on the asphalt, my legs began to tremble. I pushed my knees together and willed them to be still. Then I waved good-bye and walked unsteadily to my car.

CHAPTER 23

I slept until the alarm woke me up at 7 A.M. I felt hung over. No jog this morning and none the morning before that. At this rate, I would soon lose my wind. But work was taking my breath away just fine these days.

I cringed at the thought of facing my boss. I would have to break the news of my misdeeds to Matt Miller first, before Eastlake got to him. But first I had something else to do. Coffee cup in hand, I dialed Lily.

She sounded chirpy and fourteen. For one fleeting moment, I envied her.

"Lily, how ya doing?"

"Fine, Ms. Diamond. Tony's not here. He may be sleeping over at a friend's; he didn't come home last night. Want me to tell him you called? And what about that diary? Are we still going to solve Marina Lu's murder together?"

I had forgotten this unraveled thread in my life. "I can't talk over the phone, Lily. Too sensitive. How about in person this afternoon? And by the way, does Tony have a friend staying over?"

"How did you know? She's asleep upstairs. She won't stir before eleven."

"Maybe I can talk to her too."

"I barely can, my Chinese is so bad. And she doesn't speak English."

"Well, make sure she knows I'm a friend. Tony told me she's twitchy."

"That's for sure. She jumps each time the phone rings."

We made plans to meet at 5:30. She told me to have a nice day.

"Thanks, Lily. I'm overdue for one."

As I drove into the lot, I saw Miller's turquoise Mustang already parked in its designated spot. I slunk to my desk.

I had barely sat down when his summons came.

"I met an interesting man at a Chamber of Commerce breakfast this morning."

Relief flooded me as he handed over an embossed business card, but then panic struck in a different key.

"Reginald Lu, President and Chief Operating Executive, Golden Pacific Bank," announced the thick gold letters. Now what? I fingered the card thoughtfully, wondering how much Miller knew and fighting the temptation to tell him the whole story.

"He says you've met."

"Yes." I waited. Was this when he lowered the corporate boom and told me to lay off? Just that morning, I had noticed a big ad in our paper touting Golden Pacific Bank's low interest rates.

"He says you're a very persistent young woman."

I shrugged. "I'll take that as a compliment."

He leaned back in his chair. "Asian-American banks are springing up everywhere in the Valley. I think he would make a good profile."

So that was it. Nothing more than polite schmoozing over Chamber pancakes and hot links.

"He's the father of that murdered girl, the one who got carjacked." Miller was warming up now. All media people love gossip. The more ghoulish the better. That's why we're in the business.

"Just go easy on him."

"Right." I inhaled deeply. "Remember that brothel raid yesterday?"

Of course he did. I had called in on the cell phone, reporting that none of those arrested would talk, and Metro had passed on the story. Now I told him how I had sneaked into Eastlake to try and interview the brothel denizens and gotten caught. Miller doodled on a yellow pad while I spoke, always a bad sign. Then he tore off the page, crumpled it, and tossed it in the wastebasket, missing, which didn't improve his mood any.

"I'm going to have to tell Jane Sims. We may get a complaint."

Jane Sims was the metro editor. She was a cardboard cutout come to life, dour and two-dimensional. Her personality was gray. Her complexion was gray. Her hair was gray. I had little doubt that her heart was too. What remained of it. Sims was a reformed alcoholic and survivor of four triple bypasses. But she still came to work each day and simmered in the newsroom pressure-cooker, and it was slowly killing her. Everyone said she had been much nicer when she drank, and I could believe it. Now she was mean and sober. Jane Sims would never sneak into a locked facility to get a story. She would wait for the chain of command to deliver it into her lap. And that didn't bode well for me.

"I'm only trying to be the best reporter I can," I told Miller. The worst they could do was fire me. In which case I'd run off to Hong Kong, learn Chinese, and start my life over again. I pictured sending Mark Furukawa a postcard, informing him of my news.

"Do me a favor," he said. "Set your sights a little lower than a page-one exposé for the time being. Which reminds me." He pulled out a computer printout. "SAT scores have come in, and I need a story about how schools in the San Gabriel Valley fared in comparison with other regions. That should keep you out of trouble."

After a day of comparing SAT scores, there was one thing I knew for sure as I drove out to San Marino in the sepia light of early autumn. Lily and Tony sat smack dab in the middle of the highest-scoring school districts in Los Angeles County. But it wasn't worth a rat's ass if they ate from cardboard boxes, alone in front of the TV each night.

Lily led me out back and we sat by the pool as the light waned, marveling at the giant bird of paradise that groaned under the weight of its orange floral beaks. Damn thing looked prehistoric. The smell of chlorine rose with the heat, giving me a headache and evoking bad memories. Lily sipped a diet Coke. I drank green tea and didn't ask about the Chinese girl.

"So what did the diary say?" Lily's long legs dangled swanlike over the pool's edge. "I never read it. I stuck it up on my bookshelf and forgot. Besides, it's kind of morbid and uncool to read someone's diary, don't you think?"

That's me, morbid and uncool.

"It was a typical teenage-girl diary," I told her. "Complaining about her boyfriend. Fretting about living here alone. Hanging out with her girlfriends. Say, Marina had a friend called Alison. I met her once. Do you know what her last name is? She was very close to Marina and might be able to tell us something."

"I think it's Tsing. Her mom's on the school board."

"Great. And your guardian in the U.S.?"

"Jonathan Hsieh. He's my dad's lawyer. But he doesn't watch over us or anything. It's just on paper."

I wrote down both names.

"So where's Tony's friend? Doesn't she want to join us poolside?"

"May-li's still in her room. She's been thumbing through a stack of my magazines all afternoon."

"Can we go up and visit? You can introduce me as your friend so she doesn't freak."

"I remember how to say that, at least," Lily laughed.

Upstairs, the door was ajar and I pushed it open, letting Lily enter first.

The girl was sitting cross-legged on the floor, magazines spread out before her. She looked up as we walked in, her face a pale, questioning oval. She would have been pretty except for the fear in her eyes. Body unfurling, she moved into the shadows of the room.

Lily said something in soft Chinese as she gestured to me. I seized my cue.

"Hello, May-li. My name is Eve."

I turned to Lily. "Can you ask where she's from and how she got here?"

"My Chinese is rusty and she speaks a different dialect. I catch words like ship and sailors and village and hungry. But it's pretty fragmented."

"I have a friend who speaks Chinese and works with teens in trouble. Maybe he could come over?"

Lily was suddenly on guard.

"Is May-li in some kind of trouble?"

"I don't know," I said. "I think she might have been smuggled to America from China aboard a ship. There's a lot of Mainland Chinese trying to get into the U.S. illegally for jobs. Maybe she has relatives here and we can help her find them."

This resonated with Lily.

"OK. Hey, Tony's not back yet. Do you think I should be getting worried? He's never gone this long."

"Let's go talk in the other room so May-li doesn't think we're rude. Tell her we'll be back with a translator."

"I'll try." Lily was dubious.

She stuttered through some Chinese. May-li nodded. We left. The whiteness in Lily's room was blinding, fracturing my sight. My head throbbed. I summoned all my strength to say what I had to.

"Lily, your brother is OK, but he's in jail. The police picked him up last night. They think he's in a gang."

I left out the part about the brothel. Would she even know what one was? At fourteen, I hadn't. But kids were older today.

"Jail!" She began weeping. "I told him to stay away from those guys. But he never listens to me. Oh God, what will my parents say? This will kill my dad. How long will he be there? Can we go visit him? Is May-li part of this?"

My mind raced forward and launched into damage control.

"Lily, your brother's in good spirits. I saw him last night. He'll be out soon. But your guardian's going to have to get involved. Maybe even your dad."

As I spoke, I wished I could confer with Mark. Troubled kids were his specialty.

"How about we ask my translator friend for some advice about Tony too?"

I wasn't sold on this plan myself, but felt short on options. To my relief, she acquiesced.

"If he's your friend and you trust him, then that sounds OK to me."

She enunciated clearly and distinctly. Not a shred of Chinese accent in her. There was something so measured and adult about her voice that it scared me. But then she broke.

"Oh God, oh God." She grabbed a white stuffed bunny and rocked back and forth on the bed like an autistic child. "To-ny, To-ny."

"It's OK, Lily. It'll be OK," I amended. Just days ago, I had tried to comfort her brother.

I pulled the sheets up and she drew them to her chin, her voice muffled beneath the 300-thread-count pima cotton, the best money could buy.

"W-what's your friend's name?"

"Mark. Mark Furukawa."

"Furukawa, Furukawa," she repeated in a singsong chant. "You'll help Tony, won't you, Mark Furukawa."

I reached for the phone on her white wicker table. Mark said he was working late again, but could join us in an hour.

"How do you get yourself into these messes?" he murmured, when he arrived fifty-eight minutes later.

"Come and meet Lily," I said brightly, grabbing him by the arm and tugging him into the kitchen.

We sat on stools and I explained Tony's predicament. This time I didn't censor the brothel part. I watched Lily out of the corner of my eye, but she didn't ask what a brothel was and I didn't volunteer.

Soon, she broke in angrily. "I told him he'd get into trouble if he didn't stop hanging out with those guys. They snap their fingers and he comes like an obedient dog. And they always call in the middle of the night. Especially Jimmy Lai."

I thought I saw something pass across Mark's eye. But it could have been the evening shadows coming on.

He got up suddenly, saying he was going to leave a message on Hsieh's answering machine.

"There's more," I told him when he returned. "The night before Tony got arrested, he brought home a young woman and stashed her here. She's Chinese, possibly a smuggled immigrant, most probably Fukienese. She was a sex slave at the brothel. Can you find out her story?"

"Holy shit," said Mark, shaking his head. "You *are* looking for trouble. Fine. Let's see how rusty my Fukienese has gotten."

He rattled off something in Chinese.

"It's very vulgar, what he just said," Lily giggled, as we made our way upstairs.

The girl was asleep over her magazines, but awoke as we walked in and put both elbows before her in a defensive maneuver when she saw Mark.

"She may be afraid because you're a man," I told him.

Mark stopped and began a soothing litany of Chinese. He kept his distance and opened his arms in front of him to show that he meant no harm. May-li's eyes swiveled from Lily to me and back to Mark. She began crying. Lily ran and put her arm around May-li, conveying in a wordless language that she would be safe here. Her youth and innocence accomplished what we adults couldn't. May-li leaned against Lily's arm. Then with Mark translating, she began to speak.

CHAPTER 24

I f they find me, they'll kill me," the girl said, staring at the floor. "I've brought such shame on my family. My ancestors stir in their graves and my parents will die without money for their burial. All because we trusted the wrong person. We were poor farmers. One day a man came to my village. He was a friend of the local officials. He wore nice clothes and had been to America. He complimented my parents on how smart and pretty I was and said I could make good money in America working as a waitress. How much, we asked. A thousand a month, he answered. People in our village don't make that in one year. My family got excited. There are no sons, just me. I was their only hope. They sold their land for five thousand to pay my passage. But we still owed the smugglers twenty-five thousand. I was to pay it off, month by month. Oh, I am ready to work hard to pay off my debt, I told the man. Then I will send money back to my parents."

Mark stopped for breath, then continued translating. His voice was spare, without emotion, while the girl's words poured forth in a torrent. I shifted uncomfortably, dreading what came next.

"My parents sewed their last yuan into my coat and packed rice and pickled vegetables for the journey," May-li continued. " 'She doesn't need your peasant food,' " the man told them. " 'We have plenty to eat

167

on the ship.' I was embarrassed at our ignorance, but took the food my mother pressed into my pack. There were fifteen of us, mostly girls. I thought that was strange, since we knew it was easier for young men to find work in America. But I said nothing. For two days we walked at night, hiding by day, until we reached the coast. Then the guide gave a customs official money to row us to a big ship offshore. A terrible smell came from the lower levels where they herded us. It was dark and wet and cold and people moaned and vomited. There was only one bucket and it overflowed.

" 'At least we'll eat well on the journey,' I told them. They looked at me like I was crazy. 'Stupid girl,' they said. 'Do you see a cafeteria here?' So then I was glad for my mother's provisions. I tried hard to eat only a few bites each day, but after a week my food was gone. Then the horror started. The sailors taunted us with food, which they sold at high prices. Rice was five yuan. Water too, and we had to have water. People begged for it. We weren't allowed above deck. Twice a day people passed up yuan and the sailors lowered down rice and water. When they opened the hatch in the morning, we crowded around to see the blue sky. At night, there were stars. But only for a moment. The rest of the time, we lived in darkness.

"One night a sailor called me and two other girls to the deck. He smelled of whiskey. We were frightened and cried. One sailor sat on my hands while another held my feet. A third ripped off my clothes."

May-li broke off. She splayed her hands over her face and a long, high wail escaped her. It was the way women keen at a funeral, the type where you throw yourself on the bonfire at the grand finale. Her body shook with sobs now and she couldn't go on. We waited, sniffling ourselves, groping for Kleenex, pretending it was allergies flaring up.

Slowly, she began to speak again through her fingers. Her voice got real tiny, almost singsong, and Mark strained to hear her. Hunching her shoulders, she folded into herself like the petals of a flower in the fading sun. Soon, she was a disembodied voice hovering in the room.

"They said they were preparing us for our new jobs. When I got back to the hold, I tried to kill myself. A man stopped me. He said I must make it to America alive for my family's sake. But inside, I was already dead. Each night the sailors came for girls. It was selfish, but I was glad when they picked someone else. I lost track of time. One man said it was ninety days and nights. Finally the ship anchored and some smugglers rowed off to make arrangements. One night without a moon, they brought us ashore. We were so thin and weak, we could barely walk. It hurt my lungs to breathe. The smugglers hid us in a village for several days and then put us in a truck. We lay under boxes of tomatoes and the truck drove across a border. The smugglers told us we were crossing from Mexico into America. Finally, I thought, this nightmare will end.

"They took us to a house, where new people asked if we had relatives in America to pay our passage. They beat me when I told them I had no one. I explained the waitressing job but they only made dirty jokes. Still, they started feeding me better. 'Eat, eat,' they urged and gave me extra rice. They laughed and said no one wants food served by a thin waitress. After some days, they drove me to a place where a Chinese man in a dirty white smock made me sit at a shiny table. There was dried blood on the walls. Another man held me so I couldn't move. The first one held my arm up and shoved something sharp under the skin. I screamed and fought but they held me tight. Here."

May-li lifted her arm and all of us except Mark peered in. The underside bore a slight scar and a raised bump, as though a tiny cartridge had been inserted under the skin.

"Norplant." Mark's eyebrow rose in disbelief. "They wanted to make sure she didn't get pregnant. I've heard of such things, but never seen it until now. Probably wasn't a real doctor, either. More likely a hospital aide moonlighting for the triad. Yeah, and he'd double as an abortionist." His voice was smoldering.

Mark explained to May-li what they had done and I could see him struggle to control his anger.

"The next day, they drove me to another house," May-li continued. "It was on a busy street and beautiful, with a round driveway made of bricks and tall windows like rich people have in the city. Inside were so many rooms. When I arrived, a woman with bad skin took one look at me and yelled at the guy, saying who will want such a bag of bones. Then she gave me a towel and told me to go upstairs and take a shower. When I got out, she said there was a man waiting in the bedroom and I should go in. When I told her I didn't want to, she threatened to beat me.

" 'I already bought you,' she told me. 'You have to pay back the thirty thousand I spent for you. So get busy.' "

"It was like that each day. After the first time, I didn't care anymore. There were eight girls like me. Most were Chinese, but there were also two Thai and one Malaysian. The woman who ran the place was Tiffany. She said they'd kill us if we tried to leave. The boys who kept guard all had guns. The clients pinched my skin until it bruised. My heart flew away from my body and I became a machine.

"Then we moved to a new house with new guards. One of them spoke to me. At first, I didn't answer. But his voice was gentle. His name was Tony. No one had spoken to me that way since my mother whispered good-bye. He told me he was nervous. 'Why don't you leave then?' I asked. 'No one's guarding you.' Then he apologized and said he had to guard me for his friend. I thought that was strange. The next night we talked more. I begged him to bring me pills so I could kill myself, but he refused. The third night I hoped he would come guard me. When he arrived, I showed him some poetry I had written. I began to think about a life outside that place. I told Tony what the sailors had done. After that, he was different. He offered to help me escape. It could have been a trick—he would pretend to help me and then capture me to show his bosses what a good guard he was. But I had to take the chance." She looked at us. "By now I wanted to stay alive. So I put myself in his hands. He got the other guard drunk, then showed me how to climb out the window and down the oak tree. Then he drove me to this house. I am ashamed I left without repaying my debt. That is not honorable, and I come from a poor but honorable family. But what they did to me was not honorable either. I have no money. I don't speak English. I have no papers. I am seventeen years old. If they find out Tony helped me escape, they will come here to kill us both."

And now she was in hiding. And we were harboring a fugitive. A federal witness. An illegal immigrant. The crimes were stacking up.

Halfway through May-li's story, Mark had closed his eyes, his voice growing more dull and monotone as the girl's story got more awful. His body was rigid and he clenched and unclenched his fists. Finally he broke off translating and said something long and solemn to her in Chinese. Then he turned back to us.

"I promised that no more bad things would happen to her. I said she was safe with us. I gave her my word. None of those goons will find her, I said, because they're all cooling their heels in jail."

Lily still had her arm around May-li. Her face was buried in the girl's sleeve, but I knew she hadn't missed a word. May-li didn't look any more hopeful than she had at the beginning, but something in her eyes had relaxed.

It was midnight now. There was nothing more we could do tonight. I went to get my purse, pulling out my car keys, but stopped when I saw Lily's face.

"Maybe we should stay here tonight."

"Y-you don't have to," Lily said bravely.

"What about it, Mark? I'm game."

"Yeah, sure."

"Yay!" said Lily, in her best professional cheerleader voice. "Eve, you can sleep in Papa's bedroom. The one he uses when he visits us. Mark can have Tony's room."

We all settled in for a long night. Once Lily was asleep, Mark tiptoed to my room. I'd been waiting for him, but not the way I had imagined earlier. I was relieved to see that he just wanted to talk too.

"I've been counseling kids for twelve years and that's the saddest story I've ever heard," he whispered.

"And it's not over yet."

Soon, exhaustion overcame us. Dawn was just a few hours away. He leaned over, kissed me lightly on the lips.

"Sweet dreams," he said.

CHAPTER 25

I heard movement downstairs and smelled the aroma of fresh brewed coffee curling up the stairs.

It was 7 A.M. I threw on yesterday's clothes and walked down the hallway. Both girls were sound asleep in their beds. Good. I padded down to the kitchen, where Mark was whistling a tune and rooting through the fridge for butter. We settled for orange marmalade imported from Hong Kong.

After the caffeine woke me up, I began jotting down options on my reporter's pad.

1. Call the INS. CONSEQUENCE: May-li gets put in federal detention and could get deported.

2. Call the police. CONSEQUENCE: They might be able to get her into a witness protection plan if she agrees to testify against her captors. She might get killed if it doesn't work.

3. Try to hook her up with sympathetic Chinese community folks like Father Wong and get her integrated into L.A.'s sprawling, underground Chinese community. CONSEQUENCE:

Mark ambled over to peer over my shoulder.

"Number three won't work. For one, it's illegal. Secondly, the Chinese community may be huge but even from jail, those smugglers will have put the word out about their valuable missing girl. By now there's a bounty on her head."

"Maybe there's a legal way to do this through Father Wong. Why don't you try Hsieh again?" I suggested. As Tony's guardian, Hsieh would be needed.

Mark made a goofy martial-arts move and went off. When I reached Father Wong on the phone, he agreed to help if we took May-li to the INS and told them the truth.

"We have an arrangement with them," he explained. "We put the kids in church-sponsored foster homes pending their asylum hearings. We'll testify that May-li was persecuted in China for her religious beliefs. The whole process takes two years, and in the meantime she lives with a family, enrolls in school, learns English. Leads a normal teen-age life."

I promised to get back to him. In the kitchen, Mark was sipping a second cup of coffee and staring out at the pool.

"Here it is, everything that money can buy," he said with disgust.

I poured my own cup and asked about Hsieh.

"Smug bastard started out by lying to me," Mark said. "Said the kids live with him and he has no idea how Tony got mixed up with this. I told him I was standing in the kids' kitchen right now, making myself breakfast, so I knew he was a lying son of a bitch. Once we got that clear, it went fine."

"And?"

"Hsieh's worried. He was supposed to be keeping an eye on them. Now he has to call Tony's dad and tell him what happened."

I told him about Harry Wong's proposal, then we went upstairs and asked May-li. She was wearing black jeans and a sweatshirt that said San Marino Archery Team and would have looked right at home on campus. Mark told her about Wong's proposal while she fiddled with her sleeves, Tony's too-long trousers puddling at her feet.

"Be brutally honest in describing the INS facilities," I said. "But explain that no one will mistreat her and she'll get three meals a day."

May-li seemed to wilt as he spoke. Then she responded.

"She wants to know how can we trust the American authorities," Mark translated. "She says in China, the police and customs officers demand bribes for everything. She wants to stay here with Lily while the INS decides her case and says she'll do all the cooking and cleaning."

"Poor thing, if only it were that simple."

Mark explained the INS rules to her. As he spoke, I could see her struggling. She looked at me and said something.

"She asks if you think this is best. She calls you Miss Eve."

"We've been told this is your best chance to stay in America," I answered. It was hard to meet her eyes.

"Then let it be so," Mark translated.

I helped her pack, grabbing two valises and stuffing them full of Tony and Lily's clothes. They would never miss any of it. I went to the pantry and swept entire shelves clean, dumping them into her suitcases. Smoked oysters, chicken soup, crackers, and tuna fish. Bottled juices and dried fruits. I would make damn sure she ate well. Then I went to the ATM and got out $200.

"It's not much, but here," I said, shoving the just-baked $20s into her hand.

May-li folded them carefully and tucked them into a book. I saw that she had hollowed out part of the spine.

We agreed to rendezvous with Harry Wong at six and drive to the INS facility in San Pedro.

After Mark left, I realized my clothes smelled stale. I showered, then pulled a fresh shirt from Tony's closet. A little tight across the front, but it would do.

CHAPTER 26

That night, we watched the uniformed guard at the INS's Terminal Island Detention Center lead May-li away. She turned to look at us one last time. She didn't smile.

"When can we visit her?" I asked the surly woman behind the desk.

"No visitors except family." She didn't look up.

"I'm better than family, I'm press." I slapped down the battered ID that had saved my ass so many times already in my brief career.

"Try between five and six P.M. tomorrow," she said.

Lily wanted to come too, so around 3 the next afternoon, I told Miller I was checking out a possible school story in San Marino—which was the bare-assed truth—and picked her up. We were back on the freeway before 4 and waiting at the INS office at 5 sharp.

"Is the girl family?" the INS clerk wanted to know.

"She's, um, my translator."

"They'll bring her out shortly."

Lily and I sat and fidgeted for twenty minutes before May-li was brought in. She looked terrible dressed in the orange INS overalls that obviously weren't made for eighty-five-pound teenage girls.

"Is everything OK?" I asked, and Lily translated.

"Yes. It is fine." She seemed listless.

"Do they let you out at all during the day?"

177

"Oh yes," she replied eagerly, and started talking in Chinese. Lily gave me a worried look.

"She's saying something about how most of the people in her cell are Mexican and they can't communicate. But there are a few Chinese. Oh, Eve, I'm not sure that's what she said. I'm just guessing."

"Don't sweat it."

"Here," I said to May-li, sliding a few periodicals across the table. They were Chinese fashion magazines, all that I had been able to find on a quick sweep through the San Gabriel Mall earlier that day.

May-li started to cry.

"Why is she crying?" I asked Lily in bewilderment.

"She says we're so kind. Hold on." Lily stuck out her tongue in concentration. "She says no one has shown her any kindness since she arrived in America, except Tony and the girl who came to the brothel to look for her boyfriend."

I pictured some weird scene of revenge and retribution. But May-li's voice was warm.

"What girl?" I asked.

"She wants to say thank you, Eve."

"Wait a minute. What girl? Can you please ask May-li the name of the girl who came to the brothel?"

"Sure," said Lily, and she did.

"Her name was Marina."

I gulped. "Ask her what the girl's last name was."

Lily translated.

"She doesn't know."

"Who was her boyfriend? What did she do at the brothel? What did they talk about? How many times did she go there? When? How old was she?"

"E-Eve! You know my Chinese is lousy. Why do you want to know all that stuff?"

"Lily, she said a girl named Marina used to come to the brothel. What if it was Marina Lu? Aren't we solving that mystery together?" I reminded her, shame blooming as I threw out the old lure once more.

"Oh, that." She rested her head on her hand. "I've been so busy worrying about Tony that I forgot."

Lily stumbled through her Chinese. May-li looked on, quizzical.

But she answered my questions, I'm sure of it. She talked for five minutes. Impatiently, I turned to Lily.

"I can only make out bits of it. She's using phrases I don't understand. Her boyfriend was involved with the brothel, but he wasn't a customer. Marina was about May-li's age. She wasn't a prostitute."

"The age checks out. Marina was seventeen. We know she had an older boyfriend. But he was supposed to be a bank executive. Oh, Christ, we need a proper translator."

I looked at Lily, who wore a look of humiliation.

"I'm sorry. I'm not a good translator for you."

I pulled her to me.

"You've been great. This has been a big help."

But inwardly, I seethed. I needed to come back here ASAP with a professional interpreter.

"Time's up, honey," said the woman at the desk.

"OK, ma'am," I said. She didn't seem as surly today as the day before. Clearly, she didn't have a pleasant job. I decided to chat her up a bit. It couldn't hurt to get on her good side if I was going to be visiting on a regular basis until May-li got out.

"We're on our way, ma'am. Oh, I feel so bad for this young girl. See, she's all alone here in the United States and doesn't understand why she's being locked up. She didn't realize she was doing anything illegal. She's from a village where people think the streets of America are lined with gold and we welcome everyone with open arms."

"She doesn't look a bad sort," the woman agreed.

"I hope she gets treated well here," I told the woman. Maybe if I said it, it would be true.

"We're not ogres, you know. We're just doing our jobs."

I smiled at the lady and we left. In the hallway, I paused, dug into my purse, and pulled out a business card. Quickly, I scrawled my home number across the back. Then I walked back in and handed it to the INS clerk, noting her name.

"I appreciate your help, Mrs. Locksley. Here's my business card. In case you ever need to talk to a reporter."

Wordlessly, she took it. Maybe I had gone too far. But once before, someone I had met briefly had called months later to tip me off to a good story. You never knew where these things led.

CHAPTER 27

The next day, I picked up Mark for the drive to San Pedro. His translation would be perfect, I knew. For added insurance, I had brought a tape recorder. We were going to get this down officially. I pictured handing the tape recorder over to the police, who would enter it into the criminal docket as Exhibit A.

A new lady was at the desk when we arrived. She looked at us suspiciously. When we asked for May-li, she picked up the phone to ring the guard who handled that cell block.

"I'll hold," she said, and waited impassively for several minutes. Then, "Yeah, I'll tell them."

She replaced the receiver. "She's not here."

"What do you mean?" I spluttered.

"Checked out. Gone." The woman enunciated the words as if we were hard of hearing.

"This isn't a hotel, for Chrissakes." Mark's voice was taut with concern. "She can't just check out. Has she been transferred to another facility?"

"They didn't say. They just said she's gone."

"Can we speak to your supervisor?" I asked, which is what I did whenever things weren't going my way. "I need to talk to your supervi-

181

sor right now," I repeated firmly. "I'm a reporter, and it's extremely urgent. People's lives may be at stake."

"Just a minute," the woman said, and looked something up in a tattered but official-looking book.

At that moment, another woman walked out a door labeled "No Admittance" and came toward us. It was my friend, the INS clerk from the previous day. She headed for the exit, then saw us and stopped.

"Oh, hello," she said. "I'm just getting off. I work the early shift on Wednesdays. What a coincidence that I should run into you. It turns out that your little friend, that sweet Chinese girl, had some family in the U.S. after all."

"W-what do you mean?" I asked.

"Her aunt and uncle came by today. They were so happy to see her. They had flown in all the way from New Jersey on the red-eye, and they cried and cried when we brought her out. I've never seen such a happy reunion. They told me they had feared . . ."

"Where is she?" I screamed.

". . . something terrible had happened to their darling niece because they hadn't heard from her in so long. And they spoke such good English. What's the matter? Why are you yelling?"

"You didn't release her to them? Tell me you didn't."

"Oh, honey, I'll tell you, that little girl cried tears of joy. She got down on her knees and threw her arms around my feet and started kissing them, can you believe that, holding on like she would never let go. Her aunt and uncle had to pry her off of me."

"You let them take her?"

"Not at first, I didn't. We're career skeptics here at the INS. We've seen every trick in the book. My antenna was up right away when she didn't recognize them. But they were very patient and loving. The wife held the little girl's hand and petted it gently while the husband explained how they hadn't seen her since their last trip to China ten years ago, so it was natural she wouldn't remember them. He took a photo out of his wallet. It was dog-eared and crinkled, but you could see a little Chinese girl sitting on a dirt floor with a lady who looked like the aunt. 'Our ancestral village,' he said. 'May-li was only six here. Poor little thing, all she's been through, she probably thinks *we're* smugglers,' and he laughed with embarrassment.

"Then he whispered something to her in Chinese and the girl stopped crying and calmed down. Just sat there demurely without looking up while her relatives filled out the forms and posted the bond. They couldn't wait to get her out of here."

"Of course not!" I screamed. "How could you? Those people weren't her family. They were smugglers. She escaped from a brothel where they were holding her prisoner and forcing her to have sex with men for money and you delivered her right back into their filthy hands."

I moved toward her, but Mark reached over and grabbed my hands.

"We promised," I cried. "We promised she'd be safe if she did as we asked. We promised nothing bad would ever happen to her again. She trusted us. She believed us."

I turned to the INS clerk, who stood there uncertainly. You could tell she felt betrayed. Just yesterday, I had been so nice to her.

"Those weren't tears of joy she was crying, you idiot," I said. "She was on her knees, begging you in the only language she knew, not to let them take her. They threatened her, that's why she let up. And you sold her down the river."

The woman blanched. A look of horrified awareness was slowly dawning across her fat face.

"But what about the photo? We have their home address and phone and driver's license. They gave us a cashier's check for five thousand dollars."

"She's worth a lot more than that on the street," I said quietly now, my anger fading to a dull ache where my heart should be. "Each guy who has sex with her has to pay a hundred bucks. Do the math. They'll use her til she's sick and diseased and her teeth fall out and then they'll cast her into the gutter. There are millions more where she comes from. Rural Mainland China. And millions of grainy photos, too. Do you know what a girl baby's life is worth there? She's lucky she wasn't strangled at birth and buried quietly in the sorghum field after the neighbors were asleep. Or then again, maybe she's not."

"Can we see the paperwork they filled out before they took her?" Mark said. I was glad someone's brain was still functioning enough to think of practical matters.

"I'm not supposed to," the woman whispered. "I'll get into trouble."

"You're not supposed to let her go off with smugglers who masquerade as family members either," I snapped. "It boggles the mind that the INS, known and feared on six continents, can be so incompetent."

The woman looked around, saw the clerk who had replaced her at the desk watching our outbursts, then lowered her voice.

"I'm not a bad person," she said. "I was so happy for her. And she seemed OK with it. I thought we were doing the right thing. My supervisor had to sign off on it. They fooled him too."

She bit her lip and thought for a moment. "OK," she said. "I'll get you a copy of that document. Wait for me in the hallway. But if anyone asks, you didn't get it from me."

"Thank you," I whispered fiercely. I turned to the woman at the desk. "Never mind about your supervisor. I'll call him in the morning."

It wasn't until we were in my car a block away from the INS facility that Mark dared to look at the papers. In neatly printed block letters, the man and woman had written down their names: Randall and Daisy Hong, 175 Ridgecrest Avenue, Orange, New Jersey 01543. Next to it was a New Jersey telephone number. The Hongs had written that they were blood relatives of May-li Hong, 17, of Fujian Province, PRC. Randall was the brother of May-li's father, Zhiyong.

"Pull over at that liquor store," Mark told me.

"You need a drink that bad?"

"No, I want to use the pay phone. I want to check out the number they gave the INS. I bet all of this information is bogus."

He held up the paper with distaste, holding it between his thumb and forefinger. When I pulled up with a screech, scattering a few winos, he jumped out of the car, locked himself in the booth, and fumbled for his calling card. I hunched over the steering wheel, watching him dial, then slam the receiver down and stride back to the car in disgust.

"It's a fucking pager number," he said. "And we're not going to get a callback, today or ever. The number's been disconnected."

CHAPTER 28

T his time, I dropped Mark off at his car in the parking lot of the Rainbow Coalition Center and we went our separate ways. I wasn't sure how Mark felt, but I needed some time to huddle and brood—definitely not a team sport. I rejected the possibility that we might never see May-li again. I blocked out the image of her being led away by the smugglers, and what came afterward. If I didn't censor that part for now, I wouldn't be able to go on.

At home, I whistled for Bon Jovi and the landlady's dog came and buried his long needle nose in my chest, nuzzling me as though he knew. I petted his silky fur absently and thought about my messed-up life.

May-li was gone, swallowed up by the vast, interlinked Chinese criminal underground as though she had never existed. Tony was in jail. Marina's murder was unsolved, despite tantalizing glimpses into her short life. My relationship with Mark seemed doomed to sputter and start forever, sidetracked by calamity at every turn.

I sat slumped for hours, my mind spinning through the scenarios of horror I had witnessed over the past forty-eight hours. Outside, the rat-tat-tat of gunfire ricocheted off the hills, delivering an apt sound-track to my unfolding *cinema verité* of misery. The Silverlake Locos were warring with Los Vatos again. The crossed-out graffiti on the walls and sidewalks—the *sinverguenzas* had even spray-painted the 100-year-old oak tree in the corner lot—was proof of that. And we who lived in the hood but were not of it studied the markings thoughtfully, like urban rangers poking at the scat of some unfamiliar but dangerous large cat. What did it bode for our survival? The gang members mainly shoot at each other, we reassured ourselves, clustered around the banked warmth of neighborhood watch meetings. But bullets didn't know friend from foe. One journalist pal of mine had been feeding dinner to her baby in their Silverlake home one recent night when a bullet soared through the open kitchen window and came clattering to rest on her dining room table. Left some bad skid marks on the antique mahogany, that was for sure. The baby just stared and opened his mouth for more.

Twilight came on, and Bon Jovi stirred, whining hopefully. He often got taken for walks at this hour. A dog's hope springs eternal.

"All right. It will do me good too," I told him, shucking off my clothes for a cotton T-shirt and shorts.

I wound a neutral yellow bandanna (better to avoid gang colors) around my forehead a little too tight for comfort. Maybe it would pen in the headache that roamed inside, keep it from busting loose. A long, leisurely run was just the thing to chase away my evil spirits, so I crossed Glendale Boulevard and headed down Silverlake to the better part of town, past the bakery where the punks and artists gathered at sidewalk tables to discuss life and art over cold coffee and sugarless pastries. I would go into the hills of the rich today, jogging past architectural marvels built by disciples of Neutra and Schindler, sometimes even the masters themselves, sprinting up the secret staircase streets that interlocked this neighborhood like branching capillaries on a drunk's nose.

Rounding a 1920s Spanish-style apartment with a turret that I had always secretly lusted after because of the killer views it commanded of the lake below, I heard a disembodied moan from the second-floor window, a woman's moan, and stopped in my tracks while Bon Jovi seized the rare opportunity to investigate a clump of lavender. Jogging in place, I strained to hear it again, alert to possible trouble. Suddenly, the tenants of my fantasy abode were real flesh-and-blood people, distant neighbors in trouble. I pictured a domestic abuse scene and wondered where the nearest pay phone was. Here it came again, long and slow, floating above me until the notes rained down along with comprehension. How alike are the sounds of pain and ecstasy, I marveled. The crescendo of pleasure rang in my ears, and I felt embarrassed, a sweaty voyeur with a meager excuse (um, I was waiting for the dog to finish peeing) yet unable to tear myself away. As the two naked bodies came into focus in my mind's eye, they hovered like sweaty wraiths, coupling on a quilted bedcover, which in their need they hadn't even bothered to tear back, the woman arching her back with pleasure, head lolling over the bed as she gasped. The white muslin curtain in that high window concealed the secrets of that room only to the deaf. I inclined my head, invoking proper reverence for the transcendent. Only then did I move on, surging with carnality that made me sprint faster and longer than I had ever thought possible until I finally settled into a loping and rhythmic gait.

Up, up Redcliff I went, huffing as Bon Jovi puffed. The weather had turned humid during my reverie and the air smelled dank. A UPS truck shot past me in a stream of exhaust, and I tucked my nose into my shirt and breathed in the salty surface of my skin to avoid inhaling all that toxic waste. Five minutes later, I heard it chugging up the next street, still circling like a bird of prey for its target address. People always got lost up here. Drivers would cruise up slowly and ask for directions, feebly waving hand-scribbled instructions on a torn envelope or hoisting their maps in a silent plea. The streets dog-legged and dead-ended after one block, only to pick up a mile later.

Here came the UPS truck again. It careened behind me now, more beat-up than most of the ones I saw in this neighborhood, delivering manuscripts and L.L. Bean packages to the self-employed who had the luxury of hanging out in these delightful hills all day, taking calls and stirring the paella they were whipping up for dinner as "All Things Considered" began its familiar drumbeat and the sun descended. That was the life. One day, I too would live like that. I even had the house picked out: a big orange dump of a Spanish with turquoise trim and a cactus garden. No bourgeois lawn for me.

The truck pulled up level to me and I noticed that the UPS logo had been spray-painted on the truck's side. At the same time, a young Asian face leaned out the passenger side, twisting until his entire torso dangled in the window. Like all of them, he held something in his hand. And then I saw it. The dull, steel barrel of a gun, pointed right at my head.

Instinctively, I ducked, and the shot ricocheted past. My first thought was that it was a lot louder than the sounds that serenaded me on mean Saturday nights, going off like endless Chinese firecrackers. This was an explosion ripping up the air around my left ear. Bon Jovi lunged against the leash and whinnied in terror. Then I remembered the overgrown staircase street that loomed directly to my right. Bobbing and weaving now, I ran toward it and turned, immediately obscured by canopied trees, as more shots whistled through the leaves. Bon Jovi whimpered again as I pulled his leash, jerking him up the stairs and into the safety of the green darkness. Usually I was spooked going up this one, it was so dark and overhanging, a perfect rape-pit, but today I welcomed the cool concrete dark and mulch that squelched below my feet, all pine needles and dead leaves.

"C'mon, Bon Jovi." I groped my limbs, checking for wounds. I knew the shock of being shot could numb you to the pain. Everything seemed intact. Unless the UPS driver was familiar with these vertical back roads, he'd never find us, but I was going to hang out here for a while anyway, just to make sure.

Who was shooting at me, and why?

Bon Jovi was still whimpering, so I grabbed his fur to pull him up into the hidden recesses of someone's backyard and into an unlocked tool shed behind a copse of trees where we could crouch safely, just in case. My hand came away wet and sticky. It was covered with blood. The dog was panting now, and his eyes were dulling. Blood trickled out of his mouth. He groaned and grunted as more blood spewed forth. I petted his narrow head and whispered soothing words to him and he looked at me with the same trust I had seen in May-li's eyes. I had betrayed them both. Now I heard the scrunching of leaves, the soft step of someone on the stairs. I held Bon Jovi's bleeding mouth closed, praying he wouldn't whimper as he died, afraid to leave him and run for fear of making more noise.

There were two of them. The voices came from different places. They were speaking in Chinese. I heard a ripping noise, then the sulfur flare of a match. The air filled with acrid smoke, a singular and unpleasant smell that reminded me of Gauloises cigarettes. I wondered whether my attacker had dropped the match into the undergrowth and whether it would ignite and make the flames dance all around me and the dead dog, heating up our tin shed until the metal glowed red and I was flushed out like a frightened deer. But no. They swept right past, hissing urgently to each other, and I prayed they wouldn't stray off the path. They didn't. Soon their voices faded, and I didn't hear any more crackling. Maybe it was a trap, and they were lying in wait for me to come out and show myself. I forced myself to recall every book report I had done in the seventh grade. Hawthorne, Poe, O. Henry, and Steinbeck. The night grew completely dark. The dog's limbs were stiff and heavy against my thigh now, and no longer warm. I started shivering, although it must have been 75 degrees. When an eternity had gone by, I started doing the multiplication tables in my head. O blessed, rote memorization. When those ran out, I sat silently, listening with rabbit ears for any sound.

But all that registered was the stench of night-blooming jasmine, surging into my nostrils and flooding the back of my throat as if I had gargled my great aunt's *eau de parfum*. It was funny how your senses betrayed you. I retched, vomiting only bile. A long, slow spasm went through me as I fought to be still. I heard myself shrieking orders to my rebellious body, then realized that the sound came from outside me and I collapsed, head grazing Bon Jovi's long strands of blood-caked fur.

It was a great horned owl screeching in impending victory as it dove for food. The talons and beak connected with something warm and furry. Small, agonized squealings filled the air, and a tussle ensued on the dried leaves. I pictured them rolling on the ground together, hunter and hunted, and the thought sent stalactites creeping down my back. Nature unfolding the scenario I had just avoided, the food chain fixed and unyielding. But I refused to play mouse to their raptor. I counted to one thousand. Then I stood up, pushed open the door of the shed, and limped on trembling limbs under the buzzing yellow streetlights all the way home.

CHAPTER 29

T he false dawn was shimmering around the edges of the sky by the time I finished telling my story to the cops. They seemed convinced it was nothing more than a robbery gone awry and told me they'd be in touch. Of course, I hadn't told them the back story. How could I, since I had broken a few laws myself, I thought wearily, leaning over the tub with my last reserves of strength to crank the hot water. Easing myself into the sloshing bath, I surrendered to the liquid warmth. I must have dozed off that way, because I woke to the phone ringing. Through the bathroom window, the real dawn was now glowing on the horizon.

"It's Mark. Sorry to wake you up. I had a terrible dream . . ." he began.

"You did? Well, it's all true, but I'm still alive."

"What's true?" he asked in confusion.

"Someone tried to kill me last night as I was jogging. He missed but got my neighbor's dog. An Asian kid with a gun leaning out of a UPS truck that wasn't a real UPS truck," I said, remembering his face, and the expressionless, almost bored look in his eyes right before he pulled the trigger. Like it was some rote task he had done a thousand times.

"Good God. Stay there, I'll be right over."

"See what happens when I'm without you?"

"*You're* the one who wanted some time to yourself. You can't have it both ways."

"Ah, Mark, but I want you every which way," I said, hanging up.

Gingerly, I dried off, wrapped a flannel bathrobe around myself, made a cup of instant cocoa with tiny bobbing marshmallows that gave me immense and inexplicable comfort, and got into bed to await his arrival.

And then it hit me. Someone really had tried to kill me. My words to Mark had not been just dramatic flourish. And the assassins had failed, which meant that they would try again. That truck hadn't found me by accident. It had circled several times, quietly mapping my progress before striking. They must have trailed me from the house. This house, where I lay curled up in bed, feeling suddenly not so secure. But why did they want to kill me? And how had they gotten my address?

My mind flashed to a memory of scribbling my home number on a business card and handing it over to the INS clerk who in her ignorance had handed May-li over to the smugglers. Scrambling out of bed, I raced for the phone and began dialing. It took me seven calls to get through.

"Mrs. Locksley, this is Eve Diamond, the reporter who was down at INS detention looking for the Chinese girl yesterday. I need to know something. Did you by any chance give my address or business card to the people who took May-li away?"

There was silence on the other end of the phone. I began picking at my cuticles, prying up little bits of dried flesh with the underside of my nail.

"Mrs. Locksley, it's OK if you did. But it's really important that you tell me."

"You won't get mad?"

"I promise," I said, pulling a stubborn flap of skin.

"They said they wanted to thank the person who found May-li and took such good care of her and brought her to the INS," Mrs. Locksley said.

"I told them it was a reporter and they asked for your name. They wanted to send a thank you note. The Chinese are so formal and polite! So I went and got them your card. They copied down the address and gave it back to me. I still have it."

"Did they see the number I wrote on the back?" With a tremendous effort, I yanked the cuticle and it finally tore, exposing a jagged strip of pink skin. Slowly the blood welled to the surface and began to pool like a gigantic teardrop. I studied it with indifference, then raised the injured thumb to my mouth and sucked the salty liquid.

"Why, I don't know. They were turning it all around, holding it up to the light and admiring the embossed eagle on the card, you know, the *Times* logo."

"Thank you, Mrs. Locksley. And listen, if anyone else asks you for that card, don't show it to them, OK. Put it at the bottom of your desk under your packets of Top Ramen and Tampax and forget I ever gave it to you."

"Why sure, Ms. Diamond. I'll do that. But I won't forget to call if I ever hear of a good story."

"You're a sweetheart, Mrs. Locksley."

I hung up and stared blindly at the phone. Any moron could look up someone's address if they had the telephone number. All they needed was a Criss-Cross Directory, which worked like a regular phone book, but in reverse. We used them all the time at work.

So now they knew where I lived. And they might be back. I thought about my close call the previous night, and I groaned, remembering suddenly that I would have to break the news about Bon Jovi to Violetta. She loved that dog. She sang Hungarian folk songs to him and cooked him fried liver with onions so he'd get plenty of vitamins. From me he got only leftovers. Sometimes he slept with me, that's why she hadn't come up looking for him yet, she figured he was here. Suddenly, I missed his warm fur and cold nose more than I could bear. And I knew I had to get out of Silverlake, fast.

When the knock came, intimate but insistent, I ran into the kitchen for a butcher knife.

"Who is it?" I stood off to the side so that if a bullet pierced the wood door, it would miss me. Sure, they might kick the door in, but I would call 911 as that happened, then stab them in the heart with my knife as they came bursting through. I visualized plunging my knife into a Thanksgiving turkey, the closest I could approximate to carving a human body.

"Mark." His voice was terse. "Let me in."

I unlocked the deadbolt and he saw me blinking in the morning light with my butcher knife still outstretched. His hair was tousled, as if he had rolled directly off his pillow into the car, and the yeasty smell of sleep still clung to him, mingling with the sharp mint of freshly brushed teeth. His eyes filled with a husky tenderness.

I moved toward him, trying to inhale as much of his comforting essence as I could.

"What in the . . . oh, my poor baby." He gathered me in his arms, car keys still jingling in his hand as he gently pried the knife free.

"They . . . they know where I live," I stammered. "The INS lady gave them my business card, which had my home number on it. They got my address from it. They think I know something about May-li that's worth dying for."

He led me to the bedroom, stopping in front of my closet.

"Pack. I'm taking you to my house."

I blanched. "But . . ."

"But nothing. They've lost the element of surprise, but they're going to try again. You'll be safer at my house."

When I didn't move, he flung open the closet doors, pulled down a suitcase, and started yanking things off hangers.

"No, wait, I never wear that. And this has a spot. Here, let me do it."

An hour later, I stood in Mark's living room, fighting off a monster case of sleep deprivation. Gently, Mark pried the suitcase from my hand.

"You look like a zombie. I'm going to make you scrambled eggs and then I'm putting you to bed and staying here while you sleep. When you wake up, we'll figure out what you know that's worth killing you."

The eggs were buttery and the toast was dense and chewy and I washed it all down with whole, creamy milk, and then let him tuck me into his bed, where I fell into a deep and dreamless sleep. When I swam up to consciousness, he was sitting in the corner reading, and he raised his head as I stirred, smiled and came over and kissed my forehead as one does with a feverish child, touched my hand under the cover, then retreated to his corner. And so the day passed.

The next time I woke, the afternoon sun was dappling through the trees. Mark was outside, drinking a glass of juice and surveying the garden as I padded over to a chaise lounge and eased into it. It was hard to believe this wasn't a figment of my wistful imagination.

"You missed a whole day of work for me."

"And I'd even miss two." He came over and kissed me on the cheek. "In fact, now that you're feeling better, and I can take proper advantage of you, I think I'll take tomorrow off as well. What do you think of that?" he whispered into my ear, squeezing my arm. "Twenty-four hours and we unplug the phone. No juvenile delinquents. No newspaper deadlines. No gangs. No stopping."

My knees trembled, desire shot through with fear. Of love, death, and letting go all wrapped into one. For once, I went with animal instinct.

"Why wait til tomorrow?" I tugged his arm and pulled him along, retracing my steps down the hallway, back to the room where the dappled sunshine soon gave way to deeper hues that danced across his skin like a Balinese shadow play.

But the fear came back as the curtain fell.

"Mark." I broke the spell. "They think May-li told me something that will lead the cops to them."

He ticked off the facts. "She told us how she spent three months on that horrid ship. About how the sailors raped her. About how she was transported up from Mexico in a produce truck. About the brothel she lived in."

"Wait," I said. "There were two brothels. The first one, then the Rosemead place the cops busted. May-li said the first one had a circular brick driveway and was on a main street. I bet it's still a functioning brothel today."

I turned to him excitedly. "Maybe that's it. They're worried we could find it and sic the cops on them. Then there's the Marina angle. May-li knew Marina." I ran my finger along the plaster crack on his bedroom wall. "Marina visited the brothel at least once. She wrote about it in her diary . . ."

Something made me look up. Mark was staring, his mouth agape.

"Marina? That murdered girl? What are you talking about?"

I thought hard. I had been playing four-dimensional chess in my own head for so long, compartmentalizing what I told everybody, that I had finally slipped up.

"I know I told you," I stammered. "I found this diary . . ."

I stopped. This scenario brought everything into painful focus for me. The diary had disappeared right after I told him about it the first time. Was I holding back now because I still didn't trust him completely? And if so, then why on earth was I sleeping with him? Mark Furukawa did not exactly wear his heart on his sleeve either. His depths held depths, and his mirrored eyes only truly opened to me in bed. We were always either in bed or flailing about in this quicksand. I might as well sink a bit deeper.

"Marina Lu was the girl who was killed in that botched carjacking. I found her diary but it was stolen out of my car before I read more than a few pages. She was a parachute kid, a rich and legal Chinese immigrant, about as far removed from May-li's sad tale as you can get. But it's like they were two sides of the same coin. They both came to America for the same thing. They both ended up badly. And the parachute kid—the good little straight-A student from San Marino—had some connection to the brothel where May-li was held. I'm trying to find out what that is. And there are other things I haven't told you." Somehow, my voice stayed steady.

I started with the easy one and confessed my suspicions about Reginald Lu and Golden Pacific Bank, recounting my visit to the Vietnamese family in South El Monte who were so poor they served me hot water to drink.

"It's a Vietnamese custom," Mark said under his breath.

"What, breaking your kneecaps if you don't repay your loan to a federally chartered American commercial bank?"

"No, that's appalling." Mark sounded frustrated. "But in many parts of Southeast Asia, it's customary to serve visitors a glass of warm water. It doesn't mean they're too poor to serve tea."

"Oh." For one brief moment, I felt chastened. Then anger welled.

"Something else happened," I said, "for which I don't think there could be any possible cultural misunderstanding on my part."

I told him how I had gone to the Jade Dragon to meet Michael Ho and been drugged by a group of Asian men who interrogated me, then dumped me in my car to sleep it off.

"They drugged you?"

It sounded so ludicrous that for a moment, I wasn't sure myself. The memories had faded even further, making me wonder whether I hadn't dreamed it all during a particularly virulent nightmare. Then I remembered the touch on my breasts, the insistent questions, my nausea the next morning, and knew it had all happened, and maybe even more.

"That's right. Have you ever heard of a drug called Rohypnol? Your kids would know it as roofies."

"The date-rape drug? Oh my God, Eve, they didn't . . . ?"

"No, they didn't rape me. But I certainly felt violated."

"What happened when you went to the police?"

I started crying.

"I didn't go to the police, Mark. I didn't think anyone would believe me. They'd ask what I was doing in an Asian nightclub at two A.M. to begin with. Plus I've written about roofies. It's really hard to prove anything, the drug doesn't stay in your system. And what am I going to say, that they drugged me and asked me questions about a carjacking and then touched my breasts?"

"Yes." Mark was indignant. "That's exactly what you'd say. And it's not too late."

He reached for the phone, but I grabbed his hand.

"Wait. You don't know the whole story yet. And I need time to think this through before I tell you any more. I'm sorry."

He looked at me, waiting. Finally he spoke. "They're going to kill you."

"I'm not ready to go to the police."

"Then promise me that you won't do anything foolish, like looking for this 'brothel' house alone. These people would love for you to show up on their doorstep. Save them the trouble of hunting you down."

"I promise. But one more thing. I'm going to spend tomorrow night at a friend's house," I told him. "It's nothing personal. I just need a little time apart. Her name is Babette, and we grew up together."

"If that's what you want." He could retreat too.

We both went to work the next day after all.

CHAPTER 30

O n the way to work the next morning, I kept looking in my rearview for a UPS truck, even though I knew in the rational part of my brain that they would have ditched it once their plan failed. I had the feeling there was an hourglass somewhere with my name on it, and when the sand ran out, they would strike again. I had to move fast. My brain fastened onto something May-li had said— that the brothel was on a main street and had a circular brick driveway. Perhaps there were more clues in Marina's diary that the thieves had missed.

I had packed the pages into my briefcase the day before. Once at my desk, I reread carefully:

> September 14. Last night we followed him to a house in a skanky neighborhood, with houses and auto body shops jumbled next to each other, nothing like San Marino. Alison drank so much diet Coke that we went to the gas station twice so she could pee, which majorly screwed up our plans to watch the door til he came out . . .

It was depressing to look at the front lawn, which was about all we could do from the car, it was all yellow and dying. Maybe they can't afford a gardener and the disrespectful teenagers who live inside won't help out their parents. There were three nice cars parked in the circular brick driveway and more on the street, with lots of people coming and going. But not Michael. He stayed put. I know because his car was still there each time we came back from pee patrol. Maybe he really does have a girlfriend, although she must be boring if she lives in a place like that. I know I shouldn't be spying on my fiancé. But I can't stop now until I know.

I got out my notepad and wrote:

Clue No. 1. Mixed-use street with businesses and homes.
Clue No. 2. Yellowed lawn.
Clue No. 3. Circular brick driveway.
Clue No. 4. Many cars parked in front.
Clue No. 5. Alison.

After I wrote her name down, I looked out the window at the smog already blanketing the horizon. And smiled. Lily had given me Alison's last name. It was Tsing. I had promised Mark I wouldn't go shopping for clues by myself. I intended to keep my word. By taking Alison.

That afternoon, I left work early and headed down to San Marino High as school let out. I felt fairly sure that Alison Tsing crammed in a full load, probably honors, AP, and extracurricular activities as well to impress the admission officers at all the Ivy League schools where she had applied. Sure enough, I found her studying in the library. She looked vulnerable and solitary, a slight, wispy girl with straight black hair and a triangular cat face.

She remembered me, all right, and agreed to go with me to House of Pies to talk some more. Away from her friend Ms. Sunflower Halter Top, Alison was more loquacious, laying it on thick about what a wonderful human being her dead friend had been. I let her prattle on about Saint Marina, then leaned across the Formica table until I saw the salt from her french fries melting on her lower lip.

"Alison, I know about the spying."

"What spying? What are you talking about?" The voice was shrill, scared.

"I'm talking about how you guys would park in front of a certain house when you were tailing Michael. See, I met another girl who knew Marina. I even know that you drank so much Diet Pepsi you had to use the dirty gas station bathroom all the time. What I can't understand though, is why you didn't tell the cops?"

"Are you kidding?" If she had a tail, she'd be swishing it. Neither one of us spoke.

"It was Coke," she finally spat out. And then I knew I had her. I knew that all I had to do was sit there and fidget with my drink and sooner or later she'd open her mouth and blab until they rolled up the sidewalk in front of House of Pies and shooed us out of there like a housewife brooms away a stray cat.

So I kept my eyes averted, took a sip of ice water, and said nothing.

"My mom didn't know we were out all night, cruising bad parts of town, spying on her fiancé," Alison whispered when my water was at the halfway mark. "That would have looked real good for a National Merit Scholarship winner, huh? I'm on the waiting list at Harvard. My older sister's there, she made the Dean's List. In exactly ten months, I will be out of here. And a messy murder is not on the agenda. Marina was my friend and I'm sorry she's dead. But I'm only seventeen years old and I haven't done anything wrong. And honestly, I don't know who killed her. So why should I go to the police?"

Her ivory nostrils flared in defiance.

"Then tell *me* what you know instead. I'm much nicer than the cops, believe me. It will be our little secret."

Christ, I sounded just like a pedophile. There were no depths I would not stoop to for this story.

"We followed him a lot." Alison pushed a fry around her plate. "First it was just a fun thing when we were bored. But Marina became obsessed. She couldn't figure out what Michael was up to and it drove her nuts. I mean, they were having a nonstop party in there with cars coming and going, but there was no loud music or anything, so that was kind of creepy. And one evening, get this, he goes to a hotel and picks up this girl and they drive back to the house and go in. Marina couldn't stand it. She was wild, tearing her hair out, I'm not kidding, strands knotted around her fingers. She was ready to walk in and confront him. I talked her out of it. I said, look, he's an asshole. Call off the wedding now, while you still have a chance. The next night, I had an advanced placement chem test to study for, and then I was leaving for Hong Kong. She knew it was real important that I ace the test. I told her not to go by herself, but did she listen?"

Alison rolled her eyes. "The next day, she passed me a note in French IV and told me to meet her by the catering truck at lunch. She had something *très grande* to tell me." Alison paused.

"And?"

"She never showed. I waited for eighteen minutes—that's almost our whole lunch—and then I thought maybe I had heard her wrong. As I crossed the quad, I saw Marina getting into Asshole's Jag. She didn't notice me. The windows are tinted, see. And then Michael tore out of the school parking lot and down Huntington Drive."

Alison gave me a significant look. But this was not the payoff I wanted.

"Then what? Did you call her that evening? What was so important?"

"I paged her eight times that day but she never answered. She wasn't home, either. I was leaving for Hong Kong the next day—my auntie still has a house there and she was sick, so I had other things on my mind, like packing. When I came back ten days later, Marina was dead."

"But didn't you call her once you got to Hong Kong? You guys are always calling back and forth across the Pacific."

"Of course I did." Alison straightened up and put a haughty distance between us. "I called her at least six times more after I got to my auntie's. But then I started thinking maybe she was mad at me. For bad-mouthing Michael. Also, I met a guy."

Alison looked at me through downcast lashes. I filled in the blanks, imagining the phone calls to San Marino dwindling as the overseas romance heated up.

My mind exploded with various scenarios. Marina going back to the house alone, finding her boyfriend there, what, in bed with one of the girls? Doing drugs? Running the show? Working as an undercover cop? Highly unlikely. Marina somehow meeting up with May-li. And then what? Doing something to sabotage the operation? Threatening to tell her father? Go to the police? And ultimately, getting killed because she knew too much? Is that what had happened to my little parachute girl? Random death as a result of a carjacking gone awry was seeming less and less likely.

"Alison, do you think Michael killed Marina because she was on to something bad he was doing and was threatening to tell?"

"Don't think so." Alison leaned over her diet Coke and sucked hard on the straw. "Marina was a sweet girl. She hadn't been over here long enough to develop her assertive side. Unlike me."

She tossed back her long glossy hair. "Nope. I can't imagine Marina confronting anyone."

"So what do you think happened?"

"I think she caught him in bed with some girl. That was her big news. But she obviously didn't call off the wedding because I would have heard about it. And then she got carjacked and shot. Michael's a jerk but I can't see him as a murderer. Oh, I can't wait to get to Harvard and leave all this behind."

"Alison, would you recognize the house if you drove past it?"

She looked at me with alarm. "Nooooo," she said, but it was just a general protest. I waited, locking eyes. "I don't know," she stammered. "Maybe."

"What street was it on?"

"I don't remember. We'd have to retrace our steps from the In-N-Out. We stopped there for chili cheese fries and diet Cokes beforehand."

"Done."

"And we'd have to do it at night. So they can't see me."

"Why? I thought you said her death was random."

"I did not. I said I don't know who killed her."

"So you think it's someone who could kill you too?"

"Look, Eve, don't be naive. Anyone could get killed for anything. People don't need a reason to die."

I thought of the young man leaning out of the truck the other evening, eyes hardening with concentration as he got me in his sights. Before I could check the impulse, I looked over my shoulder. An empty booth. Somehow, that made me feel worse than if it had been filled with people.

"You're right," I said. "So we'll go at night."

We took my car. Alison crouched down low in the seat. She wore a big floppy hat and sunglasses, even though it was dark. She looked ridiculous and her disguise attracted more attention as we drove down Valley Boulevard than if she had been dressed normally. For that matter, I should be the one wearing a disguise. No one had tried to kill her.

We drove slowly up and down the streets of Rosemead, which I had learned was the only city in the area that allowed mixed-use—homes built next to businesses. Alison thought we were in the right general area. She also thought the house was on a street named after a tree. Maple, Elm, Chestnut Street. Up and down we drove, through suburbs that looked like they had sprung out of the cornfields yesterday, with snap-on turrets and prefab sod you roll out and tack down for instant lawns. Many of these streets dead-ended into gated communities and cemeteries, which was something I didn't let myself dwell on.

Then we retraced our steps back to that burger joint, where the smell of grease was beginning to curdle my stomach. I had seen a few circular driveways, but not the one that Marina described.

"Alison, you sure we're on the right track? Maybe you stopped at McDonald's, not In-N-Out."

Alison closed her eyes, and I knew I was sinking lower and lower in her esteem.

"I don't eat at McDonald's," she said. "We're close. I can feel it. Trust me."

Without anything better to go on, I did. Soon we ditched the tree streets and moved on to bigger avenues. Methodically, we passed houses on Rosemead Boulevard, Del Mar, Garvey. "There," Alison said triumphantly. "That's it."

It was a shabby stucco house on South Garvey Avenue with a circular brick driveway and an auto body shop across the street. My stomach tightened. But this was no street named after a tree. And the grass was green. Oh well, maybe they had replanted.

"You sure?" I whispered.

"Yes. That's it. That's it."

"Positive?"

"Ee-ee-vve," she whined.

I rested my forehead against the steering wheel. "Thank you," I said, to no one in particular.

"No prob," said Alison, rummaging through her purse and pulling out a cell phone.

"Let me call my mom and tell her I'll be home in twenty minutes so she doesn't worry. Hey, I'm thirsty," she continued. "Can we stop at In-N-Out for a diet Coke before you drop me off?"

CHAPTER 31

As Alison yakked on her cell phone, lying through her teeth to dear old mom with the glib expertise of all teenagers, we drove right past the Rainbow Coalition Center and I fantasized about calling to see if Mark was still in. I didn't, but after dropping Alison off at her two-story Spanish home in the ritzy part of San Marino, I still couldn't get Mark Furukawa out of my mind. Now that I had the brothel house nailed down, I felt magnanimous. I realized that I owed Mark a major explanation. The look on his face still resonated—"Don't you trust me?" Besides, an idea was forming in the back of my head about how to infiltrate the brothel to see if May-li was still there, but I needed Mark's help. Also, I missed him.

Ready to confess all, I pulled into the lot. Mark often worked late. A slim Vietnamese man buzzed me in, took note of my briefcase, and led me to Mark's office. I was right. He was still in the building, his keys atop his Filofax.

"You wait here, please," the skinny guy murmured, then disappeared.

I settled into the plastic chair, wishing I had brought something to read. True readers are rapacious that way; it doesn't matter if we're holding *Jane Eyre* or the folded-up instructions to a bottle of Tylenol, we just need the alphabetic fix. Mark's desk was bare except for manila folders with Asian names. His troubled young "clients." Temptation beckoned, but I refrained.

A medallion on Mark's key chain caught my eye. Disgusting. It was a scorpion, a real one, embedded in a shiny laminated resin. I knew a liquor store in Silverlake that sold these key chains. They were popular with the Mexican kids. Morbidly fascinated, I leaned over the desk to take a closer look. Could you see its stinger? I heard a door open down the hall, a perfunctory conversation in Chinese, then footsteps heading toward me. Mark's counseling session was over. Embarrassed now, I straightened up, willing myself not to blush. He would think I had been snooping. As I turned to greet him, my eyes traveled across an open Rolodex stuffed with dog-eared business cards and I couldn't help but notice the last call Mark had made today. Even before I saw the name, I recognized the logo, that white, embossed pillar superimposed with Chinese characters, signifying wealth, purity, and trust. And my blood congealed. Golden Pacific Bank, the card said. And in Chinese and English, the name "Michael Ho, Senior Vice President for Finance."

"Hey, you," Mark walked through the door. "I thought you were at your friend's house. Did you get the five messages I left for you at work?"

He leaned over to kiss me and I was too frozen to move. All I could think of was that he had to be in on it. He had set me up. And blinded by his attention, I had been too oblivious to see.

"Hello, Mark." My heart pounded.

"I came by . . . ," I began, then just couldn't go on. Maybe Mark had gone to Golden Pacific Bank for a loan. Maybe he had a drug habit and Michael Ho was his supplier. Maybe Mark was even part of the triad. But then why hadn't they just killed me? Mark had had plenty of opportunities. And in his own backhanded way, he might even be in love with me, I thought, recalling the previous night's fever. As I was in love with him, I realized in an unforeseen rush.

"I came by just for a minute to see you, and now I'm going to go." I forced a sick smile. Let him think me an idiot. I couldn't come up with anything more coherent right now. And I was too heartsick to confront him, too vulnerable. One must attack from strength, not weakness.

"What's wrong?" He seemed bewildered, alarmed. "You look terrible. I think this is finally all catching up with you. Please come home with me tonight. I'd feel so much better."

I bet, I thought. Where you can have me under your thumb, under your scrutiny, so you can file your reports and make sure I don't learn anything more than you want me to.

He grabbed the scorpion keys and jingled them in his hand to illustrate the comfort of his home, and I wanted that antediluvian sand monster to lift its tail and sting him right through the resin.

"I can't." I headed for the door, keeping my head averted from the Rolodex so he wouldn't even dream that I knew. "I'll be OK tonight."

"But I don't understand. You drop in for one whole minute and then tell me you're taking off?"

And then I threw out the ultimate red herring, which was all the more powerful and distracting because it was true, and he knew me well enough to know that it wasn't said lightly or without cost, and it bought me the time I needed to get out of that room.

"I'm falling in love with you and it scares me," I said, focusing on the spot between his eyes. And then I was running down the hall and flinging open the car door and barreling down the street like a Saturday night drunk, heading for the oblivion that only an eight-lane highway at night can bring when you can't go home and your destination's unknown.

CHAPTER 32

I t wasn't until I was headed back to L.A. on I-10 that I realized I had never gotten around to calling my old friend Babette. And I couldn't go home to Silverlake. No sir, I didn't want to stand on my front porch in the dark, sticking my house key into the lock and wondering what had slithered in ahead of me. As the great interchange of downtown L.A. neared, I swung the car into a long, cool right and headed for Eagle Rock to throw myself on Babette's manicured mercy.

I breathed a sigh of relief when I didn't see any cars parked in front of her fifties dingbat apartment. But then I realized that didn't preclude the possibility she might be dating some loser without a car. I hadn't seen her since our Millie's breakfast and that was eons in Babette's world, where things moved fast.

Babette slid her peephole open on the first knock, then undid her triple locks, stepping out to reveal hair perfectly curled, her perfumed person trailing fluffy Day-Glo mules and a peach negligee.

"Eve, come in, what's the matter?" she asked, instantly perceptive.

"Oh, Babette, you look like you're expecting company. I'm sorry to drop by without calling. It's just that I was on the freeway and . . . Is this a bad time?"

"Company? Why, no," she giggled.

When I was home alone, I wore a ratty T-shirt and sweatpants from my college track days, which just shows you the hopeless couture chasm that lay between us.

"Well, don't just stand there, come in, come in." She grabbed my arm and yanked me inside.

"Oh, Babette," I said forty minutes later, when I had finished telling her about my week. "Do you see what a mess I've gotten myself into? And the worst thing of all, which I just realized tonight, is that I'm in love with him."

"Girlfriend," said Babette, "you don't do things halfway, do you. So you got involved with him. You guys have great chemistry. That's good. But he could be double-crossing you. That's bad. There's a lot you don't know about this man. Or maybe you know, deep down, but won't let yourself think about it. You need to get to the bottom of these crossed signals you're receiving. And sending out too. Oh yes you are," Babette said, as I opened my mouth to protest.

"I know you, Eve. You hide your heart. Maybe he thinks you're just using him. You need to step back from this relationship and contemplate it in tranquillity. Which is Wordsworth's way of saying, just relax. Remember ole William Wordsworth from high school? It's one of the few things that stuck to this Teflon brain. But say, I've got just the thing for relaxing. You remember Patrick—he was a doll but I'm not dating him anymore, he had too much hair on his back, it was like sleeping with the Wolfman. Anyway, he brought over some Perrier-Jouët and beluga a few months back and we never even opened it, he was such a beast that night! Let's nip into it tonight. You look like a little caviar would do you good."

Caviar and champagne on a weeknight sounded decadent enough to whet my appetite. But I questioned whether this would lead to the inner contemplation Babette suggested. In fact, I thought I might be going a little crazy. Every time I mentioned that someone was trying to kill me, people told me to relax and offered me something to eat. It made me want to scream. Did I sound that delusional? I wondered, remembering that even paranoiacs have enemies.

An hour later, Babette's pink tongue was delicately picking out the last of the black globules and the Perrier-Jouët bottle sprawled drunk-enly on its side. My troubles seemed dim and far away, like the Caspian Sea where the sturgeon spawned their sinfully salty eggs. And with that, I slept.

CHAPTER 33

My head felt fuzzy the next morning as I navigated to my desk, sank into the privacy of my cubicle, and propped my head up with one hand. I used the other to punch in the code to my answering machine and heard two appeals from Mark.

"Damn it, Eve, what was up with you last night? I was so worried I drove by your house and pounded on your door, but the lights were out and I didn't see your car. I hope you're really with your girlfriend. Call me."

"Eve, it's me again. It's 9:45 A.M. Where are you? God, I hope you're OK."

Tough beans for Mr. Furukawa, I thought. I'll call him when I get around to it.

I heard a snicker nearby and knew without looking that Trevor Fingerhaven was upon me. Shooting him a dirty look as he towered over my desk, I willed him to go away.

"... said it was really important that he reach you as soon as possible. I told him to try again at ten, and he said he'd call right back. Big story brewing, eh?" Trevor's large Adam's apple bobbed with enthusiasm and he gave me an admiring look.

"What was his name?" I snapped.

Trevor put his hand up to his mouth, as if to impart a secret. "Wouldn't say." He was practically leering.

"Oh, well." I was determined not to play along. "Let's see if he calls back."

But my anonymous source played coy. At noon, I gave up and went to lunch. Trevor, who usually wolfed down a potted lunchmeat sandwich at his desk so he wouldn't miss any calls, sidled up as I walked in.

"Your friend called back. He sounded real disappointed you weren't here."

Trevor's voice was accusing, but I had sat through too many obsessive diatribes from nutcases who wanted an *L.A. Times* reporter to write about the secret camera the government had installed in their toilet. Besides, in the back of my mind, I figured it was probably Mark, using a different ploy to get me on the phone.

I sat down and the wires caught fire with news of a gang shooting after a high school graduation party in South Pasadena. The bash had been thrown by a good kid, ethnic Chinese from Vietnam, the kind who wore tennis whites and took honors classes. His parents were both home, chaperoning the event. No alcohol had been served. It didn't matter. Around the time that Babette and I got down to business with Messieurs Perrier and Jouët, some sixteen-year-old party-crashers had been turned away at the door. They returned early the next morning, loaded for bear. Rejection can be an ugly thing. Now the Yale-bound host was headed six feet under.

My thankless task was to interview the parents. But I had done it a hundred times before, so I gulped two aspirin and headed out.

When I rang the bell, the dead boy's mother opened the door. Her thin black hair stuck out like a punk rocker's and she clutched a red silk robe tightly around herself. For a moment, she looked out in bewilderment. Then she spied the press pass dangling like a laminated albatross around my neck and her eyes hardened into hatred, as though she'd like to stomp me into a slithering mass in the corner.

"You not come when I fax press release about how he accepted Yale," she spat in broken English. "Principal say, you write *L.A. Times*. Your boy good story. So I write. I say how Jonathan born seventeen years ago on boat in South China Sea. Where too many pirates. They come on boat, want throw baby overboard if my husband not give them gold. He one day old. And we think only, please, God, help us reach America. America safe country. We dream come here."

I feel your pain, lady. It's shitty American luck that your son got offed by some animals. But we don't do stories just because a kid gets accepted to an Ivy League school.

"I'm sorry about your loss, Mrs. Tam," I said. "I know you're in pain."

"You not cover debate tournament when he win," she shrieked. "You not write he 4.32 GPA. He good boy. He play cello. He volunteer animal shelter. No. You only come now he dead. Shame."

She pointed a trembling finger at me. My heart ached for her. But it would sound trite to say so. Like I was a conniving reporter just pretending to feel sympathy.

So I stood there, knowing she was right and her son's principal was wrong and that tragedies did make better copy than successes. Mrs. Tam hurled the door shut. I turned and walked slowly to my car, admiring the clay tennis court in the backyard. I shook my head. Coming penniless from Vietnam, they had clawed their way up to affluence. That was the Overseas Chinese for you. But none of it would do Jonathan any good now, and it was a pity too, that nice clay court going to waste. They had no other kids.

Once inside my car, I called Miller on the cell phone.

"Family isn't feeling very chatty. Got the door slammed in my face."

"Did you knock again? Did you tell them we're doing the story whether they talk or not but we'd prefer to get their cooperation? Yell through the window if you have to."

I winced, glad for the distance between us. I was losing my stomach for this line of work. I wondered what Mark was doing and whether I dared go home tonight to Silverlake. Then I banished the thoughts. Another teenager was dead and I had work to do.

"Yeah, yeah, I tried all that." I lied. "No dice."

"Then come back and start writing. Luz is at the cop shop and Trevor's on campus, talking to classmates. They'll call you with feeds."

At the office, the A/C was out, which didn't help my mood much. Thank God for good colleagues. Luz phoned in with ten clean grafs that I stuck right into the story. Trevor was another matter, and it took me fifteen precious minutes of questioning to get anything useful out of him. After that, I lost myself in the suspended space of deadline writing, where you are agonizingly aware of each minute ticking past and yet loose enough in your head to let the words flow.

At one point, I saw that Trevor had returned and was gesticulating wildly. "It's him," he mouthed, pointing to the telephone receiver in his hand.

My mystery caller again. Too bad. "Trevor, I have thirty-five inches to file in the next ten minutes and I'm still writing the lead. Tell him I'm on deadline and get his name and number."

I could see he was crushed. He lived vicariously through the exploits of other reporters and now hoped to get a ringside seat at whatever scandal might be brewing on my beat. But he relayed the message and hung up.

"So did he leave his name and number this time?" I asked at 5:02 P.M. after hitting the string of computer keys that sent my story pulsing to the Metro desk downtown.

"Nope," Trevor said. It was an accusation.

"Oh well, that's life in the big city." I sauntered to the kitchen, where the lone pot of afternoon coffee had been reduced to thick black syrup. Glad that no one was around to watch, I filled a Styrofoam cup halfway with the molten matter, swished it, and sniffed. Nose of burning rubber, with light tar accents. I topped it off with Sparklett's, then nuked it. Kills the germs.

When Luz yelled in that Metro was on the line with questions, I knew it was time to gulp down my medicine. They wanted a rewrite for the home edition and the hours ticked by. At 9 P.M., after a final call to the cop shop to confirm there had been no arrests yet, I was done. Even Trevor had given up and gone home.

Offices are depressing places to be in by yourself late at night, with all those empty desks and only the hum of computers and fluorescent lights for company. Every noise seems magnified. As the adrenaline ebbed, I heard the roar of the 210 Freeway just a stone's throw from the office—the *Times* always placed its suburban bureaus near the freeways, where they could broadcast their presence to commuters with big burly signage—and realized the back door must be open.

Damn, I hated that. Made me feel so vulnerable. We were always getting memos from management to keep the doors locked at night, especially after they caught some homeless guys scrubbing down in the bathroom one Saturday afternoon. But with the air-conditioning out, someone must have propped the door open to catch the afternoon breeze and forgotten to close it when they left for the day. That meant anyone could have strolled in while I was on deadline fugue, oblivious to my surroundings.

And then somebody did. "Why haven't you returned my phone calls?" Mark said. "I've been worried sick."

He loomed over me, smooth arms planted on either side of my desk, so close I could see the blue veins rippling. He wore black jeans, a tight black T-shirt, and a Dodger's baseball cap and smelled like he had just come out of the shower, waves of lavender sage that slowly expanded into the stale, institutional air. We were alone. If he really was an emissary of the triads, no one would hear my pleas for mercy. I pictured myself slumped over my desk, blood spurting out of my carotid artery and pooling on the keyboard until the keys jammed. With my luck, Trevor Fingerhaven would discover my body and have the story of his life.

Determined to dispel this morbid scenario, I blinked hard. "So you're tired of me already, huh?" Mark was saying. It was a petulant, hectoring question, and I saw him push back the bill of his cap as he asked it.

"Hey, that's usually my line. How did you know I'd still be at work?"

"I know Jonathan Tam was murdered last night. I was at the school all day, doing grief counseling. I figured you'd be working late on the story so I took a chance and swung by on the way home. You're not going to slip away from me two nights in a row. What in the hell is going on?"

If I had been half-scared before, his words turned my fear to anger.

I stood up. "No." I whirled around now, jabbing him in the chest with my finger the way Mrs. Tam had done with me earlier that day. "It's you who have to level with me. About Michael Ho of Golden Pacific Bank."

He blanched, and I saw that shadow come over his eyes, although I have to hand it to him, he controlled himself quickly.

"Eve, you sound like you're going off the deep end."

Although the words made me gasp, I think that even then, I wanted him to fold me into his arms and tell me I was wrong and it was all a crazy coincidence. But I knew I would only mistrust him more if I gave in to my emotions. I was actually glad of his bracingly harsh words, and met them with some of my own.

"You've been lying to me since we met."

I didn't tell him that my instincts were utterly at war with themselves, squaring off and prepared to do battle over whether this was really true. Instead I said:

"If you don't tell me how you know Michael Ho, I'm going to the cops right now."

"Hey, hey, calm down. It was I who urged *you* to go to the cops at Lily's, then again after you got shot at. If I had anything real to hide, why would I have done that?"

He spread his hands wide like a Chinese fan. But I had found the tear I needed and rushed in to rend whatever illusions remained.

"What do you mean, if you had anything *real* to hide?"

"Eve, I work with screwed-up kids. I can't break the therapist-patient oath of confidentiality . . ."

"Fuck your oath." My fingers slid over my cuticles and I felt the sharp rush of pain as I plucked off the living skin. Oh, I wanted to make it hurt bad. "Doesn't your relationship with me count for something?"

Mark walked over to an office chair, sat down, and pulled it level with mine. He took the baseball hat off and ran his fingers through his hair, wet now with sweat. Then he reached for a stray reporter's notebook and began to absentmindedly tear out blank pages.

"OK. Yes, I was counseling Tony. He was so desperate for a father figure. He reminded me of myself at his age. Alienated. Confused."

Mark gave me a weak, hopeful smile but I held my scowl.

"And I had two parents at home growing up, he's got neither. For a while, we made headway. Then he started skipping sessions. Told me he had some new friends. And told me a *gwai lo* reporter wanted to interview him for a story about parachute kids. I told him to avoid you. I said you'd sensationalize his story, because that's all reporters were after."

I stirred in protest, but he overrode me. Despite his harsh words, I felt a rush of tenderness for Mark, knowing that he, too, had tried to protect Tony. Even if that meant warning him away from me.

"You don't know how fragile this kid is," he continued. "Say your story runs on the front page and you get a pat on the back from your editor, maybe even some award or promotion, but Tony's life goes on as before, or maybe it gets worse, because your story forces him to hold a mirror to his life. You're a good reporter, see, and you've wormed your way into his confidence and coaxed all these intimate details out of him and he doesn't like what he reads, he's ashamed, but it's too late now because bam, you're gone, chasing the next hot story, and I'm left to pick up the pieces when he falls apart or turns to his new 'friends' who have all sorts of ways to make him feel better."

Then he was talking about how even good kids got sucked into gangs, how the lines got real blurry when you were an adolescent because gang culture—the music, the clothes, the beepers and earrings—was cool teen culture, and then pretty soon with some of these kids, it wasn't just acting anymore, but the real thing. Especially if they came from another country and didn't fit into the American mainstream. Gangs were a way for them to feel instantly powerful, totally connected. Mark's voice was low and urgent and something in the tone struck me.

"Are you trying to dissuade me from joining or to recruit me?"

He looked startled. "You're very perceptive," he said softly.

"How's that?"

He was busy folding the notepad pages into dozens of little creases, his brow furrowed with concentration. He didn't notice the Kleenex I had plucked to dab at the blood on my fingers.

"I feel for these kids because I was one myself. Gangs, I mean. Luckily, I got out by sixteen. Only a passing phase. But that's why I can walk the walk and talk the talk. I've been there."

My jaw dropped. Then I scooted my chair over, grabbed his knee, and found my voice.

"I had you pegged as some bleeding-heart liberal who got into this line of work after taking a deviant psychology class at your Ivy League college."

"Wrong-o, pal." He took my empty Styrofoam cup and smashed it in his fist. "It was Cal State L.A. Took me eight years, working full-time. And just because I don't have a dragon tattooed across my chest doesn't mean I haven't been scorched by its breath."

I swallowed hard. "But you're Japanese," I said. "They don't have gangs."

"You grow up in the San Gabriel Valley and look like me, you get recruited sooner or later. It happens in junior high. They come to the playground when school lets out, driving nice cars, flashing bills. They've got their little intermediaries to talk it up. Oh yeah. The Black Hand, they take all comers. Chinese. Vietnamese. Filipino. Latino. Japanese. Anything but white boys. And by the way, all that Japanese law-abiding shit you were throwing out. That's a stereotype. Don't forget the Yakuza."

"So what did you do in this gang?"

"What is this, an interview for the latest Eve Diamond exclusive, 'Youth Counselor Recounts Formative Gang Years'?"

"I just want to know."

"Robberies, mostly."

"You—you mean, like home invasions? Where people get tortured into giving up their valuables?"

Mark's eyes caught mine, then glanced away, and he went back to creasing his papers.

"Only one," he muttered. "That was what convinced me to get out. It was hairy, man. Here I was, sixteen years old and toting a semiautomatic around, handing over duct tape so they could bind an old lady's wrists together. When my pal got out the lit cigarette, I started losing it. That could have been my grandmother, you know."

I rolled my chair away from him. "So what did you do?"

"Created a distraction. It wasn't real brilliant, but it worked. I walked over to the window and yelled 'Fuck, two cop cars just drove by real slow.' I told my friends the old bitch must have tripped some kind of security alarm, and we'd better run for it. I knew they wouldn't kill her. The folks we picked on were too scared to go to the police. It's a cultural thing. Besides, we always took a picture off the mantel just in case. One of their children. They knew what that meant.

"So my friends took off. I made sure I was the last one out the door. And right before I left, I untied her hands. She saw me coming at her and tried to scream, but it was more like an Edvard Munch number. Maybe she thought I was going to slit her throat or rape her or something. I already knew a little Chinese, just from hanging with my homies, so I whispered to her, 'It's all right, Granny, we won't hurt you any more.' Then I begged her forgiveness, bowed, and ran out to the waiting car."

"Jesus."

"It was pure sick. And there was no excuse. I was sixteen and more than a little bit wild. But that day in Rowland Heights, my reptilian conscience finally kicked in. I realized I'd end up getting iced, and probably by my own homies, unless I pulled out."

"Is that how you know Michael Ho? Was he in the Black Hand too?"

"Golden Pacific Bank is a corporate sponsor of the Youth Center," Mark said stiffly. "They donated $250,000 last year."

"That's not how you know Michael Ho."

Mark groaned and kicked out his legs. "That's the only official way. Golden Pacific Bank brought him over from Hong Kong, he's the rising young star, plus he was marrying into the Lu family. But unofficially, I hear things. Successful businessman by day, shadow overlord by night, where he's known as Jimmy Lai. It's not uncommon . . . And when Michael's organization began recruiting Tony, I told them to back off or I'd bring some heat down."

"Jimmy Lai is Michael Ho? Now I'm beginning to get it. What did he want from you in return?"

"Oh, I keep my ear to the ground for him. Don't look at me like that, the cops do it with informants all the time."

I dug my heels into the carpeted floor and pushed my chair to the wall of my cubicle.

"So which are you, cop or informant?" I asked the calendar on the wall. "What kind of things do you tell them? And taking money from Golden Pacific Bank at the same time. What kind of shitty ethics is that? You're using the money that Golden Pacific Bank gives you to ransom the kids back from the gang that Golden Pacific Bank's new hotshot lures them into in the first place."

"I don't tell them anything important." He grabbed my chair and whirled me around. "L.A. County is broke, they keep slashing our grants each year. Or haven't you been reading your own newspaper? Golden Pacific Bank is huge in the Overseas Chinese community. They cohost the Chinese New Year's Parade. They donate money to the mayor's race. If they offer us a cool quarter mil, the Rainbow Coalition Center's not going to turn its nose up at it."

I was suddenly bone tired. "I've always admired your devotion," I said wearily. "But you're so blinded you don't realize you've crossed the line."

"I've never asked them for anything before. Just for Tony. I'm not going to see him wind up dead." He paused, as if he had just thought of something. "Spend the night with me," he said. "I'll tuck you in and won't lay a hand on you. I promise. But we'll both feel much safer, especially after all that has happened."

I didn't want to spend time with him out of fear. I wanted to spend the night with him because I couldn't stay away. But all I felt right now was exhaustion.

He grabbed my arm. I turned away.

"Goddamn it, Eve, I wouldn't be standing here with my hat in my hand if I didn't love you. I wouldn't be pounding down your door at midnight and calling you five times a day if I didn't care more about you than I've ever cared about anyone in my whole life."

His words caught me like a left hook and left me gasping for air.

"Come home with me now. I know these guys. You're not safe."

I gave in. I was so tired I couldn't see straight. "Give me five minutes so I can gather some sensitive files. I don't want to leave them here tonight."

Mark went out to his car to make room for my stuff. I walked over to get some water but stopped in my tracks. On the desk where he had been sitting were four tiny but perfect works of origami, as if a magician had been sitting there, transforming a reporter's dross into art. An angular cat. A bird. A frog. And a dagger. Put them together and you had some twisted nursery rhyme. How could Mark have had the presence of mind to create such intricate creatures as he told that story? Was he able to compartmentalize so well? I was disturbed by his confession, but worried for him too, which made me realize with a rush of relief that we were still on the same team. Mark was a lot more complex and flawed than I had ever imagined, and that made me feel better. None of us were completely whole; we all carried our little private hell inside of us and wrestled with it each day. Those who denied it were lying.

Gently, I swept the origami creatures into the palm of my hand and placed them on the top shelf of my desk, next to my red enamel Chinese dragon lady who bestowed good luck, the green plastic cactus from Mexico, and the bottle of Sriracha hot sauce from Vietnam which I doused over everything and sometimes even licked off my fingers.

It took me a moment to register the noise coming from the corner office where Matt Miller usually sat.

"Oh, God," I said. Someone had overheard our entire conversation. As I opened my mouth to scream for Mark, Trevor's long nose peeked around the corner.

"*Fuck*-ing *scan*-dal," he croaked, waddling out. "Couldn't help but overhear," he apologized. "*Big* fucking scandal."

My blood boiled. "Trevor Fingerhaven, what were you doing in there?"

"Ah, just talking to my folks. After hours and all. They're in Rome, seeing the sights. Wanted the privacy of the boss's office. You know."

"I do not," I retorted. "And if you ever breathe a word about this to anyone, I will immediately report your unauthorized, long-distance personal calls to the suburban editor and he will fire your sorry ass. And on the off chance that he doesn't, I will make life in this bureau a holy living hell for you. Every day will become utterly miserable in a hundred large and small ways. Is that clear?"

Trevor squealed in dismay. "But I'm on your side. I think you have a lot of guts. And I can help you in your investigation. I know a lot about Chinese gangs, and in fact, several of my sources have already told me in confidence that . . ."

He stopped when he saw the murderous look in my eye. "OK. Not a word. There there." He reached out a hand in an awkward attempt to soothe me. I flung it off and stomped out to meet Mark.

CHAPTER 34

I startled awake, straining to remember where I was. The mattress was firmer than mine and lacked the contours sculpted by nights of restless sleep. Outside, an autumn breeze swept the leaves and whipped through a nearby wind chime, which tinkled like a melancholy bird. The digital clock said 7:02 in big red numbers. I saw the arched window framing a banana palm. The indigo cloth. The weights in the corner. On the bed's far edge, Mark slumbered in a black T-shirt and boxers.

I barely recalled him driving me here last night. With little preamble, I had stepped out of my skirt, crawled into bed, and passed out. When I looked in the mirror now, my cheek was creased, like I had slept hard on it. A few more years of this living and the lines would be permanent. The creases made me think of Mark folding and refolding those notebook pages into origami as he told me the secrets of his youth. I threw on his robe, knotted it around my waist, and walked into the kitchen, where the cat jumped down from the chair with a mew of welcome and wound himself between my ankles. We have to stop meeting like this, I told him, pouring more food. I brought him fresh water and got the coffeemaker going. As it dripped, I made toast and spread it with some crystallized raspberry jam from the fridge. I gulped down two cups of coffee, poured a third, and took it in to Mark.

"I hate to wake you, but you'll be late for work."

Mark groaned, rolled over, and reached out, grasping blindly for my hand, then shaking it back and forth. "It's Saturday."

Damn if he wasn't right. A day of rest. Other people my age were heading for the beach. The Farmer's Market. The German Expressionist show at the County Museum. Once, I too had spent my weekends like that. Now, I felt like a separate species from those lotus-eating leisure seekers.

"I made coffee." I extended the steaming peace offering. "Couldn't find any milk or sugar, though."

"S'fine." His eyes were still closed.

I gave him three sips before I started talking. With two cups of coffee inside me, I can be ruthless.

"I have an idea how to get May-li out of that horrid brothel."

Like a human mood ring, Mark's face went from sleepy to alarmed as I piled on the details, describing Marina's diary entries, the late-night stakeouts. Finally I laid out the plan I had been hatching. And for that, I needed a man. An Asian man.

"You want me to what?"

"They won't suspect. I went through the court records the other day. All the johns heard about the brothel during Asian Night at local clubs. A man with bad skin walked up and gave them a business card that said 'Dan's Towing, 24 hours a day' in English. And in Chinese, the characters read 'Here for your pleasure, day or night.' Then he wrote a number on the back and said: 'This place has beautiful girls.' "

"So you want me to walk up and tell them I heard about it at a nightclub?"

"They're not even going to ask. When you get inside, ask to see the girls. Tell them you want to pick. Isn't that what the guys do? Or do they just go into any old bedroom?"

"I'm sure I don't know," Mark said. "But what if she's not there?"

I glanced sideways at him. "Then you'll have to fake it with another girl. Pretend you have a foot fetish or something. I can give you a stiletto heel."

He laughed despite himself. "You're a sick puppy."

"I'll be even sicker if we don't find her."

"If she's there," Mark said, "we go into a bedroom and I tell her we're calling the police to shut the place down. If she's not, I'll tell the Mama-san I like her girls so much I want to visit another house. I'll run through every Chinese brothel in the Valley until I find her."

The phone rang. I sighed in irritation. The shrill electronic beast had a way of shanghaiing any important discussion I ever had. I fully expected that if a man ever got around to proposing, we would be immediately interrupted by the telephone. Mark wavered, looked at the digital clock, then reached over me for the receiver.

"Yeah. No. Oh, great," I heard him say. "Jesus. That's all I need." Mark stared out the window. "That was Tony's guardian. The kid's gone AWOL. Hsieh got him out of Eastlake but he didn't come home last night."

I tried to swallow but only seared my throat. First May-li. Now Tony. Disappeared in plain sight. I flashed to my brother, floating in the pool, floating for eternity. My brother with Tony's face. With difficulty, I pushed the image back. "Where could he have gone?"

"I bet he's holed up in a Black Hand safe house somewhere in the San Gabriel Valley right now."

"Somebody called me a bunch of times yesterday at work," I told Mark. "Wouldn't leave a name or number and never did get me live. I assumed it was you."

Mark looked thoughtful. "I had a few of those myself yesterday. But in my line, that's not unusual."

"That poor kid was trying to make contact."

"He'll call back. And when he does, don't let him off the phone until he agrees to meet with us. He's got to turn himself in."

Either way, I thought, another life had hit the skids. I wondered about my obsession with Tony, Marina, and May-li. Three troubled kids. See how they run. More than ever, I was convinced they were all linked like a daisy chain. But each time I almost broke through, the chain closed in on itself, leaving me standing forlornly on the outside.

"You should check out the brothel while we wait for Tony. Today. And go early, because this place keeps office hours."

Mark yawned and surveyed his closet. "How does one dress for a brothel?"

"Like you're a businessman going home to your wife and kids who just dropped by for a quickie," I replied, thinking of the johns I had seen.

"I must have a suit in here somewhere."

Late that afternoon, with my directions in hand, he left.

CHAPTER 35

I switched on the TV, but punched it off after five minutes, annoyed by the inane hum. I tried to read a book but couldn't concentrate. Mostly I played with the cat and sat in Mark's backyard, watching the night fall and listening to neighborhood children play, then wail as parents began whisking them inside for evening baths.

I went inside too and prowled through Mark's house. At an old newspaper stack, I stopped and fished out a *New York Times*. Scanning the headlines, I saw that a cheating ring had been busted at Harvard. That was where Marina's friend Alison was headed. I wondered if Alison's older sister was involved. The pressure to succeed at those places started before you even got in. Look how hard Alison was driving herself. She would not allow anything to derail her plans, not even her friend's death. But would she go as far as to cheat, to lie? I thought for a moment. Then I put down the paper, ran to my car, and flipped through the notebooks until I found what I wanted. She answered on the second ring.

"This is Eve Diamond. You didn't tell me the whole story the other day, Alison." My voice was quiet and steady.

"What are you taaaalking about?" Her voice radiated disbelief tinged with boredom.

"You are a lying little sack of teenage shit. So we're going to sit down over pie again and you can tell me what really happened to Marina before she died."

"Look, Eve. I'm really busy."

"The choice is yours. Either tell me the truth or tell it to the cops. Then you can kiss your Harvard career good-bye. There's a name for what you've done, *chica*, and that's obstruction of justice."

"Don't do this to me."

"Ten A.M. tomorrow at House of Pies. Bring your appetite." I knew she'd be there. I had her by the jugular. How could I have been taken in by her? She was a manipulative little liar trying to save her ass, and it had taken a newspaper story to bring it home. Of course Marina had told Alison what happened at the brothel. Alison had been lying because she didn't want to get involved. Well, she was involved. Up to her slender, swanlike neck.

I had just settled back onto the couch with the paper to see what other revelations might befall me when I heard a key in the door.

Mark walked in and locked the door behind him. "She's there," he said hoarsely.

He moved slowly around the living room, touching the books, straightening a frame that already seemed perfectly hung. It wasn't until I saw him go to the sideboard and pour himself a scotch that I saw his hands tremble so hard that the bottle clinked against the glass. He took a slug.

"I went up and knocked and they let me in, simple as that."

"Were you scared?"

"Yeah, I was scared. They led me to the living room. I lit up a cigarette. There were other men sitting. We watched TV. It was like waiting at the dentist's office. The girls come downstairs once they're free."

"Are they like, dressed?"

"In negligees. They look about fifteen."

"Just like that bust I went on."

"I didn't see her at first. Two other girls walked down to pick up customers, and luckily, there were other men ahead of me. But I was getting nervous. Then May-li came down. 'I'll take her,' I told the houseboy."

"Did she recognize you?" Somewhere in the pit of my stomach, a rat was gnawing a hole.

"Yeah. I followed her upstairs and she shut the door."

"Jesus! What did you say?"

"I grabbed her hands and told her there is no way in hell I could apologize enough for what had happened. I said we were going to get her out of there."

I clenched my fists. "Good."

"She cried. She didn't want to believe me. It had cost her too much the first time. They threatened to slit her throat and kill her parents in China if she tried it again. She showed me her back—it was like raw hamburger. They left her face alone but beat her where the customers wouldn't care. She told me to go away and forget about her. I told her that wasn't possible. I told her the police would come tomorrow. Then I pulled my shirt out of my trousers, walked downstairs, paid the houseboy a hundred bucks, and left."

"So who should we call?"

"I'll call a cop friend of mine and get some advice. We have to make sure they don't treat us like crackpots."

But Mark's friend was on vacation. He left a message on the cop's answering machine, then slammed down the receiver. I tried several cops I knew too. It was Saturday night and no one was around.

"What shitty timing," I said. "But we've waited this long, one more day won't matter. Your friend can get us to the right people and make them move quickly. If we don't hear back from someone tomorrow, then we can call the sheriff. They have an organized crime unit."

We sat in silence, sipping our drinks, until I remembered about Alison. "Hey, I made some progress tonight too. Without ever leaving the house," I added, seeing his worried look. "How would you like me to buy you breakfast tomorrow at the House of Pies?"

CHAPTER 36

It was 10:20 in the morning and I was beginning to think Alison wasn't going to show. While Mark read the Sunday *New York Times*, I fidgeted with the lace paper doily under my coffee cup and watched the pies spin around in their glass carousel. I wanted the purple berry one with the oozing fruit. But I ordered bacon and eggs, protein to make my synapses fire. Each time the door opened, I craned my head in vain.

"Check out this story about illegal Chinese immigrants," Mark said, sliding Part 1 of the *New York Times* across the table. "This one guy works eighteen hours a day at a restaurant and sleeps in the kitchen at night. He only spends ten dollars per month for stuff like postage stamps and toothpaste. So far he's saved eight thousand to bring his wife and kids out. Figures the whole family will take fifteen years if each smuggling trip costs thirty thousand."

I read. The next thing I knew, Alison stood before me, alarm metastasizing across her face as she saw Mark.

"Who's this dude?"

"My, um, partner. He's cool. Sit down."

"He wasn't part of the deal." She crossed her arms and sulked at the floor.

"Relax, he's not a cop. He's an adolescent psychologist. He did grief counseling at your school when Marina was killed so he knows all about it. I'd tell him anyway so he might as well hear it without operator assistance."

She gave Mark a searching look. "Yeah, maybe I saw you on campus."

Used to dealing with kids who wore their fear like a shield, Mark cleared away the newspaper, scooted over in the booth, and patted the vinyl seat beside him.

"Are you going to sit down so we can have a nice, civilized chat or are you going to stand there and block my view of the pies?"

Something in her face collapsed. I'd like to think she was forcing back a smile. Then, for someone who didn't weigh more than 105 pounds, she sat down with a loud thlump. Maybe it was all those heavy secrets she'd been keeping.

"I'm hungry," she said.

"Good." Mark pushed over a menu and gave her a lopsided grin, bringing on a pang of jealousy that surprised me. I had thought he reserved that smile for me.

We did the yak-yak until she ordered and the waitress ambled off to another table.

"Now tell us what happened the night Marina went into the mysterious boyfriend house," I began. "And don't give me any shit about how you left for Hong Kong without talking to her. It doesn't fly."

She reddened but didn't disagree. "How do you know I saw her?"

So they had seen each other, not just talked. "C'mon, girlfriend, you're smarter than that," I said. "You two were best buds."

Alison looked at me, then Mark. He studied his plate like he was unlocking the DNA sequence of his bacon.

"It was early morning," she began nervously. "I got sick of waiting up after I finished studying for my test and went upstairs to sleep. She knows where we keep the spare key to the service porch. Next thing I know, she's standing next to my bed, big tears running down her face. I thought I was having a bad dream. Someone had beaten her up bad.

She was crying and holding her hand to her mouth. When she took it away, her lip was purple and split. It was still dark so I went to turn on my bedside light, but she was all like 'Don't.' "

I had slid my notepad out and was taking discreet notes. Alison didn't even notice. The House of Pies had receded. She was back in her own bed staring at the wraithlike apparition of her friend.

CHAPTER 37

I asked if Michael had done this to her, and she just turned away," Alison told us. "So I cleaned up her face and put a nightgown on her and stuck her under the covers. Then I told her we should call the police.

"She just shook her head and hugged her elbows. She was shivering so much her teeth chattered.

"She said it wasn't that simple. She said there was evil in the world that I couldn't imagine and that she had come face-to-face with it that night."

Alison started shivering quite a bit herself. She took a paper napkin, folded it in four, and dabbed the corners of her eyes, which had suddenly gotten shiny.

"Michael was at that house all right. After I dropped her off, she snaked over to a side window and saw him watching TV with some guys on a couch. Marina said it looked like someone had just moved in and forgotten to unpack the furniture. A guy was leading a girl up the stairs, and she was crying."

Under the table, I nudged Mark with my knee and felt him return the pressure. It sounded exactly like his experience at the brothel and I knew we were finally getting close to the truth.

"Did Michael see her?" Mark asked.

"Nobody saw her until she got upstairs. Then she met a girl. Not the crying one. This one was singing."

"Slow down," I said. "How did she get past Michael and the guys in the living room?"

"She snuck in through the back door when someone was taking out the trash," Alison told us. "Marina scored 1560 on her SATs, but sometimes she doesn't act that smart. Or else she would never have run up the stairs. But she did. All the doors were shut, except for one bedroom where a girl was brushing her hair and singing a song in Fukienese. Fujian, that's on the Mainland, where both our families are originally from too. So Marina the spy decided to introduce herself and try to get the 411 on her fiancé. The girl told her she was in a brothel. All the girls were smuggled in from Asia and guarded so they couldn't escape. Michael was hanging out each night in some jail-like whorehouse."

Alison's voice quavered. She frowned and pressed her water glass methodically against the *New York Times*, leaving damp rings on the newsprint. When she spoke again, the quaver was gone.

"At first, Marina didn't believe her. She explained that Michael Ho came from one of the best families in Hong Kong. She still wanted to defend that asshole.

"When the girl heard his name, she told Marina that Michael wasn't a customer, he was the *boss*.

"Then Marina finally gets it—all those late nights, the boxes of condoms in his car, what she had seen downstairs. Like I told you, Marina was kind of naive.

"Just then they heard someone walking down the hall and the Mainland girl said it was a customer and shoved Marina into a closet.

"Marina opened it a crack and watched a white guy with a cowboy hat get undressed. He made the girl kneel in front of him."

In the next booth, a baby was crying, the snuffling whine of a hungry infant. Alison lowered her voice, then went on.

"Marina came out and yelled at him to stop. This pissed the guy off and he grabbed her arm and twisted it. Then he threw her on the bed and raped her. He raped Marina."

Alison's voice started shaking. "If I had been with her that night, none of this would have happened. I'm the one who got her all excited about spying on Michael. We were bored and it seemed like fun. But when stuff came down, I wasn't around, and she got raped. Now she's dead. And it's my fault. It's all my fault."

Alison sobbed quietly now. I put my arm around her, but she stayed hunched over, quaking. I had never seen her lose control like this before. It made me like her more.

"Marina tried to fight him," Alison said. "She scratched and bit. But he slugged her and she blacked out. When she came to, he was gone.

"The girl told her he freaked out when he saw her tattoo."

Alison looked up at us, cheeks red and glistening. "Michael talked her into that. Black hand with a red heart. He said it symbolized their love. Some love."

"After the place closed down for the night, the girl showed her how to get away by climbing down a tree outside the window. Marina tried to get the girl to go with her, but she was too scared."

"Of what?"

Alison shook her head. "It's all blurry. I blocked it out for so long that now I don't remember." She rubbed her eyes with her fists, forgetting the napkin. "I think she was afraid the police would find her and bring her back. They came there to have sex with the girls too, that's what the guards told her. And there was something about her ancestors."

"She had to pay back her smuggling debt to avoid dishonoring her ancestors?" Mark asked.

"That was it, how did you know?" Alison scrunched up her eyes. "OK, it's coming back. The girl gave Marina some poetic line about being born into your fate, how she and Marina were sisters separated by a sea who have grown apart. The girl told Marina she wasn't Chinese anymore, but American. Marina was really upset by that because she knows that to the Americans, we'll always be Chinese."

Alison sighed. "So finally it gets quiet and Marina escaped like the girl showed her and drove straight to my house. And I'm getting really scared for both of us, so I run around the house making sure all the windows and doors are locked."

"Let's see if I have this straight," I said. "Your fiancé is in a murderous gang called the Black Hand and he runs a sex slavery brothel. You were raped by one of the johns, a white guy who saw your tattoo and got scared and ran off after knocking you unconscious. You can't tell your fiancé because he might kill you to shut you up. You can't call the police because they're in on it too. Where does that leave us?"

"But Marina just started crying and wanted a hot bath. I told her she'd destroy the evidence—we learned that in health class. You have to get tested to prove it's rape.

"But she insisted, so whatever, she takes her bath and then we lie on the bed for a long time without saying anything. Finally it got light. I told her I wanted to help but I had to go take my AP test and then leave for Hong Kong in a few hours, my aunt was dying. And Marina sighed and said she guessed that meant she was on her own."

CHAPTER 38

The lunch crowd had come and gone at House of Pies as Alison spun her tale. My shoulders were now hunched somewhere near my ears, radiating pain down my back. The stakes had gotten really, really high.

"So then what happened?" I asked.

"We slept for a few hours, then I got up and packed. My mom drove me to take my test before I went to LAX and Marina went home. By the time I got to my auntie's in Hong Kong, Marina was dead."

Her face sagged with exhaustion. "May I please get another diet Coke?"

"You want a burger too?" I felt bad for her. But not so much that I forgot who I was or why I was there. "So what day did you get to Hong Kong?"

"September fourteenth," she said.

"Marina wasn't killed until the sixteenth, Alison. Is there anything else you want to tell us?"

I saw the hesitation in her eyes.

"C'mon, take us to the bitter end."

Alison gave me a beseeching look. "She called five times before I got to my auntie's."

"And? What was up? What did she do after she left your house?"

"She went home that morning and called her dad, but he was traveling in Malaysia and wasn't at the hotel. She left an urgent message for him. Then she called me.

"She had decided that no matter what her dad said, no matter what it meant for Michael, she was going to the cops. She knew Monterey Park had an Asian gang task force—it was in all the Chinese papers—and she thought that would be the right place to go.

"I told her to be careful and write down what had happened in her diary. So there would be, like, a record. And to tell someone else too, just in case. Like Nick Madigan. He's our history teacher but he's really cool. He cares about us as people."

"And did she?"

"I don't think so. She sat at home waiting for a callback from her dad that never came. Meanwhile, Michael's calling her, all lovey-dovey, wanting to come over, and she has to pretend she's too busy running errands to plan the wedding. He still thinks they're getting hitched. As if!! The next day, she calls me again totally hysterical . . ."

Alison broke off. Her hand shook as she lifted the glass to her mouth, and water sloshed onto the table.

"If I tell you this part, you have to promise . . . ," she began. Her eyes begged us. "You have to promise you'll protect me."

Mark grabbed her hand. "You got it. Just tell it to us straight."

I could see her struggling.

"It was Monday, and Marina wasn't feeling well so she skipped school. Maybe she was embarrassed about her face. Instead, she drove Colin to his Chinese school. It's in Montebello and he usually takes the bus. After she gets home, Colin calls to say he's forgotten his lunch, and it would be no big deal but he has an ear infection and has to take this antibiotic four times a day and it's sitting in his lunch bag on the kitchen counter. So Marina says she'll run it down to him . . ."

"Alison, will you please cut to the chase," I said with exasperation.

"This is the chase. You'll see in a minute."

"So she's speeding a little because she's afraid she'll miss Colin's lunch period, and then of all the crappy luck, she gets pulled over by the cops.

"There are two of them, one Asian, one white, and the white guy walks over and she notices something familiar about him as he gets closer. He's ditched the cowboy hat and is wearing a uniform now, but it's the same guy who raped her two days ago, and her heart starts pounding because she realizes the Mainland girl was right, he is a cop, and what if he recognizes her?

"So she pulls her hair over her face. The white cop leans in the window and makes some joke about being surprised to see a 'nice little Asian girl' breaking the law in such a badass car he could never afford on his salary.

"Then he asks for her driver's license, and she's afraid he'll recognize her photo and learn where she lives. Then he'll come looking for her. But what can she do, she hands it over. When he gives it back with the ticket, she doesn't think he's caught on, but she's not sure. The cop tells her she can go, so she takes off, totally shaking now, totally spacing on Colin's lunch and his medicine. For hours, she drives around, afraid to go home.

"So," continues Alison, "she's majorly wigging, and finally she stops at a pay phone and calls me in Hong Kong. It's the middle of the night, but I have my own phone so it's OK. Marina's losing it. I can barely hear her with the traffic whizzing by. Now for sure she can't go to the cops. Her dad's in fucking Malaysia, unreachable, and she's dodging Michael. And I'm on the other side of the globe and won't be back for a week. I don't have any bright ideas, anyway. Finally, I tell her again to go find Mr. Madigan at school. He's an adult. He will know what to do. I tell her that maybe she'll have to enter some kind of protection program and get plastic surgery and a new name and testify for the feds from behind a screen and I'll never see her again. She doesn't think that's too funny. She's not completely sold on Madigan but I make her promise she'll call him. Finally, we hang up. And I never hear from her again. I swear to God. She was killed the next day. And I don't know who did it. I swear I don't."

"I believe you. Now tell me, what city was she in when she got pulled over?"

Alison looked blank. "She never said. Why?"

"There's about thirty of them in the San Gabriel Valley, each with its own police force. When you got back to the States, did Michael Ho try to get in touch with you?"

At this, Mark leaned forward.

"Yeah. He had sensed something was up when Marina wouldn't see him. First he tried to sweet-talk me. Then he threatened me. He knows we were best friends. But I couldn't tell him the truth, could I? Because if he killed Marina, then he'd kill me too. And if he learned what I knew, then I'd be dead meat anyway."

"He didn't need you to tell him. I think he knows, because Marina took your advice and wrote it all down in her diary. I'm almost sure of that. Right after she died, her brother gave the diary to his friend Lily Hsu. He didn't want his parents to find it and read all about their lonely lives in the U.S.A. Lily stuck it on her shelf and forgot about it. I ran across it when I interviewed her and Tony for a story about parachute kids. I had covered Marina's murder, so I was curious to read it. But before I could do more than skim a few pages, it was stolen out of my car. I think Michael sent his thugs for it, though I'm not sure how he traced it to me."

"How did he know Marina even kept a diary?" Alison asked.

"He probably saw her scribbling."

Alison went pale suddenly and gripped the table. "Then he knows how Marina came to my house after the rape and told me everything."

"I don't think so, Alison." This time it was Mark who answered. "He read the diary weeks ago. If Marina had mentioned you, we'd be laying flowers on your grave by now."

CHAPTER 39

Mark and I didn't talk much on the way back to his house. My mind crawled with images: May-li brushing her hair, Marina bursting out of the closet, the cop in his mirrored shades approaching the girl who crouched, trembling, in her Lexus.

When we got home, Mark lowered the blinds and locked all the doors. We looked, but there were no messages on his machine. I took a tumbler and poured three fingers worth of Tres Hermanos, a tequila I drank like a Southern sipping whiskey.

"No wonder Alison was scared shitless to tell us."

"You think the cop killed Marina?" Mark had his own tumbler now.

"Either he or Michael. Did you call your cop friend?"

Mark grimaced. "Yeah. He's on vacation until next week."

"Great. Well, I'm out of ideas right now. Although I know there's something real basic here that we're missing."

"I get that feeling too," Mark said. We sipped and went around and around what we knew. But in the end, we agreed to revisit it in the morning when we were fresh.

All too soon it was Monday morning and we had both overslept. At the office, I brought a steaming cup to my desk and placed it precariously atop a stack of reporter notebooks, the only free space I could find.

247

Once, I had been the most organized of journalists, filing away all notes and scraps of paper like a diligent pack rat. Now, the mess on my desk echoed the clutter in my brain. In disgust, I swept away the files, city council agendas, and press releases. I needed room to think.

But what popped into my head was Tony. He was still alive and needed my help. I called his guardian but Tony had not shown up. I called San Marino High and spoke to Nick Madigan, but Tony had been absent for a week. No surprise there. I told him Tony had disappeared. Nick was a nice guy but I didn't know whom to trust anymore. And I noted with cold detachment how easily the lie tripped off my tongue.

"N-Nick," I said. "Did you have a senior named Marina Lu in your class?"

"You mean the girl killed in that carjacking? Yeah, she was mine. Real studious and quiet. Why?"

"Did she ever talk to you about any personal problems?"

"Can I ask what this is about?"

"I'm working on a backgrounder and looking for anyone who might have known her. I thought she might have opened up and told you stuff."

"This is off the record, but I think she was a parachute kid like Tony."

"That I know. Anything else? Did she ever ask for advice or seem like she was in trouble?"

"Not that one. She was reserved. Seemed almost sad. She was an A-student, by the way. Scored 800 on her English SAT, there's something for you. Oh, and I heard she was engaged."

"Tell me about the fiancé."

"Another immigrant Chinese from Hong Kong. He was older than her. That's all I know."

So she hadn't told him about Michael and the brothels. How, then, had she spent her last hours? I couldn't dwell on it, however, because important news was breaking. A samurai bunny had attacked a kid in La Verne and stolen his Halloween candy, and Metro wanted a story. I did a double take when I heard that one, not because of the samurai bunny—we journalists are used to surreal tales trickling out of the suburbs—but because for a minute there, I thought that things had been so crazy I had missed one of my favorite holidays.

"No," said the bored cop on the other end of the phone, audibly picking his teeth. "The school threw the kids an early party, since Halloween falls on Saturday this year. The perp snatched the candy as the kid was walking home. Got himself part of an ear, too."

"Oh yeah?" It was best not to show too much enthusiasm with cops. Made them clam up.

"Let me get the report." He shuffled some papers. "Here it is."

"Three P.M. Kids are pouring out of Harcastle Elementary, dressed as ghouls and witches. A tall skinny guy, about nineteen, with scraggly facial hair, according to eyewitnesses, walks northbound down the street. He's wearing an Iron Maiden T-shirt and carrying a huge samurai sword like you'd see in a museum. On top of his head is a stuffed animal, a rabbit, that he's sliced open and is wearing like a Davy Crockett hat. He's clutching a trick-or-treat bag, trying to blend in with the kiddies. Trouble starts when a neighbor sees the freak and yells out, 'Hey, aren't you a little old to be trick-or-treating?' "

"Makes sense to me." I gulped a mouthful of coffee.

"Well, that pisses off our samurai bunny." The cop was warming up to his tale. "So he brandishes his sword, gives a war cry, and charges the man, whacking him across the ear. Lopped off the lobe, had to be surgically reattached. Then he plunges into a group of kids, snatches a bag of candy, and runs off down the street. We caught him, though," the policeman concludes smugly. "A samurai bunny is pretty hard to miss."

"Did the kid get his candy back?"

"We confiscated it for evidence."

"Beware of cavities," I said.

I spent hours crafting my samurai bunny story, knowing that a deadpan delivery would best preserve its bizarre humor. I had almost forgotten about Tony when the phone rang.

"Eve?"

My heart jumped.

"Tony, where are you? Mark and I have been trying to reach you."

His voice sounded far away. "I've been staying with friends." He sniffed, like he had a cold.

"What do you mean with friends? You're under court order to stay with your guardian and you're blowing it big-time." I stopped and caught myself. "Are you OK?"

"I need to talk to you. You're never home. And when I call you at the office, someone else picks up. I'll call you back at five. I can't talk from here."

"Tony, wait. What do you mean, you . . . ?"

But he was gone. I looked at my watch. 4:40 P.M. Mark was in counseling. I left an urgent message, then looked around and saw Trevor fussing with some papers, his body angled like a question mark. Creature of the media that he was, Trevor had a sixth sense when something was up, and right now, his antennae were quivering.

Miller buzzed me. Other than the samurai bunny, it was a slow news day and he wanted to discuss story ideas. We batted around a few and I told him I was waiting for a phone call, but five o'clock came and went without a ring. Bastard, I thought. He's playing games again. At 6:30, Miller left for his son's T-ball game. The phone rang.

"It's Tony."

"Talk to me."

"Someone was following me, but I lost them. I'm at a pay phone."

"Who was following you?"

"I'll tell you everything. Can we meet at 8 P.M. at the Rowland Glen Estates? You know, up the ridge from the big Buddhist temple? Go to 18484 Pepper Tree Lane. My parents were going to buy that house but changed their minds. It's still empty. I'll be behind the garage."

"Wait." I grabbed for the spiral phone pad at the receptionist's desk. "Give me that address again. It sounds creepy, Tony. Why not at a McDonald's or something?"

"Too public. The whole San Gabriel Valley is too public."

"Then let's meet somewhere in Hollywood."

"I'd get lost. This is safer."

It was the same with all these immigrant kids. Anything outside the Valley was *terra incognita*. It might as well have been another country.

I tore off the address I had jotted down and ran out the door with just enough time to make it. Inching my way up the freeway on-ramp, I merged anonymously with the commuting hordes making their weary way east to the far suburbs. If I had to live that way, I'd die, I thought, vaguely aware that I could die anyway and for reasons more traumatic than commuter stress. Daylight savings time had ended and the shadows were lengthening. I felt I was driving into some gloomy black pit. Was Tony setting me up? I couldn't let myself believe that.

By sheer coincidence, I knew exactly which housing development Tony was talking about because I had written about it. Built strictly for Pacific Rim buyers who paid in cash. There was nothing under $450,000 and it went up from there. The average gringo wouldn't have noticed anything unusual about these digs, but the sales agent, a thin, elegant Chinese woman from the Philippines who spoke eight languages flawlessly, including English, initiated me into its secrets. They had good *feng shui*, the ancient Chinese metaphysical art in which direction, space, and flow are combined for good luck. The *chi*, or life force, had to flow freely through a house. Bedrooms should face east. Make sure the street addresses and telephone numbers have lots of numeral eights, which signified growth and expansion, and avoid fours, which symbolized death.

Yes, I had been here before, I thought, crawling along with my fellow man on Interstate 10 until finally I turned right and headed for the mountains as Rowland Glen caught the last rays of sunlight and shimmered like a golden Oz. Up above the suburban congestion I climbed, into the serene privacy that affluence brings. The city had even put a new elementary school and community center into this eagle's aerie. I saw a hawk hunting overhead, its red tail spread out, and the fallacy of my analogy hit me. There were no more eagles here, hadn't been in a long time. I wondered where the hawks would go when the field mice gave way to lawn statues and automatic sprinklers. Could they beat a retreat further into the wilds on their big wings? Or would they expire here, their eggs cracked by pesticide residues, their young deformed from chlorinated pool water?

The road smelled of freshly paved asphalt and the street lamps stood sentinel, lighting up only a half-built guard station. The bile green Porta Potties installed at regular intervals along the ridge for the convenience of the construction crews were so new they hadn't even begun to smell yet.

It was dark when I pulled up in front of 18484 Pepper Tree Lane and killed the engine. I studied the spray-painted numbers on the curb.

Someone had goofed with that address all right, putting all those 8s and 4s together. Growth and death entwined, twice. No wonder Tony's parents hadn't bought this house. I shivered. For a city girl like me, darkness and silence were not friends. I liked crowds, not the eerie feel of a place emptied of people, as though an invisible bomb had gone off. There were no other cars. Tony would have stashed his and cut through the half-landscaped yards. If anyone else came up here, I'd see them arrive.

I got out, holding my keys between my fingers, points extended, like I'd learned in self-defense, but my shoes gave me away, scrunching loudly on the gravel driveway. I stood there, unwilling to disappear totally into the night.

"Tony?" I called.

A slim shape detached itself from the wall and moved toward me. I tensed, ready to jab my keys into the eyes of evildoers.

"Eve," he whispered. "You came."

He stood half in shadow, one side lit by the distant glow of a street-lamp. His face was thinner than I remembered, his shirt creased as though he had slept in it for days. At his temple was a nasty purple welt that was crusting over. I reached out a hand to touch it.

He shied away. "Do you have anything to eat?"

I rummaged through my bag and pulled out soup crackers and a bruised banana. He wolfed down the food, and I swallowed the saliva that came unbidden to my own mouth. Suddenly I wanted a bowl of comforting noodles in a tart meat broth spiked with star anise. The idea of sitting down with Tony in a well-lit noodle shop was a civilizing and soothing one. Unlike the arid dance now unfolding between us.

He looked up for more, but all I found was a crumpled pack of gum. "Look at the city," he said instead, pulling me over to the bluff. "That's the temple below, see all those big lights. There's Rowland Heights. And Hacienda Boulevard. The realtor said you could see the Pacific on a clear day. I bet they tell all the homesick immigrants that."

We gazed at the panorama below, the cars like brightly colored Chinese lanterns strung out along the major arteries. A light wind was blowing, flapping my skirt around my knees and making me realize it wasn't summer anymore.

"It's just as beautiful as I imagined it would be, when I was on the other side of the world," Tony said, then fell to his knees as a small sound escaped him. "But nothing has turned out right."

I stepped forward then and knelt in the soft black loam beside him, two penitents praying for forgiveness. I pulled him to me and stroked his head gently, smoothing back the hair, making sure to avoid the ugly gash on his temple. I could smell the banana on his breath.

"Where did you get that nasty wound?" My knees sank further into the dirt.

"I'm sorry, Eve. I screwed everything up."

"Don't be sorry. Talk to me. What's happened to you since you went AWOL?"

But he only sobbed louder. "I'm sorry, Eve. They made me do it."

"Do what?"

I was still staring down into the valley of jewels below when his words registered and a flicker of fear ran through me. And then, without taking my eyes off the view, without removing my hand from Tony's head, I knew where he had gotten that ugly gash and exactly what they had made him do. I stroked his hair sorrowfully now and let the silence envelop us, mourning for what could have been and now never would be. Out of the corner of my left eye, I saw something move and knew it wasn't a bush swaying in the wind. I had walked into a trap.

"Finally we meet, Ms. Diamond."

The voice had British colonial accents, clipped and proper. But the gloating was pure animal.

With slow, deliberate movements, I hoisted myself up, pulling Tony with me. I wasn't sure whether I intended to use him as a shield or vice versa. I felt a great emptiness inside, large and churning as the Pacific. I didn't blame Tony. He was nothing more than a trapped animal. Well, that made two of us. I dusted off my skirt and smoothed down the hem, cursing the fact that I hadn't told anyone where I was going, hadn't at least left Mark the address. Was it because I still didn't quite trust him? Because I wanted to rescue Tony all by myself? Maybe it was more simple; I had just rushed out the door in my usual scatterbrained hurry.

"I don't think I've had the pleasure."

"Michael Ho, at your service." He bowed deeply. It was an affront, but I took his cue and bantered in a way I did not feel.

"I've read so many nice things about you in Marina's diary."

He cocked his head, puzzled for a moment. I took in the suit and still-knotted silk tie. He had a strong chin, planed cheeks, and black eyes, gleaming and calculating as a panther's. It was the same face that had peered over me, then disintegrated into a thousand ripples at the Jade Dragon when I had been drugged. It was the same face that had given me the penetrating stare at Eastlake, sending chills up my spine, when Wong and I had gone to talk to Tony. Marina had been right. He was handsome. And deadly as belladonna.

"In that case, Tony, you've done even better than you know by bringing this little rabbit to me tonight."

As he spoke, he put his arm around me and my skin crawled. I didn't look at Tony. I knew he'd be hanging his head. All my thoughts and energies were now concentrated on Michael Ho. If I had to die, I meant to go to my grave knowing as much as I could about this whole dirty business. I guess I was still vain enough to wonder whether I had been on the right track.

"I know you killed Marina," I said evenly. "I've written a story all about it, with names and addresses. If something happens to me, my editors will give it to the police."

His lips made an *O* of mock horror. He shook his head.

"Now why would I kill my fiancée?"

"Because she knew about the brothels and was going to tell the police and her father."

He laughed. "Her father?"

"Yes, her father." I didn't get what was so funny.

"I have no secrets from Reginald Lu."

"He's a banker," I said.

"Yes. A respectable profession. You'll find no dirt under those fingernails."

"Are you telling me he had his own daughter killed?"

"We don't know who killed Marina," Ho answered. He was solemn now, pensive. "It may be as your newspaper reported—a 'senseless' murder—I believe that was the term—committed during a carjacking."

"Yeah, well, I bet it was some of your goons who jacked her car. Did you ever think of that? Which means that indirectly, her blood is still on your hands."

Michael's thin lips creased into a smile. "It was not one of ours. The appropriate inquiries have been made and there was a substantial incentive for those with information to come forward."

"Well, then, if you're so innocent, why did you lure me up here?"

"For the view." He laughed. "You won't find any better in the Valley. The privacy is an added bonus. It's so remote that no one comes up here unexpectedly. I've walked the grounds many a time myself, since Golden Pacific Bank loaned the money that built this subdivision. But back to you, Ms. Diamond. You're a meddler. You tried to change the rules. That is unacceptable."

"So you used Tony as bait to get me here? What made you so sure I'd come?"

"You've exhibited great weakness when it comes to our young friend here. But your foolish emotions have betrayed you. Stick to saving your own people, Ms. Diamond. You know nothing about us and our affairs. Tony is mine. Still, I'm sorry we didn't meet under other circumstances. I have found you rather . . . interesting."

Michael eyed me with clinical detachment. I was desperate to keep the conversation going. I knew what would happen when it ended.

"Tony reminds me of my little brother, who died. I wanted to be his friend, OK, and if that's what you call a 'weakness,' then I'm guilty. But if you find me so 'interesting,' " I said, "why did you try to have me killed? I'll bet you were real crushed when I got away from your hit men."

Michael's eyes flickered. "We'll talk about that some other time."

I sensed a weakness. I knew something he didn't, but what? I would keep the rapist cop card to myself for now. It was my only ace, and maybe a potential bargaining chip. I kept talking.

"That was pretty clever of you, getting my address from the INS lady and tricking up the brown truck like a UPS job. It would have looked like just another drive-by shooting. But how did you know I'd be jogging that evening in Silverlake?"

Now Michael's face was blank. "UPS? What are you talking about? I never ordered anything in Silverlake."

"Since you're dumb as a fox, Mr. Ho, I'll spell it out. Two young Asian men tried to kill me last week as I was jogging. Maybe that was their initiation into the Black Hand. I didn't stick around to find out and haven't been home since."

Now he dropped all pretense. "If you are lying, we'll find out. If what you say is true, then someone else wants you dead too, and that makes you even more valuable to us, little *gwai lo* reporter."

"Then you'd better not kill me until you find out."

Michael laughed again, and for the first time I noticed he held a gun almost concealed within his large palm. "Kill you? Ms. Diamond. Hardly. I'm going to escort you to the man who almost became my father-in-law. It is he you'll have to answer to."

So it all came back to Marina's father, the first stop in my investigation all those weeks ago. I had felt the silent undercurrent of power eddying around us but had foolishly taken it for the dark aura that surrounds many of the world's successful men.

"Then your usefulness to him will be over," I said. "He'll ship you back in pieces to Hong Kong on a slow-moving cargo ship as a sign to all those who would skim a little off the top and hope no one would notice."

The smirk left Michael's face. So my desperate guess had been right. A crook was a crook, no matter what language he spoke.

Suddenly, another voice broke the night stillness.

"Drop the gun, Michael."

A look of anger crossed Michael Ho's face. Maybe he didn't recognize the voice, but I did. It was Mark. I had no idea how he had arrived here, on this godforsaken mountain, but I didn't care. I felt overwhelming relief.

"I said drop or I shoot." Mark stepped out of the bushes twenty feet away, covering Michael Ho with his own gun. "Just enough to maim, not kill. So that you'll have to watch your back the rest of your days in prison after the cops bust the Black Hand and your pals figure you're the one who ratted them out."

Michael was no street tough. I saw him calculating the odds, considering his options, caught up with this new and unexpected threat while still trying to digest the one I had made.

"Don't shoot." Michael lowered his arm, then leaned forward to pitch the gun gently to the ground. But as he did so, his body followed his arm like a coiled spring and slammed straight into the gleaming new Porta Potti three feet away. With violent grunts of exertion,

Michael now toppled the Porta Potti and it fell forward, creating an instant bunker behind which to hide.

At the same time, I hit the ground so I heard but didn't see whose gun went off. I heard two shots, then moaning, and smelled the harsh cordite curling on the night breeze. Squinting in the dark, I saw a figure on the ground where Mark had been standing. Oh no, oh please, God, I prayed. Closer to me, I heard the moan again, and realized it came from Michael Ho, who was also down, clutching his leg and inching through the dirt toward something that gleamed dully just feet away. It was his gun. Next to it stood Tony, shaking and shell-shocked, like a zombie in a cheap B movie who feels dawn approach.

I opened my mouth to speak, but someone beat me to it.

"Tony, pick up the gun." It was Mark, and my heart gladdened, because it meant he was still alive and conscious, although his breath came in ragged spurts and I knew he too was hurt.

From the writhing pile on the ground near me, I heard a deep chuckle. "That's an excellent idea, Mark. Yes, little brother, fetch my gun."

Tony startled to life. He looked around at the voices as if to fix them in time and place, then reached in slow-mo for the gun. When his fingers finally closed around the weapon, he scooped it up with an ease that made me realize he knew exactly how to use it.

"Thank you, Tony," said Michael. "Now, I want you to go over to our friend there and kill him. I'd do it myself but I'm temporarily indisposed. He has played his part well, but as the game draws to a close, he proves himself a Judas. And death, Tony, is what awaits traitors."

Tony didn't answer. He stared at the weapon in his hand, as though committing it to memory. I thought he might be in shock.

"You're doing it for me, Tony, your *dai lo*. We back each other up, right, bro? I know I can count on you."

Tony looked at him.

"Tony," Mark panted. "I want you to put the gun down. Think of everything we've talked about in these past months. Look into your heart, Tony, and listen to what it tells you."

Tony shook his head. He stared at Michael, who looked up smugly, wounded but confident of the end game. He looked into the darkness

that concealed Mark. The events of the last six months had led inex-
orably to this moment when Tony would have to choose. He had
always been here, on this windswept ridge, with a gun in his hand.

I held my breath. But six tiny words kept hammering through my
brain. "He has played his part well." What part had Mark played? That
of my lover? That of a counselor? Of both? I feared I had been
betrayed twice this night. Who, in the end, was the Mark Furukawa I
knew except a construct of my desperate imagination? And for all my
spun-sugar dreams of saving Tony and turning him into my new little
brother, I knew I had no sway over him compared to the power exerted
by these two men. Saying the wrong thing now would tip the scales
that already teetered precariously in this war for his soul. What if I
urged him to listen to Mark, and my words only pushed him into
Michael's arms? When I looked up again, I saw there another battle
raging outside of me.

A tear crept down Tony's cheek. He aimed the gun and took a step in
Mark's direction. I opened my mouth to speak, but as my brain groped
for the right words, Tony pivoted, his gun arm still extended, and
trained the gun on Michael Ho.

And then I heard the wail of a police siren.

CHAPTER 40

Much later, I sat in a brightly lit room in the Rowland Heights Police Department and insisted that Officer Steven Zhang of the Monterey Park Police Department's Asian Organized Crime Unit be present before I told my story. The Rowland detectives harangued me, saying that the shooting had occurred on their turf and was outside of Zhang's jurisdiction, but I asked what made them think the triads stayed within their puny city limits. After what had happened that night, I wasn't afraid of the cops or anybody else.

I had been puzzling it out on the way to their headquarters, and felt pretty sure of my instincts. If I had to recount my Great Wall roller-coaster ride without sounding like one of those crackpots I myself shied away from as a reporter, I had to have someone there who knew the world I was sketching and might even corroborate crucial parts of the story. And despite whatever bad blood might have existed between them, Vittorio Carabini had trained Zhang well. Plus he was George Ling's friend, and that counted for something.

Somewhere around 2 A.M., Zhang showed up, sleepy and rubbing his neck. He didn't give me more than a perfunctory look, but it didn't matter. I eased up on my cuticles and asked for a cup of hot coffee. Once we were all sitting down like proper gentlemen across the table and the tape recorder was running, I began to speak.

I started at the beginning but didn't bury the lead either, making sure that I highlighted my suspicions of Michael Ho from the start. After covering Marina's murder, I told them, I probably would have written up the story, filed it away under *T* for tragic, and forgotten about it if I hadn't met Tony and Lily Hsu.

I told them about the diary that Marina's brother had given Lily for safekeeping and how I had sweet-talked it out of her hands.

"We could prosecute you for withholding evidence," a fox-faced cop barked.

"What evidence is that, Officer? According to your colleagues, Marina Lu's death was a random carjacking and you've never given the media any information to indicate otherwise. Besides, I had no idea that the police were interested in her diary or that it would contain anything other than schoolgirl ramblings."

"And did it?" a pasty-faced cop wanted to know.

"Some. I never got to the end, it was stolen out of my car in a restaurant parking lot that very night." I blushed then, realizing I wasn't going to tell them the whole story after all and might even still be covering for Mark. I would deal with that soon enough. The way I preferred to do things. Alone. The way I saw it, my relationship with the youth counselor was none of their goddamn business. I was giving them enough.

I told them about the diary pages that had fallen out and how Marina had followed her boyfriend, Michael Ho, to a strange house and learned what lay hidden behind its nondescript exterior. I described her conversation with May-li and the rape. I gave them the address and urged them to hurry and bust the brothel before the gang learned about Michael's arrest and fled. I explained that a similar sex slavery operation had been busted the previous week.

"Isn't that right?" I asked Officer Zhang.

He sat with his hands tucked into his armpits. Now he nodded silently.

"If what you say is true," one cop demanded, "then why didn't Marina Lu file a police report?"

"She was scared, for one. And she was immigrant Chinese, didn't trust the police, for two. They might be corrupt, like the cops back home."

At this, the white cops began murmuring among themselves. You could tell they felt insulted. Again, they looked at Zhang.

"It's true that some Overseas Chinese won't report crime," he responded. "But many more realize that in America, the police are the only place they can turn to for safety."

"I have another idea why Marina didn't go to the cops," I said, then bit my lip and looked at Officer Zhang. "It was a police officer who raped her."

The cops looked momentarily startled, then a wave of suspicion flooded the room as they closed ranks.

"A cop?" said Fox-Face.

"A white cop."

"What made her so sure about that?" asked Mr. Pasty.

I explained how a white cop had pulled Marina over in her daddy's Lexus and she had recognized him as her attacker. Now I looked full on at Zhang.

"She was pulled over for speeding in the West San Gabriel Valley two days before she was killed. And if what she told her girlfriend is true, this cop might just be on one of your local forces."

"Get a load of that," one cop said, turning to Zhang. "Got anyone who'd fit the bill?"

"I don't think such speculation deserves an answer," Zhang said.

"Why would Marina Lu make up such a story?" I asked.

"'Cuz she was working as a hooker on the side and her boyfriend caught her," one of the cops in the back chimed in.

"Fine. Don't believe me. There's no way to prove it anyway. The girl's dead and whoever raped and killed her—and it might have been the same person—certainly isn't talking."

I gazed at the hard-faced men around me. I would have liked to have seen just one woman. Maybe Marina's story would have gotten a more serious reception then, but maybe the empathy got hammered out of them in cadet school, regardless of sex.

"Look, I can understand why you wouldn't want to pursue this. It could be quite a scandal."

"We investigate any and all legitimate allegations," Fox-Face said, making it clear mine wasn't.

I wasn't making any friends, and I didn't care. I was hopping mad.

"There's a lot more." I went on, telling them everything that Michael Ho had told me on that windswept hill about Reginald Lu. I even told them how the Golden Pacific Bank thugs had busted in on the Vietnamese colonel, demanding repayment of their loan.

The cops looked skeptical. Anyone connected with civic life in the San Gabriel Valley knew about Golden Pacific Bank's sterling reputation. Why, I bet they even contributed to the Rowland Heights Policemen's Retirement Fund. Still I persisted. And was glad I hadn't gone to them for help any sooner.

They kept interrupting, trying to trip me up, but I held my ground. They were especially dubious when I told them about my drugging. And when I described the UPS attack in Silverlake, they wanted to know why I hadn't told the LAPD the whole truth. I said it was because I feared the reception I was getting now, after a whole lot more had gone down and Michael Ho was in custody with a warm revolver ticketed as evidence. But that did nothing to mollify them.

The last thing I did was plead for leniency for Tony. I told them how Michael Ho and Mark Furukawa had fought over him up there on that desolate ridge, but that in the end, the boy had made up his own mind to turn to the light. I told them that should count for something, even though Tony had been an errand boy for the Black Hand and skipped his parole hearing and gone AWOL.

It was 5 A.M. when we finished. The sun would be coming up soon. I told them I'd be available for as much questioning as they wanted, and Fox-Face smirked and said weren't they lucky, and added that I'd hear from them soon enough.

I knew I should go home and get some sleep. Home was safe now, with Michael in jail. But what if he had been telling the truth about the UPS thugs, and there was a second predator still on the loose? Ultimately, I was too wired to sleep. And I knew I had to find out what Michael meant when he called Mark a Judas.

Zhang offered to stroll me to my car, making a feeble joke about how it might not be safe to walk to the parking lot at night, even though we were in a police compound.

"Yeah, especially after that story I told in there," I said. But I accepted his offer for the olive branch it was and let him accompany me.

"Thank you for coming out in the middle of the night," I said as we reached my car. "Zhang, I didn't mean to put you in the hot seat against your fellow officers back there. But I desperately needed a backup, someone who could confirm that I didn't hallucinate this."

He didn't say anything. After I unlocked my door and slid into the seat, he stood by my car a fraction of a second too long, until something made me look up into his face. He fumbled for his wallet and pulled out a business card.

"Here," he said. "Why don't you give me a call tomorrow, after you've rested."

I opened my mouth to speak, then stopped when I saw the look on his face. I was beginning to suspect who had killed Marina Lu, and I didn't want to wait any longer to nail it down. But I couldn't push him either. Better to make a graceful exit, my first in the last twenty-four hours.

Hepped up on adrenaline now and a desire to confront Mark, I drove to Rowland Memorial where they had taken him after the shooting. The hospital parking lot was surprisingly busy for so early an hour. I sat in the car, wondering how to pull this one off. Only immediate family would be allowed in, and visiting hours were still far away. Then I strode through the automatic doors, down the pastel carpet, and up to the sleepy young Latina at the front desk, transferring an amber ring on my right hand to the second finger on my left and turning it around so only the gold band showed.

"My husband's in here," I lied. The words felt thrilling and dangerous on my tongue. "His name's Mark Furukawa. Is he still in surgery? I know visiting hours haven't started yet but I was giving my statement to the police. We were almost killed. I've got to see him."

"You're his wife?" the woman behind the counter looked me over. "Can I please see your ID?"

"Sure." I handed her my driver's license, trying to look as distraught as I felt. My whole world had just collapsed like a Northridge apartment building, although in retrospect, the Richter scale had been off the charts for some time now.

"This ID says Eve Diamond."

"I kept my maiden name when we got married."

I stared steadily at her, thinking what an archaic word "maiden" was. Did I still qualify as one?

"We have to check," she apologized.

"No prob." I was gracious as a duchess. "I'm sure you have all sorts of people trying to sneak in."

"Lady, you have no idea." She buzzed upstairs and asked the nursing supervisor whether to let me in.

"She wants to talk to you first. Second elevator on the right. Get off on the seventh floor. He's in Room 717. Post-op. He's heavily sedated."

"Oh, my poor baby."

I repeated my story to a white, middle-aged nursing supervisor who radiated suspicion. Is it because we're different races that you find it so hard to believe we're married? I wanted to ask, but held my tongue.

Finally, she let me in. "Twenty minutes and that's all. He's too fragile for any more."

Mark was hooked up to more tubes than a generator. He was out. I sat there and prayed. It seemed like so long since I had sat still. Out in the hall, the night shift went home and the day shift began its work. *Sayonara* to that bossy nursing supervisor. I hoped she wouldn't remember to tell her replacement to shoo me out.

I must have dozed off. When I woke up, a nurse was adjusting the IV and the sun was streaming in through the shutters. "How's he doing?" I asked.

"Amazingly well, for someone with a punctured lung."

"How much longer will he be out?"

"Couple of hours. Then we'll turn down the Demerol and see how he responds."

I realized I would be here a while. "Is the cafeteria open yet?" I asked.

"In the basement." I stood up, wobbled, and had to grab the edge of Mark's bed. She looked at my ashen state and took pity on me. She was young and still not jaded by her profession.

"I can get you a half a sandwich from the nurse's station if you'd like. Turkey OK?"

After eating, I curled up on the sofa with those thin institutional blankets the hospitals hand out and tried to catch a little more sleep, but the nurses' steady visits in and out kept me from drifting off. Finally Mark opened his eyes and saw me.

"Eve," he said with some difficulty. "Am I dreaming? Are you really here?"

"Yes. It's me. How do you feel?"

"Terrible. My head hurts. My chest hurts. I can hardly breathe."

"You have a punctured lung. But it appears you'll live."

He cracked a thin smile that was painful to see.

"You sound disappointed."

"I'm not. You saved my life. But how did you know where I was?"

Mark looked surprised. This was not what he had been anticipating. But hadn't he heard Michael call him a traitor? After that, did he expect Florence Nightingale? I waited, and the story came out in dribbles as Mark struggled for breath and I held mine.

"When you called yesterday afternoon . . . yikes, it hurts," Mark said, after an almost imperceptible effort at shifting his weight. "I was at Eastlake doing psych evals. I called you as soon as I got free. Someone named Trevor answered. He said you had run out in a hurry.

"I asked if he knew where you'd gone or when you'd be back. I told him I thought you might be in trouble. He explained that you were investigating something really big—he called it a 'fuckin' scandal'— and to hang on. I waited a long time. I didn't know what the hell he was up to. There was a lot of banging and muttering. He must have been going through your desk."

Mark stopped for breath. I hated myself for making him continue, but then, I also wanted to make him suffer, now that I knew there was no danger of him dying. All he had was a punctured lung. I had a punctured heart.

"Finally he came back on the line and told me in this conspiratorial tone that you had gotten a phone call right before you left and scribbled something down and he had flipped through the message pad on the receptionist's desk and found an address followed by the letters R.H. that were real faint, he could barely read them on the duplicate. I took a wild guess and figured that must mean Rowland Heights. So I came looking for you. I was afraid you might be walking into a trap. I told Trevor so. He said I should call him in an hour or else he was going to call the police and give them the address you had left behind. He didn't even wait that long. He must be some reporter, that guy. He saved us both."

"Tony saved us," I insisted. "Our fate was in his hands and he chose." Even now, I begrudged Trevor the credit I knew in the meanest, blackest part of my heart that he deserved. Besides, what had he saved me for? The opportunity to learn the extent of Mark's betrayal?

But Mark didn't hear the petty tone in my voice.

"I love you. Thank God I got there in time."

"So you knew where I was because of Trevor, not because you were in on this from the start with Michael and the Black Hand?"

"God, no."

But the shame in his eyes told me more than his words.

"You worked for Michael, didn't you, Mark? Are you a Black Hand too?"

"No," Mark rasped. I could tell this was wearing him out, but I couldn't stop palpating the wound.

"Then what did he mean when he said you had become a Judas? You were sleeping with me and reporting back, weren't you? That's how he knew I had the diary."

"God forgive me, Eve. I never told him anything after that first night."

"So it's true." Suddenly nothing mattered anymore.

"In the beginning, yeah, I told Michael there was a reporter snooping around and he said keep an eye on you. But anything that happened once you spent the night, that was strictly between us. He had nothing to do with it."

"He didn't order you to seduce me, huh? You thought that one up on your own. How very clever. Did you file reports each time we had sex? Did you tell him what you whispered when I was on my knees?"

"I fell in love with you, goddamnit! And then everything changed. Michael even tried to blackmail me but it didn't work. See, I had a little coke problem a few years back and the Black Hand found out about it and took advantage."

"No one can take advantage of you unless you let them." I said dully, repeating what I had heard a thousand times from recovery-speak.

"They didn't deal drugs back then, but they made an exception for me." He tried to swallow and almost choked, his mouth was so dry. "They even delivered it right to the Rainbow Coalition office."

"So what was the pound of flesh they extracted?" I asked, knowing in advance. His life had nothing to do with mine anymore.

"Not much, at first. And I was so greedy and lost I couldn't say no. Then I was just a pair of eyes and ears on the street who could pass on things I heard."

I felt his self-loathing. And this time, he couldn't pace or punch his fist through a wall or even fold up teeny origami animals. All he could do was lie there, tethered to his machines like some high-tech martyr.

"Then I came along."

"Then you came along," he agreed. "They were especially interested in what you knew about Marina's murder. And yes, it was I who told them you might have the diary. You hinted as much that night at Bahooka's. You were drunk. It was easy to slip away and make a phone call."

"My car. You told them where it was and they broke into it and took the diary."

"Yes."

"How could you?" I had tears in my eyes.

He hadn't heard me. "And then we spent that night together. After that I told Michael the deal was off. So Michael drugged you to find out what you knew. But I couldn't tell you that without revealing my own complicity. Then after Alison's story, I was sick with guilt. I had told May-li nothing bad would ever happen to her again and I broke my promise. I was trying to help Tony, and that wasn't working. Then you almost got killed because of me. I didn't think Michael was a killer, but what almost happened on your jog proved me wrong. That really shook me. I wanted to go to the cops, remember? But you were so stubborn. Eve on the scene, determined to resolve everything yourself. That's why I insisted you come stay at my house. For God's sake, Eve, why would I have come barreling up to Rowland Heights with a gun if I didn't love you? If I wasn't scared shitless about what Michael Ho and his boss Reginald Lu might do to you?"

I laughed bitterly. "I suppose I should feel flattered. Funny how I just can't muster up the emotion anymore."

At that moment, the day nurse came running in. Mark's vital signs were going nuts.

"Mrs. Furukawa, whatever you're saying is exciting him too much, and that's bad for his heart. I'm going to have to ask you to leave and return later in the afternoon after he's had some rest."

"That's OK, nurse, I was just on my way out." I walked over and kissed him gently on the forehead. He looked so helpless and shrunken, with all those tubes and bandages, his eyes dilated from pain and shock and who knows, maybe even love.

"Good-bye, my own dear heart," I whispered. I had never meant anything so sincerely in all my life. And then I turned and walked out.

CHAPTER 41

I went home, to the only real home I had, back to Silverlake, where I stood in the doorway, scanning for signs of intruders and sniffing the air. I figured that after all the windows being closed up tight for a week, I would smell it if anyone had been here, smell the acrid cigarettes or the perspiration or the unwashed hair. But there was nothing, just a faint dusty smell and some oranges molding silently on the kitchen table, green and furry.

I got myself some juice from the fridge, then walked to the back porch to see if Bon Jovi was around before remembering that he was dead. Violetta had cried and cried when I told her, when the Humane Society had sent a truck to pick him up and cremate him. She was going to scatter his ashes in the yard he had once patrolled for squirrels.

I finished the juice, rinsed out the glass, stepped out of my clothes, and crawled into bed, where I curled into the fetal position and slept for ten hours straight. It was night when I woke, groggy and disoriented.

I got up, took a hot shower, and ordered in green curry and *tom yum gai* soup from the twenty-four-hour Thai place around the corner. When the guy rang the doorbell, I peeked out through the mini-blinds to make sure he carried a plastic bag. Then I opened the door and overtipped recklessly.

While I ate, I read three days' worth of papers that Violetta had thoughtfully piled on the porch for me. Then I made barley tea, took it to bed, sipped it while I finished the Sunday *Times* magazine and fell asleep until morning.

I was up by six and ate again, hot oatmeal with Violetta's homemade apricot jam and lots of coffee. I called and left a message on Miller's voicemail that I'd be at work that afternoon. I knew that Trevor, exulting in his hero's role, would have filled him in on the previous forty-eight hours.

Not wanting to sound overeager, I waited until 10 A.M. to call Officer Zhang. But my voice cracked and betrayed me anyway when I gave my name to the receptionist. He came on the line immediately and asked how I was feeling.

"OK, I guess. At least I've had a good night's sleep and a few decent meals since we last talked."

"Glad to hear it. How'd you like another? I've got several things to do this morning, but should be breaking loose around lunchtime."

He named a small place on Valley Boulevard and gave me directions. I hung up and decided I'd best burn off my excess energy with a run. Even though it had been a while, my feet skated along the asphalt like it was newly groomed ice. Some days it just comes easy.

At noon, I sat inside the 3.6.9. restaurant, eyeing the barbecued shrimp and Szechwan eggplant on the menu. Officer Zhang walked in a few minutes later.

I wondered whether he might not want to be seen here with me in uniform, but kept that thought to myself. We ordered jasmine tea and he asked if I liked spicy food.

"Can't work in this valley and not."

"You'd be surprised." He sipped his tea. "Vittorio Carabini told me you could keep your mouth shut."

I bowed my head and counted the flecks of loose tea leaf in my cup. Carabini was long buried, but he was still reaching out over six feet of earth to shake things up.

"I was no fan of Vit's, you should know that." He stopped. "You really care about that kid Tony."

"Yeah. For all the good it's done."

"I'm sure it meant a lot to him. I was a parachute kid too, and I can tell you, I wish someone would have shown an interest in me at that age."

"No shit, Zhang. God, they're everywhere." I looked at him sitting there, so normal-like. "You turned out OK."

"No visible scars, anyway. Listen," he leaned in now. "I believe everything you told the Rowland PD the other night."

"Oh, yeah?" Here it came. Every fiber in my body was on red alert.
"Yeah."

"Even about the crooked cop?"

"Yeah."

"Is that right?" I leaned back in the booth and waited. In the last month, I had become good at waiting.

"When I told you I was no fan of Carabini, that was an understatement. He was a racist who didn't trust guys without an epicanthal fold. This used to be a white man's valley, he'd say, when we cruised around in the patrol car. You left something out of that story about Marina getting stopped by the white cop, didn't you?"

"He had an Asian cop with him," I said. My hands were tingling. "Go on," I whispered.

"I didn't even remember that traffic ticket until yesterday. But you brought it all back in Technicolor. He made some awful jokes that day."

I hadn't mentioned any jokes to the cops. "Tell me what he said."

Zhang looked off in the distance. "He made some crack about how he would never be able to afford a Lexus on his salary and how shocked he was to find a 'nice little Asian girl' like her speeding."

I pressed my hands down flat on the fiberglass table until I felt my fingertips sweat.

"He killed her, didn't he? It wasn't Michael."

"I didn't realize it myself until I heard your story. And then it began to make sense why he never let us interview Reginald Lu. He was so secretive about that investigation. I thought it was because he didn't trust us. When in reality . . ."

"*He* was the one on the take," I said. "He was at that brothel getting paid in girls as well as money. Sample all the merchandise. Keep him sated and sluggish, so he'd turn a blind eye."

"Carabini was always strapped for money. After the divorce, it must have been a huge temptation, especially if he had a chance to get his kids back. He loved those kids. They became an obsession. And that was the opening the Black Hand needed."

Officer Zhang's words made me think of Marina's little black hand and heart tattoo. And that association made me gasp, because it brought up something I hadn't thought of.

"Carabini tried to have me killed too. But it got flubbed. That Silverlake UPS truck that shot at me. He was behind that. He must have been. He knew I was on to Marina's diary and feared she had described the cop who raped her. They tried to whack me after I told Carabini about Marina's tattoo. Stupid twerp that I was, I thought I was doing him a favor. But he must have been afraid I'd put it in one of my stories and Michael would figure out who had been at the house that night and have him killed. So he had to kill her first. And he knew plenty of petty-ass gangbangers he could put up to it through fear or intimidation. He ordered the hit, then died before he could see it carried through."

"It was too late for him anyway," Zhang said. "Because Michael Ho stole Marina's diary out of your car and read it and found out that his paid white boy had raped his precious little girl, upstairs in his own whorehouse. It must have been him who had Carabini killed."

As he spoke, I visualized it all. Check. Check. Checkmate.

"We all knew it was a gang hit," Zhang was saying. "But we thought it had to do with his undercover work in the casinos."

"That was some major gambling. Stake your life."

"Now it all makes sense. It's something Ho would do. Absolutely. Everyone in Asian law enforcement has heard of him, the leader of the Young Turks. They pattern themselves after the Italian Mafia, only smarter. Don't fuck with my woman. Oh yeah, he'd get his revenge."

"Wait til he finds out that the rapist cop he offed was the same one who killed his fiancée and aced him out of the extremely affluent Lu clan," I said. "He'll want to dig up the corpse and pump a few dozen more bullets into it."

"He'll never know. No one will. We never had this conversation."

I looked at him, aghast. Here he had just fingered two murderers to a reporter, then claimed I couldn't write about it? "Aren't you going to tell your bosses?"

Zhang ran his index finger along his chopstick. "My 'boss' was Carabini's best friend. He gave him a hero's burial, remember?"

"You mean, he's in on it too?" I flashed suddenly to Carabini's boss, Sergeant Latham, trying to weasel the brothel addresses out of Lieutenant Redman prior to the raid and growing sheepish when I overheard him. My toes curled.

"Exactly," Zhang said. "I'm green, Eve. I'm the 'Chink' recruit. I've got to watch it. You heard of the code of silence? They would drum me out of the force so fast I wouldn't have time to tuck my tail between my legs as I ran."

"Then I'll go to your boss's boss and I'll tell *him*. I'll write stories about it. We'll break it that way."

Zhang tried to smile but all I could see was the sadness in his eyes. "None of what we've discussed here today would ever hold up in court, or even against your editor's scrutiny. You can't use a third-hand source in a police report or a news story, especially when it comes to murder. And the only two people who could tell us for sure, Marina and Carabini, are dead. Even the Black Hand doesn't yet know the whole truth. Michael Ho thinks he was avenging a rape."

"Oh, Zhang, I knew Carabini was a racist, but a rapist and a killer? It doesn't track."

I told him about the bottle blonde at the apartment and her two kids. The waitress at Santori's. Our long, alcohol-soused talks.

"Maybe at one time, he was a decent guy. But somewhere back there, he crossed the Yangtze. Maybe it started out as a scheme to get his kids back. He needed money for good divorce lawyers, whatever. But it got out of his control. And he began hating himself and everyone around him, blaming them for his fall even as he took payola for it. He grew desperate. And a desperate man is a dangerous man."

I thought back to our last conversation before his death. There had been something hard in him, something brittle and unpleasant, which I had ignored because it hadn't fit in with what I wanted to see. And the next time I encountered Vittorio Carabini, it was to write his obit. There hadn't been any time to mull over the nuances, grasp those delicate tendrils of doubt and trace them to the source. We're not big on nuance in the news business, anyway. It gets in the way of the story.

EPILOGUE

I spent the next week trying to explain my nightmare on Rowland Ridge to everyone at work. The only one who didn't find my behavior that night utter lunacy was Miller. He knew me. To him, it made perfect sense that I'd risk my life to meet Tony.

In the end, it proved simple to satisfy the curiosity of my tribe—that pack of yammering, skeptical reporters—and also keep my secrets. All I had to do was tell the yarn about how I had run afoul of Asian organized crime in my unorthodox pursuit of a story, leaving out the parts that were too outlandish to believe.

For now, I blotted that out, and wrote a gazillion stories. Brights and obits, evergreens and round-ups. I volunteered for everything. I worked Saturday and Sunday shifts downtown and was never in a hurry to go home. I already spoke rudimentary Spanish. Now, I signed up for Chinese at the local junior college and was surprised to see Asian faces at the desks around me also struggling to get their tongues around the unfamiliar sounds.

I continued to puzzle over what Officer Zhang and I had discovered. As far as I could tell, we were the only ones who knew the whole story. Even Mark was out of the loop on this one. Each time the cops hauled me in for questioning, I brought up the possibility that Carabini had killed Marina Lu. I couldn't tell if they were truly ignorant or knew the foul rot in their own midst and were merely playing cover-your-ass. Hell, for all I knew, some of them were on the payroll too. Still, my allegations must have registered somewhere up the chain of command, because pretty soon they brought Alison in for a talk. Struck with remorse for her dead friend and feeling safer now that Michael Ho was in jail for trying to kill Mark, Alison described the rapist cop to them as best she could from Marina's telephone calls. With two of us now singing the same song, the top cops had a police artist draw a composite, but in the end, only one person could have judged the drawing's accuracy, and she was dead. Still, it must have looked enough like Carabini that eventually an internal investigation was launched. I knew because Zhang would call from time to time and discreetly let me know what was up. The probe wasn't surprising, considering the piles of dough that had been found in Carabini's apartment. Where else would he have gotten all that money except from the Black Hand?

Zhang says the police investigation has been inconclusive. If you ask me, they're hoping to drag it out until everyone forgets about the case. So I call them every couple of weeks and needle them, playing dumb reporter sniffing for clues, but so far I haven't written anything. Zhang was right, it's just too speculative. Sometimes the best stories stay in the shadows. I'm learning that's just the way it is. And that seeing your story in print isn't everything.

But there was some consolation. My piece about parachute kids finally ran. The wires picked it up and it went all over the world, including the *International Herald Tribune*, where I hope my exboyfriend Tim saw it in Singapore and choked on his morning noodles. I don't care about getting back together with him anymore, which is funny, since that's why I wanted to find out who killed Marina Lu in the first place. Still, the story got me noticed. The L.A. Press Club gave me an award. Graduate students call, wanting to do their doctorates on parachute kids. I also got a flurry of media interest, everyone from the *Today* show to Montel Williams. They all wanted a piece of my little parachute kids, wanted me to bring Tony and Lily on national TV to tell their stories. But I was careful to protect their identities, putting up buffers, directing journalists to school officials and youth counselors and Asian-American groups instead. Let them do their own damn reporting.

As for the parachute kids themselves, Tony's out of trouble for now. His influential father flew in for the court hearing, armed with a handful of letters from me, Father Wong, Mark Furukawa, and Nick Madigan attesting to Tony's high intelligence, lack of criminal record, and potential to contribute significantly to society. In a tearful appeal before the judge, Mr. Hsu asked that Tony be released into his custody and promised under oath to escort his son back to court the day the trial started. To show good faith, he even put up $100,000 in a special bond that his fancy lawyer drew up. And Tony walked. But not far. Taking no chances, Daddy Hsu stuck him on the first flight to Hong Kong, a one-way ticket back to the former Crown Colony. For once, I didn't blame him. I've learned the hard way that you can't trust the American system of justice any more than that of the Chinese. The only difference is that the Chinese know it. Tony can't come back to the States now—there's a warrant out for his arrest. But we e-mail a lot and he wants me to visit him in Hong Kong. I'm thinking seriously about it; I've got a lot of comp time saved up.

Lily and I keep in touch. She stayed in the United States after Tony left, convincing her dad to let her finish high school here. The Hsus sold their ranch house in San Marino for big bucks to another immigrant Chinese family and Lily moved in with a family from school where she could get some real supervision. I visit her from time to time. The other weekend, we went roller-blading down at the beach and ate taquitos. We looked out over the Pacific and the horizon stared back, calm and empty. There were no freighters crammed with Chinese immigrants running aground today. The sun was glinting through the clouds. Winter was almost here and a cold wind was blowing.

It made me think I was finally starting to get over Mark. He had called nonstop from his hospital bed but I refused to get on the phone. I needed to put some distance between us. We'd been through too much together—too much death, heartbreak, and betrayal. Our paths crossed briefly, but that time has come and gone, even though Babette keeps telling me to give him a second chance, arguing that he came through for me when it counted and why can't I see that. She's right, of course, but still I can't forgive him. Call me stubborn that way. Besides, ever since Mark testified at Michael Ho's trial and helped him get five years, he's dropped out of sight. I hear he's no longer at the Rainbow

Coalition Center, and that's too bad. The kids have lost a damn good counselor. I suspect the cops relocated him under their witness protection program, afraid that the Black Hand had put a contract out on him. Maybe he'll resurface one day and try to reach me. I'm not sure what I'd say.

Michael Ho never got charged with running those brothels. In that first week after the shoot-out on Rowland Ridge, I called the cops each day with mounting hysteria, demanding to know when they were going to raid the house where May-li was kept. Soon, soon, they kept telling me. They had the place under surveillance and had sent an informant over to check it out and confirm my story. But by the time they finally raided it, after Michael Ho had had a week to warn his cohorts, the house was empty, the smugglers having long ago moved the girls to another safe house, ensuring that the only witnesses who could testify against Michael Ho would never be found.

Once his sad little birds had flown the coop, there was simply no sex-slavery case anymore, and none of the other names or bank accounts seized during the brothel raid I had witnessed were ever traced back to Michael Ho or Reginald Lu. It made me wonder whether Michael was just bragging to me that night on Rowland Ridge about Lu's involvement with organized crime. Maybe by the time Michael comes up for parole, they will have pulled a sex-slavery case together. I think Zhang is working on it. He promises he'll give me a heads-up if something does break, but I'm not holding my breath.

I never saw May-li again. Despite all our promises to her—mine, Marina's, and Mark's—no one saved her. She joined the throngs of nameless whores plying their trade on a sin-city route from here to New York. Every time I spot a thin, scared-looking Asian girl with downcast eyes—and all of a sudden, I'm seeing them in every corner of this sprawling valley—my heart jumps until I realize it isn't her.

I wonder whether they'll really let her go after she sleeps with three hundred men and pays off her debt or if they'll prostitute her until she wastes away and dies of AIDS. If that's the case, I hope she finds a sharp knife.

It's thinking about May-li that really sends me over the edge. Marina was dead before I ever met her; there was nothing I could do except maybe help unmask her killer. But Marina's unfortunate twin, that little Mainland girl, was another story. Sometimes late at night when I'm feeling desperate, I get in my car and cruise up and down Valley Boulevard, driving by the Asian streetwalkers real slow so that they run over to the car all hopeful until they see it's just another woman behind the wheel. Then I yell out, asking do they know a girl named May-li from Fujian, China. But they just look at me like I'm crazy.

And in those hollow hours, the recriminations start. Why did Mark and I let the INS take her? Why didn't I go to the cops once we found the brothel and Mark saw her there? Why did we wait so long? Thinking about the life we condemned her to is almost unbearable. I know I have to come to terms with it or I'll lose my mind. But even when I banish her from my waking hours, she returns at night to haunt my dreams.

ACKNOWLEDGMENTS

I would like to thank the Silverlake Fiction Writers Group, without whose friendship, encouragement, and criticism this book would never have been written: Kerry Madden-Lunsford, Marlene McCurtis, Donna Rifkind, Lienna Silver, Judith Dancoff, Diane Arieff, and Diana Wagman.

A special thanks to Ellen Slezak and Donna Rifkind for their editing and writing notes at a time when I needed it most, and to Donna for paving the way to the Borchardt Literary Agency.

I would like to thank Anne Borchardt for her faith in me, and Susanne Kirk for her thoughtful editing and suggestions.

Thanks to Marissa Roth, my onetime partner in travels and journalism.

Thanks to the real Eve Diamond, whose name evoked gumshoes and glamour.

Thanks to my former editorial colleagues at the now defunct San Gabriel Bureau of the *Los Angeles Times*.

Thanks to my mother, Helene Hamilton, my late father, Edward, and to my siblings, Marc and Noelle.

Thanks to David, Adrian, and Alexander for their patience and love.

And thanks to my myriad sources in the San Gabriel Valley and to the parachute kids themselves, who opened their lives to me.

About the Author

DENISE HAMILTON is a Los Angeles–based writer/journalist whose work has appeared in the *Los Angeles Times*, *Wired*, *Cosmopolitan*, *Der Spiegel*, and *New Times*. As a Fulbright Scholar, she lived and taught in the former Yugoslavia during the Bosnian War. During ten years on staff at the *Los Angeles Times*, she covered the disintegration of communism in Eastern Europe, the break-up of the Soviet Union, and youth movements in Japan. But the bulk of her *Times* career was spent in the suburbs of Los Angeles, where she used her overseas experience to cover the city's exploding immigrant Asian communities. The recipient of various grants and fellowships, Hamilton has done consulting for New York University's Institute for War & Peace Reporting and Washington, D.C.–based Search for Common Ground. Hamilton lives in a coyote-infested Los Angeles suburb with her husband and two young children. *The Jasmine Trade* is her first novel.